AF374444

The Steps
She Took

Megan Eik

To my son, Jesse

Chapter One

I don't know if I should be telling you this or not. So, let's keep it between the two of us and I won't go to jail.

Deal?

Everyone sees what they want to see. A woman in a clean house, tucked into the end of a quiet cul-de-sac, where everything looks orderly and well-kept. The kitchen is modern. The kids are well-dressed. The holidays come with routines and ribbons. No one asks what it costs to keep it that way.

But no one sees the silence behind those walls. No one sees how I sit in my car for ten extra minutes after school drop-off, gripping the steering wheel like it's the only thing keeping me from flying apart. No one hears the thoughts I wrestle with at 2:00 a.m., lying awake in a king-sized bed that suddenly feels too big, cold, and empty. No one hears the screams, thuds, and violence that go on behind our closed doors.

I smile at the other moms at the PTA meetings, laugh

at the correct times at dinner parties, keep the house spot-less, the meals organic, and the calendar full. I play the role so well that sometimes I forget it *is* a role.

But beneath it all, I am empty. A vast shell of a woman. Every day, I whisper the same words under my breath like a prayer or a curse: *Just keep going. Smile. You're fine. It'll be okay.* But it isn't OK. And pretending isn't working any-more.

This is the story of how I unraveled, how I stopped pretending, how I walked through the ache, the guilt, and the truth before finding something tangible on the other side. It took years. And even now, there are days when the emptiness knocks at my door, uninvited and persistent. But I no longer open it out of habit.

For the first time in a long time, I feel something like… me. This is how it happened.

It all started in the late summer, five years ago, in a small town in Virginia. I had been very careful with my cof-fee that morning; he hated the smell of it. I had brewed it outside on the back porch to decrease the smell as much as possible. I even drank it while it was lukewarm, just in case having warm coffee could make my breath smell more like coffee. *Crazy, right?* That morning, I had been fed up with the extremes I had to go through to enjoy a cup of coffee in the morning. A nice warm cup of anything in the morning was something everyone should be able to do if they wanted to. Coffee was my vice, my secret morning indulgence, and I hid that from my husband.

My children, Lilly and Jack, had been away at summer camp for the last two weeks, living their dreams and hopefully getting into a bit of trouble as children should. Most summers, when the children went off to camp, my husband, Henry, and I would fly to a new country, trying our hardest to hold on to the last bit of love we had for one another. Our love started disappearing shortly after our son was born, so these days, there is little left.

Henry spent all his time at home tied to his computer. I saw very little of him between his two offices (home and away) and all the business trips in between. That summer, his firm had sent him on twelve visits, and he was packing for yet another one that morning. After hiding the evidence of my coffee and brushing any smell from my teeth and hands, I made my way upstairs. Standing in the doorway of our bedroom, I observed him fold each shirt so there was no wrinkle in sight, before placing them in his suitcase.

"Leaving again?" I asked, trying to hide the pain in my voice while keeping my breath shallow enough to keep the smell of coffee from entering the air.

Henry was still just as handsome as the day I married him. You would think his looks would have faded when his personality did, but alas, he still looked as dashing as the day I met him. I often wondered why he bothers to pack for these trips; he wears the same thing daily. Just as he is now, in slim black trousers with a tight white button-up. The only difference each day is his tie, which today's is draped across his shoulder. His suit jacket was neatly placed on the bed next to his suitcase. He has had the same hairstyle since the day I met him, too, dark brown silky straight hair perfectly combed across the left side of his forehead. The lack of change always made me wonder how often he had it cut or perhaps dyed. I can't remember seeing any gray hair on his head in the last twenty years that I have known him.

"You know I have to. The board trusts my opinions. I can't change the number of trips I have this year, even if I wanted to." He said between tightened lips and a sharp 'stay out of it' stare, screaming at me over his shoulder.

Henry enjoyed these business trips more than anything in the world. I suspected he signed up to go on these trips instead of the company sending him. He never liked being home anymore, now that the kids were older. Especially not alone with me, he detests me. I gave him his children, and then he was done with me, in more ways than one. When Lilly was younger, I often saw Henry and Lilly running in the backyard, playing tag until the sun fell. He once tried to build a swing set for Lilly, back when he made an effort as a father. She was over the moon and spent all day talking about the jumps and tricks she would learn to do as soon as her dad had finished. Halfway through the building, Henry's hand slipped, dropping one of the posts, and he lunged forward to keep it from falling on Lilly, breaking his wrist in the fall. He never did finish building the swings, and it sat there for months as a reminder of his failure. One morning, I woke up to find the swing set in pieces on the ground, shards of wood scattered everywhere. When he went to the office that day, I called a handyman to clean it up and put a proper play set with swings in its place. Any attempt at being a handyman stopped after that. Henry felt his role in our family was to be a financial provider and nothing else, which just happened to coincide with the birth of our son, Jack.

"I just thought we could spend one day together when you aren't packing or unpacking for a trip," I began as my body shook from speaking my mind, which I rarely did anymore to him.

"How about you go on a trip yourself? You might enjoy your life outside of this small town." He said, cutting me off mid-sentence by slamming his suitcase shut, before zipping it and tossing it on the ground.

I could sense the tenseness emanating from him. He fixed his tie, tightened it, and straightened his collar before draping his jacket over the suitcase handle. I watched as his chest rose, almost in slow motion. When he looked up from the suitcase, his eyes were piercing into mine, his pupils dilated, and sweat built up on his eyebrows. He came barreling towards me in the doorway; my knees weakened as he got closer.

"I do not want to go on yet another trip by myself. If I kept going on trips every time you had a business trip, I would have seen the whole world this summer! We have a house and children to care for, you know!" I shouted as loudly as my slight act of bravery would allow me, as I watched him get closer and closer to me.

I clutched the doorknob and squeezed my eyes shut as he passed me, as if this would secure me from his abuse. I let go of the breath that I had been holding in once he was far enough away from me to know I wouldn't get hit. I watched as he made his way down the hallway, slow step after slow step, pausing at the top of the stairs. He stood there momentarily, then dropped his bags beside him, slowly turning around. I could tell from the stiffness of his body as he turned that he was coming back to do damage to me.

In that split second, my mind had made a decision I was not fully aware it had made. I let go of the doorknob and ran full speed at him. Hitting his body felt like a brick wall, throwing me backwards in the process. I watched as his tense body toppled down the stairs, arms over his head, and skipped many steps on his way down. Something no architect thinks about when building the largest home in the neighborhood is that there are more stairs to *accidentally* slip or fall down.

Later that night, my once nearest and dearest friends gathered for our monthly book club. I have been hosting these events for three years now, and I have come to realize that my contribution to our book club has dwindled over time. My patience for these women who live off their husbands' paychecks and inheritances was something I never wanted to be a part of. They wander around town in their most expensive diamonds and pearls, with no real purpose in life, except to spend their husbands' money.

But here I am, fifteen years into this marriage, where my husband's inheritance paid for the biggest house in the neighborhood, and his job pays for our entire lifestyle. From the outside, I was just like any of the shallow women in my book club. Except, I got a job for myself! The pay is shit, and I have only started a few months ago, but it lets me cover my nail appointments without having to use Henry's card. That simple act gave me my first taste of freedom in years. And I wanted more. This job gave me purpose aside from my children, who have never seemed to need me between nannies, school, and their friends. I went back and forth between job ideas that would make me happy when I saw a help-wanted ad for our local publishing house in my small town of Gloomridge, Virginia. The name of our village alone would drive anyone to depression. Thankfully, this job lets me read manuscripts daily, where I can escape into different worlds and envision my life differently.

That night, the conversation flowed as smoothly as the wine, from superficial to profound, from earnest to scandalous, before inevitably drifting towards the more salacious corners of their lives. Their children, husbands, and who's maid forgot to leave a flower-shaped tissue on top of the tissue box. They never talked about the books we were supposed to read that month. I honestly do not believe any of the women have ever read one of the books on our list. The books merely became trophies for their bookcases more than anything else. These monthly meetings are simply another social engagement on their calendar. They come mostly sober and leave wasted from the alcohol and all the fresh new gossip.

I tried to keep up with the conversations and keep a smile on my face, but it was all fake. My mind was always elsewhere, especially tonight, my mind flickering between my husband's body tied up in my basement and what my plan was next.

"Emma," I heard Marsha say for the second time as she shook my shoulder. "Do you have any more bottles of wine?" She asked, shaking the empty bottle in the air. Of course, I did. They were all aware of my wine cellar.

Finally, a break.

"I'll be right back, ladies," I shouted over the laughing women and exited the room with the few empty bottles near me.

We kept our wine in the cellar, far away from the prying eyes and ears of the ladies. As I walked through the kitchen towards the basement door, I spotted Gwen, my partner in crime, confidante, and right-hand woman, grabbing a fresh bag of crackers from the kitchen. If she needed more wine, she would grab it herself as she knew where to find it. She felt at home here, as she always had. She never had to ask me to get something; she would just do it. Gwen has been my best friend since college, and she knew me before I met Henry. She once tried to talk me out of marrying him, saying he wasn't good enough for me and that I deserved better. As always, she was right, and I should have listened to her warning, but that was then, and this is now.

"Come with me," I whispered, grabbing her elbow and dragging her toward the basement door.

I could hear crackers falling to the ground behind me and decided to ignore them. I had more important things to worry about than spilled crackers. Besides, I always hire someone to come and clean the house after these gatherings. The ladies might be rich, classy broads, but they sure do know how to make a mess, especially when it is not something they have to clean up.

The first half of our basement was beyond gorgeous; it mirrored the wealthy aesthetic the rest of the house had. We had a lovely bar and wine room that was perfectly temperature-controlled to ensure the wine would last as long as possible. We had a cabinet of blankets in the corner, so I was always comfortable when I spent my evenings reading with a glass of wine. However, the other half of the basement was untouched. The air turned colder the deeper you went, and the lights dimmed. The deepest room in the basement was pitch-black, a yawning abyss beneath the shine of perfection. The walls in this part of the basement were bare, lacking any personal touches, and barely had paint on them.

The walls were covered in large wooden shelves that housed clear storage containers from the floor to the ceiling. Each container is labeled to make finding what you need easier.

"Wine's this way, Emma," Gwen said, pointing towards the cellar. I kept walking, though, straight to the last room in the basement.

When I finally reached it, Gwen was standing behind me with a confused look on her face. She had never been in this room, let alone this part of the basement. We never had a reason to go past the comfort of our bar, where we spent a lot of our time together. I took a key from my bra and slipped it into the lock. Before I turned the key, I looked back at Gwen again, took a deep breath, and unlocked the door. With a flip of a switch, the dark room came alive. Once our eyes adjusted to the light, we saw a grotesque parody of a star taking form in the middle of the room. Henry was tied up spread-eagled on a bare mattress, his expensive suit covered in blood and creased, his face a mask of bewildered terror.

The three of us stared at one another. I could see Henry trying to clear his eyes from the sudden shock of the light, but he was unable to, as his hands were tied rather tightly. Gwen's jaw dropped; she would not stop looking between Henry and me. When his eyes fully adjusted, he stared wide-eyed at the two of us standing in the doorway. He tried to scream, but the duct tape around his mouth muffled the sound.

Gwen has always had a crystal-clear face that you could

always tell what she was thinking, so I looked towards her, hoping she felt the same way as I did. To my surprise, I could not read it this time. Her eyes were the widest I had ever seen, yet they were vacant.

However, it did not take long for her to return to herself. Once she closed her mouth, I caught a slight gleam of a smile.

"Henry, you know Gwen, right? Only my best friend for many years & would do anything for me." I began before turning back to Gwen. "I guess this is a sight you don't get to see every day, huh?" I asked her, a slight laugh escaping as I spoke.

She stood there like a ghost; the only part of her moving was her lips. That faint smile grew ever so slightly with each second that passed.

"Finally got him, huh?" Gwen chuckled. "I have always envisioned doing this myself; I never thought you would have the balls to do it, though." She began to come back to life as she spoke, leaving the comfort and safety of the wall and circling the mattress on which Henry was spread out. His eyes followed her every movement, ignoring my presence completely.

When she finished her round, Gwen turned back towards me and nodded. I shut the door and locked it from the inside. As I turned back towards the two of them, I could see Gwen standing above him, straddling his waist as she reached down and tore the duct tape off of his lips.

"What the fuck is happening?" Henry shouted at the

top of his lungs. "You have to let me go. Someone will notice I was not on the plane and come looking for me." He began to say before Gwen placed the tape right back on his big, whiny mouth.

"Now listen here, you bastard." I heard Gwen shout back at him before slapping him in the face as hard as she could. "I don't know what you did this time, but I can assure you it will be the last time you ever lay a hand on your wife. Is that clear?" She asked him.

Gwen stood above him, waiting for an answer, and when one did not come, she asked the question again, this time with her heel pressed against his balls. He shook his head once. Gwen and I could see that he was not sincere about his promise, and once he was let go, he would come after me, and most likely Gwen, once he was done with me. With this knowledge, she put more weight on her heel, waiting for his response. When none came, she put all of her weight down, and he began shaking his head profusely. Gwen grabbed the duct tape by the corner, ready to remove it before changing her mind, and smacked it back onto Henry's mouth with as much force as possible. Throwing in an extra slap across his cheek for good measure.

"So, what is your plan here?" She turned towards me, her foot still on his crotch.

"I have thought long and hard about this for quite a while," I began as I leaned up against the door, tossing the key to the room between my hands, "I'm not letting him go free, that is for certain. He has caused too much pain in my life to give him the satisfaction of thinking he still owns me after this. No, I think it's time to end his torturous ways once and for all."

Henry began to shake, becoming more frightened than I had ever seen him. He's never been one to show his emotions in front of others. A few times within our marriage, I had walked in on him alone in various parts of our home, shaking with a single tear streaming down his face. In these instances, he often would stand up rather abruptly and slap himself across the face before taking a deep breath and walking out of whatever room he was in. He was never one to speak of anything that bothered him to anyone.

This was not like that. His body was covered in goosebumps, and his face was blotchy and drenched in sweat. You could hear him pleading underneath his duct tape as he tried to shake his arms and legs free of the ropes holding him down.

Gwen ripped the duct tape off his mouth. "Did you have something to say?" She asked in a singsong voice and began to chuckle. You could see small bits of skin on his lip that were ripped off from the tape and still hanging on with all its might.

"You bitch!" He shouted at Gwen, "Both of you!" This time, looking at me. "What makes you think no one will come to look for me? I mean a lot to this community and my company; everyone will come looking. And when they do, they will find out that my wife kidnapped me, hid me from the world, and tied me up just like Annie Wilkes did to poor Paul!" He continued yelling, arms and legs flailing and dripping in sweat.

"You still think she is just kidnapping you?" Gwen laughed. "Henry, this room is the last room you will ever see in your entire life. I hope you got a good look at the outside while you had the chance. Maybe even had an affair or two while out on business trips. We all know you weren't the perfect husband, so we won't be shocked if some young blonde calls looking for you."

"I have never cheated on my wife!" Henry yelled, the skin on his lips wiggling as he spoke.

"Henry, really," She giggled, "I have a hard time believing you have never had a mistress. Your wife is just as gorgeous as the day you met her; you wouldn't have a valid reason to have a mistress with her looks. I don't know why you are even trying to lie." Gwen asked, getting closer and closer to his face.

I grew tired of their back-and-forth arguing, knowing they could go on for hours, if not years, if I let them. "Honestly, at this point, does it even matter?" I asked as I walked over to them, "It doesn't. You have hurt me for the last time. Was it worth it?"

"Are you asking me if I were to do our marriage all over again, would I change anything? The answer is no, even if doing it all the same still wound me up on this floor at the mercy of the two of you." He said, whimpering. "I had a great life, and I know you did too. I gave you everything you could have ever asked for! I never once asked you to work,

I didn't ask you to raise our children without the help of a nanny, I didn't ask you to make dinners, or to keep our home clean. I gave you the best possible life you could have asked for. And this is what I get in return? A wife who hates me this much and would rather torture me than do anything else." He stopped, pausing to catch his breath and his thoughts as his head was pulsing. "You know, I stopped loving you many years ago. There was never a reason to leave you; you would have taken half of my money, and I would have had to take on a true fatherly role for our children. I wouldn't be able to travel as much as I wanted to. My life would have changed for the worse. It made sense to stay with you." Henry said quickly while gasping for breath, the final words in a wheeze.

Gwen placed more weight down on her heel, squeezing his balls with every ounce of pressure she could muster. I bent over Henry's chest to look him in the eyes to see if anything that he just admitted was the truth. Honestly, he became harder to read over the years, so this was useless, yet I still felt powerful doing it.

"Tape him back up," I told Gwen as I straightened up and headed towards the door. "Be right back."

Once on the other side of the door, I leaned my back against the door and began to take in as many deep breaths as I could before I hyperventilated. Bending over at the waist, I placed my head into my hands and rested them on my knees. *Were we really doing this? Fuck, I can't turn back now.*

When I finally caught my breath and stood straight, my confidence soared. I began marching towards the shelves on the other side of the room with more force than I knew what to do with. The shelves were stacked with forgotten items from the early days of our marriage. On the very bottom shelf, tucked away behind our wedding album and a box of my childhood mementos, sat a black lock box. I pulled it out, wiping the top with my hand to reveal a keypad below the years of dust. I keyed in the date Henry and I met and unlocked the box. Once open, the smell of metal filled the air. I lifted the black velvet cloth that adorned the contents of the box. Inside sat a handgun that I had not seen in years. I took the magazine out of the base of the gun to reveal a full clip before snapping it back into place, shutting the box, and putting it back on the shelf. With the weapon in my hand, I headed towards the room, grabbing a large, fluffy comforter from the shelf closest to the door. I unlocked the room, walking back in with the gun tucked under the comforter so my left hand was free to lock the door again.

"I hated when you bought this gun all those years ago," I told him as I began to walk closer to him, waving the gun in my hand. "You said it was for my protection when you went away on business trips." Taking a seat beside his head, I moved a strand of his dark brown hair off his forehead.

The day he brought that gun home is still ingrained in my brain. He came waltzing into the front door, swinging the gun around his pointer finger as if he were in a Western about to fight someone in a saloon. Henry shouted at the top of his lungs to get me to come and look at the gun up close. Instead of gaining my attention, he got Lilly's, who began violently screaming at the sight of it. It took an hour of rocking my sweet seven-year-old child while she ate too many croissants slathered in cinnamon butter to calm her down, explaining over and over again that Daddy would never hurt her with the gun he brought home. That was also the moment I realized that our nanny was allowing our children to watch movies that were not age-appropriate. Once she was taken care of and wrapped in her bed with one more croissant for safekeeping, I asked Henry for an explanation. That was when he told me it was for my protection while he was on business trips. Which, at that point, had only been once a year. The number of business trips steadily increased over the years.

"Little did you or I know that the only time I would ever shoot this gun was to protect myself like you wanted, but from the real threat to my life. *You.* You have said enough for today and the rest of your life." One more strand of hair had fallen into his vision. I rubbed the tip of the gun across his forehead, moving the hair as well as increasing his heart rate. I watched as his eyes followed the delicate procedure above them. "I would love to tell you that you were a wonderful husband. That I feel horrible for doing this to you, or that we could try again. Alas, that would all be lies, and you know it. The truth is, you were a horrible man from the day I said, 'I do.' Something in that psychotic brain of yours activated that day. You had secured your bride and would soon have heirs to live on your legacy. I was trapped in newlywed bliss, and I ignored all the problems and focused on building our lives together." I paused for a moment to readjust myself and decided to unbutton his shirt.

As each button came loose, I could see the fresh bruises on his chest. Each one a mark, revealing the path it took to get him into this room. After the fall down our main staircase, he was out cold, his dead weight difficult for me to move. I grabbed a golf club from his office, whacking him on his head to ensure he stayed knocked out. Then I managed to get him rolled onto a blanket and dragged him throughout the house to the cellar stairs, where his body took another tumble, head over heels, down the stairs. From there, I grabbed the rope and a pair of shears from the shelf around the corner, tossing them onto his chest with more force than was needed. I dragged him into the room and tied his arms and legs to sturdy items in each corner of the back room. In a corner sat the golf club.

"What did you do to him, Emma?" Gwen asked as she examined the damage to his chest.

"This all happened to him by *his* own doing. I had nothing to do with it. If he were a better husband, he would never have these injuries. Like I said, his own doing," I scoffed. "Now, as you know, Henry, tonight is my book club and I have many women upstairs waiting for me to bring more bottles of wine; so, you must excuse my hurry. If I take too much longer, one of them will get brave enough to come down here and grab a few bottles themselves. Although highly unlikely, they are much too high and polite to do that. You've met some of them before, darling. I'm sure you would agree." I told him before getting to my feet and walking over to stand beside Gwen.

"You're going to do it, aren't you?" Gwen whispered into my ear.

You could see the excitement slowly leaving her mind, her body stiffening, awaiting my answer. I turned to her, my mind fully committed, and nodded my head.

"Then together it is, I have always told you I would be there for you through everything. And if that includes murdering your husband, count me in." She said as her shoulders relaxed.

I reached down to grab the comforter from the floor and drag it towards my husband, where I stood over him with one foot on either side. I wrapped the comforter around the gun in my left hand.

"I do not believe this is fully necessary to conceal the sound. This room is rather soundproof, and the ladies upstairs are too wrapped up in themselves to notice the sound as something other than a pan dropping in the kitchen. Nonetheless, it will help muffle any sound that does come out and at least protect Gwen and my ears." I laughed as I finished wrapping it around my arm to hold it in place, "I'll make this quick, my dear."

Gwen approached me to stand on my right, ready to help however she could. I looked down at Henry to see his bright blue eyes wide open, lost in the fear of his impending death. At that moment, I could sense his life playing back within his mind as if in a movie. However, it was unclear if the life that flashed before his eyes was filled with the joyful moments he spent with our children or the countless hours he spent working that filled almost every waking moment of his life. The anger that filled me at that very moment was like nothing I had ever felt. I could feel Gwen staring at me now, waiting for the exact moment I would do it.

"Wait, don't do this!" Henry's voice quivered.

I placed my pointer finger over his mouth, "It's already a done deal." I whispered.

"Even if you kill me, you will never be rid of me, not truly." He fought back.

Waiting any longer was not a choice I had. It was time. I straightened my arm out in front of me, using my right hand to stabilize the newfound weight of my left arm. I closed my eyes for a split second before bending over and placing the muzzle on his forehead.

"Goodbye, my love, if only you weren't such a horrid, abusive husband, it would have never ended this way," I said before taking a deep breath and pulling firmly on the trigger.

"Wait, no!" He shouted.

Henry's eyes bulged even wider than I thought possible. His chest, which just moments before rose and fell with exceeding speed, became flat and motionless. All signs of life had dissipated as his eyes turned milky and unresponsive. Although all the signs that the shot killed him were there, I couldn't trust it. The thought of him taking another breath and coming back to kill me was stronger than I would like to admit.

"One more for good measure?" I asked Gwen, pleading with my eyes to gain the unnecessary acceptance to move forward.

"If that is what you need, then I think it is necessary. You can never be too sure." Gwen said, grabbing and squeezing my shoulder.

With that, I positioned the muzzle of the gun to sit above his heart, took a deep breath, and fired twice. The gun clicked empty on the second shot. As the sound of the weapon softened around us, I began laughing. My voice billowed throughout the room, echoing off the walls. My laugh faltered as I made eye contact with Gwen before I fell to my knees and began to hyperventilate. Gwen grabbed my arm, unwrapped the comforter, and grabbed the gun. She placed the gun by the door and shook out the comforter, covering my husband's body. She sank to the floor with me, embracing my body within hers as I began to catch my breath that I had not realized I was holding.

Gwen helped me to my feet and led me out of the room, turning the light off and grabbing the gun on our way out. She reached into my shirt, grabbed the key to the room, and locked it just in case, then helped me lock the gun back in its case. Before we rejoined the party, we stopped in the wine cellar and poured ourselves a glass of one of my favorite Bordeaux wine in silence. I chugged the first glass, barely tasting a thing before filling the glass again. My heart began to level itself halfway through the next glass of wine. Gwen never took her eyes off me, worried about what I would do next. As my heart rate leveled, I began to sweat, my mind catching up with my body.

"He can never do anything to me again, can he?" I asked Gwen before pulling my legs up to my chest.

She came to sit beside me, placing her glass on the coffee table and wrapping her arms around me. "He's gone. He will never be back. He will never hurt you or the children ever again." She whispered.

We stayed there for a few minutes before my breathing returned to normal. I wiped my tears and got to my feet and grabbed two bottles of wine from the shelf where I kept my lesser wines before heading out of the room.

"Just grab two bottles from the shelves on the right. I do not want high-quality wine wasted on already wasted women," I told Gwen.

"**Have** a great night. Tell the kids I said hello!" I told each woman as they stumbled out of the house, most with heels in their hands instead of on their feet. Staggering toward their husbands, who were waiting to place their extremely unsteady, blurry-eyed wives in their cars.

As I turned away from the door, Gwen stood swaying in her spot, a smile plastered on her face.

"Not now," I muttered as I walked past her into the kitchen. I could hear her bare feet following behind me, the soles slapping the tile as she walked.

I blindly turned on the oven as I walked past, barely stopping to ensure I had the correct temperature. Then, I went into our butler's pantry and grabbed a pizza out of the freezer.

"How could you possibly be hungry at this moment?" Gwen asked, her voice sounding rushed.

"I did not eat during the book club; I was too nervous." I paused. "And now, I couldn't care less about the perfect hors d'oeuvres that I had made for today. What I want is a nice greasy pizza and a glass of gin. Once I have fully finished those, then we will talk," I told her before walking to the bar and grabbing a heavy pour of gin.

Alcohol right now was the only thing keeping my mind from screaming out of my body. It soothed me, numbing my nerves just enough to keep me from having a panic attack. I finished the glass in one swallow, coating every taste bud and cleansing me as it went down. Without a moment to consider, I poured another glass, took a small sip, and headed back to the kitchen.

We didn't speak to each other while waiting for the pizza to cook. Gwen sat there silently, drinking straight from a bottle of wine, watching me as I slowly and quietly stuffed my face. I took my time, spending at least a solid thirty minutes only gazing at my plate or the spiraling bottom of my glass. There was only a sip left of gin; I was just too exhausted to get up and pour myself any more. Honestly, my liver probably thanked my body for forcing me not to have any more.

Time is a fickle thing. One minute, I'm worried about my children and how much nutrition they are getting or if good influences are surrounding them. Next, I'm pushing my husband down a flight of stairs and murdering him with my best friend. You never think this is how your life will turn out, but here I am, sitting in my kitchen, frozen. I have a body in my basement that I have to get rid of somehow without causing any notice from the neighbors, and a best friend who will not stop looking at me, waiting for my response. You wouldn't think this was her first time killing someone, the way her eyes lit up with enthusiasm.

I finished my food and questioned if I should make more just to prolong what we had to do. Knowing there were still untouched desserts from the book club, I stood up from my seat and headed back to the bar. These women never ate anything sweet so they could watch their figures, but your party would be the talk of the town the next day if you failed to have desserts.

Fuck my liver. I thought as the sweet nectar of the gin gods flowed into the glass in my hands. I refreshed my glass and walked to the living room. Gwen followed close behind, a little too close for comfort, like a predator stalking her prey. I often did not indulge in desserts, like many women my age, because they go straight to my hips. *But to hell with my hips today!* I birthed two children out of these hips, and if someone wants to talk about me putting on a few pounds, they might as well end up where my husband is.

Circling the dessert table, contemplating if I should get a plate or not, I started at the first tray, no plate in sight. I grabbed each dessert one by one, and slowly ate till I couldn't eat any more. Then ate a few more macarons. At first, Gwen stood there, shocked by my actions. Eventually, as she always did, she fell into line and indulged right with me.

"I haven't done this since my honeymoon!" She gleefully cheered, chocolate from the brownie smeared across her lips.

She kept pace shockingly well. We started with the brownies, then moved on to the madeleines, followed by the cupcakes, the tiramisu, and finally the macarons. Come morning, we might regret eating all of this, but for now, there was no regret. Murdering your husband really made you hungry.

"God, I'm starving," I chuckled as I remembered a strange and fond memory of childhood. "You know, I went on a field trip once in high school to watch open-heart surgery. We had to wake up extremely early to be there for an eight am operating room call. I had a scant breakfast that my parents handed me before heading to school and hopping on the bus for the two-hour ride to the hospital. At first, most of the girls were squeamish and freaked out, watching the scalpel cut through the skin as smoothly as it did. I was one of those girls at first, but soon became as fascinated as the boys were. At the same time, some boys became as squeamish as the girls. The girls and some of the squeamish boys hovered over the dome, where you had a bird's-eye view of the surgery, while the boys and a few girls watched the monitors and would peek over the dome every so often."

"Get to the point already, Emma," Gwen said, squirming from the story and the amount of sugar pumping through her veins.

"Okay, okay. At the end of the surgery, it was just after noon, and everyone was starving. You never would have known how seeing a body opened up like that would make you feel. My entire class was starving. We got Mexican food for lunch and then went to the ice cream place next door for dessert. However, we quickly learned that those two do not mix well with any lactose-intolerant folks in my class. It was an uncomfortable two-hour ride back to the school for many of us." I finished the story and found a spot on the couch.

"Interesting, I had the opposite effect. I haven't wanted any food all afternoon until right now. Seeing you devour the treats, let me open up and do it, too." She said, falling onto the couch behind her and licking chocolate off her fork.

We sat there for a bit, catching our breath and gaining the energy to walk downstairs and deal with my husband's corpse. When we finally decided to make our way to the basement, we took our time getting down the stairs. We were laughing and stumbling the whole way to the last door of our home. Between laughs, the sound of the door lock clicking open could be heard. Opening the door and seeing the cloth that draped over my husband sobered the two of us right up. I straightened my back, lifted my chin, and began to walk towards his body.

"Any ideas?" I asked Gwen, hoping that in the time that I spent stuffing my face, she had thought of something.

"Only one, and I am not too sure how well it will work. I have only heard of this happening in a true crime show, and that woman got caught, but it wasn't because of how she disposed of the body." She stated as she shuffled into the room.

She told me her plan, not certain if the booze was leading to my willingness to try it or the lack of any other ideas, but I agreed to it. We left the room, locking the door behind us, and drove to Gwen's house.

"We need to use mine in case your house gets searched. My husband won't notice these are gone, since he never uses them." She loaded up a bag of every tool she could think of and threw it in the back of my car.

If we had been pulled over on the short drive to and from her house, we would have probably been arrested just for the fact that we reeked of alcohol. The tools would have made the police scratch their heads, but we could easily say there was a good deal, and we got them for our husbands. Nothing bad ever happened to anyone in this boring town, and it wasn't going to start now, according to the cops.

When we got back home, Gwen lugged the bag to the basement, spreading the assortment out on the floor. There were drills, saws, hammers, nails, metal shears, and so many more tools we had no idea how to use. We pulled containers from my storage room down, consolidating what we had that would be useful. Gwen grabbed two tarps from a container and threw them in the room. I grabbed the twine, rope, and trash bags and placed them in the corner of the room for when we were done with what we needed to do.

"We just need one more thing," I said, and ran upstairs to grab my laptop to display our front door camera while we worked. This was not a time to be surprised by anyone, and we clearly wouldn't be appropriately dressed for a visitor. I placed this on a stool in the corner of the room and locked the door behind us.

Gwen rolled out the tarps, overlapping them as they were too big for the room. Shoving my hands under his back and shoulders, I helped lift and roll Henry onto the tarps to make our cleanup easier. Blood, sweat, wrinkles, and all. Then I removed his shirt and his pants, shoving them into a trash bag.

"You do the honors, it's your husband after all," Gwen said, gesturing towards the layout of tools on the floor.

My heart pounded in my chest as I took in the scene before me. Gwen's plan seemed insane, but just the right amount. I have had zero practice with any of the gadgets in front of me. Closing my eyes, I grabbed the electric chain-saw and plugged it into the plug behind Henry. "Here goes nothing," I said before putting my goggles on and straightening out my elbow-length gloves that I used for the dishes.

In that moment, I realized this would be the last time I would ever see my husband naked, and it filled me with joy. Not for the reason most wives get when they see their husband naked, lying there for them. *Should I even still call him my husband?* For me, it was the last time I would ever have to see the nude body of the man who constantly held me down against my will. The man who would have his way with me, because after all, he was my husband. He believed it was owed to him the second I became his wife.

Turning on the saw, the room filled to the brim with noise, and Gwen and I were unable to speak to one another. She gave me two thumbs up and took a deep breath. I followed suit, taking a deep breath before making my first incision on Henry's leg. I moved the saw closer and closer to his body until I hit flesh, unsure how it would cut through. I braced for traction. To my surprise, it went through, not as easily as a hot knife through butter, but closer to a frozen knife through a frozen stick of butter. Catching pieces of bone here and there, causing the saw to bounce back. Blood began to exit his body as the saw went through, and before I knew it, my shoes were sitting in blood, and his leg was no longer attached to his body.

I turned the saw off and looked at my shoes, shrugged, and told Gwen that she might want to cover her shoes if she didn't want to be swimming in the bodily fluids of my ex-husband. It was too late for me; the blood was beginning to soak through my shoes and into my socks. I could feel it squishing between my toes. *These would need to be burned when we were done.*

Feeling a sense of accomplishment, I took another deep breath and took the other leg off while Gwen wrapped trash bags around her feet and tied them up with the twine. "Your turn." This simple phrase sounded more like tagging in your buddy for their turn at a chance to win a prize at the claw machine. Not something you say with glee as you hand off a saw to your best friend to dismember your late husband.

"Arms next?" she asked, even though she didn't need to. She could do whatever damage she wanted to do to him, and I wouldn't bat an eye.

For a woman who has never held a saw or any tool before, she handled this like a pro. She was leveraging her body in the best way possible to ensure she wouldn't hurt your back in the process. She cut his left arm off first and began to cut his wrists next. Watching as she struggled to get the hand detached, I could see she was starting to tinker with needing to cut smaller body parts off first. His hand flopped about on the tarp till finally it separated from the forearm. From there, she cut each finger at its knuckles, leaving little chunks of fingers scattered across the tarp, and continued to the right arm to do the same, but in a better order this time.

When she finished, I wondered what to do next when a sudden bout of rage entered me. I grabbed the hammer and three nails, took the first two, and placed them in his eyes, thankful I had goggles. His eyes squished under the weight of the nails, almost deflating in his sockets, spraying my face. Before moving on to my last nail, I took the sleeve of my coat and wiped off the goo that came out of his eyes.

"Ha! Are you really going to do that?" Gwen asked when she saw what I was doing.

I had grabbed his penis in my hand, "looking mighty small there, sir," I joked before placing the nail at the tip, almost screwing it in so it would stay, before I got the hammer there. The nail would only go so far before it got stuck, but at least I knew he wouldn't be able to use it to torture any other woman where he was. "Toss me two more," I exclaimed.

"Let me help with this if you are about to do what I think you are," Gwen said, kneeling beside me.

She held a nail above his left testicle as I hammered it to his penis, just missing the other nail. I handed her the hammer and shrugged to indicate that she should do the other testicle. She nailed the right to his inner thigh, making a ringing sound as it hit a bone deep within.

"You don't get to do that too often." She said, giggling like a schoolgirl.

"No, you don't, that should be our one and only time to do it. So do not go doing it to your husband." I laughed right along with her.

"Yeah, yeah, yeah," she said, waving her hand at me to say it had never crossed her mind, although I am sure it had.

Gwen was married to a wonderful man, who looked and acted nothing like Henry. He is what I would want in my next husband if I choose to marry again. Vince was kind and sweet, the most considerate and generous man you have ever met. If Prince Charming were real, a picture of him would appear with every Google search. Gwen lucked out in the husband department. They met when they were both very young. They would tease one another on the playground in elementary school, and they started dating the summer after high school. Their mothers always said they tried to convince their children to just start dating because they could see the perfect match the two of them were from infancy, but Gwen and Vince insisted that they wanted to wait till after high school. As Gwen put it, she did not want to marry her first boyfriend; *it wasn't fair to herself.* So she dated around a bit in high school. Vince, however, did not. He waited till the day after graduation to ask Gwen out for his very first date. Ever since then, they have been inseparable and entirely in love.

We quickly finished dismembering the rest of the body, taking the toes and fingers off one by one, cutting up each limb ten different times to spread the body out, and chopping his torso with the wire shears. What we had not planned for, *then again, none of this was planned,* was the head. Gwen and I sat on the floor, dumbfounded about how to make the head completely unidentifiable. While we racked our brains, we each took a set of fingertips and began burning them to remove any part of his fingerprint on the off chance he was ever found.

Finally, we decided just to wing it. We grabbed a roll of duct tape and began wrapping his head as tightly as we could. Leaving not even a centimeter of his skin visible. With the chainsaw, we cut up from his neck, splitting his head in half, then adding another layer of duct tape to each hemisphere. When we were finally satisfied with the husband's haul in front of us, we began to split his body pieces between twenty different trash bags. Doused the tarps with bleach, threw them in their own bags, and started cleaning the room. We filled spray bottles with bleach and any cleaning products we could find and scrubbed the ceiling, walls, and floor twice. When we were done, the room smelled like bleach and looked exactly as it had before I trapped my then-husband in there. Barren and empty.

Hauling the bags up the basement stairs, through the garage, and into the back of my car was a workout. Gwen and I had both worked up a sweat and needed to clean the blood off ourselves. Gwen went to our guest room to shower while I headed towards my bathroom. I clutched the shower handle, turning on the hot water as high as possible. My reflection stared back at me as I stood before the glass door, undressing and waiting for the water to warm, sending shivers down my spine. The glass began to fog, taking away with it the blood-smeared woman before me. Stepping into the shower, the water started to tap my skin. *Tap, tap, tap.* Until all at once, a waterfall fell over me. I watched as the blood began to trickle down my arms, my stomach, and finally my legs, where the water pooled around my feet. So much blood was leaving my skin that I could not see where the line between blood and water began.

Standing in the steamy shower, I began to relax, *finally*. Taking deep breaths as I lathered my body with soap, I began to replay the day's events. The day felt like a week-long, between sneaking coffee in my backyard, murdering my husband, hosting a book club, and dismembering his body with my best friend.

My heart slowed. My head pounded. My eyes began to

blur.

I fell to my knees, water splashing all around me. *What am I doing?* I thought as the water continued to run down my face. My thoughts were like bullets running into your mind, impossible to stop. Before I knew it, I was crying. The tears ran down my face just as fast as the shower did, indiscernible from one another.

"Emma," Gwen shouted from the opposite side of my bedroom door. "Are you doing okay in there? We should get going soon." She continued.

"Yeah…" I murmured, "Almost done. Meet you downstairs!" I shouted back.

Slowly, I got to my feet, stumbling a few times but making it. I continued to wash my body and hair as quickly as I could, dried my body off, and got dressed. My clothes rubbed against my body, aching with every bit of movement. I had scrubbed my body raw, trying to take any trace of his blood off, but most importantly, trying to clean what I had just done from my body and mind.

"Oh, good, you are ready," Gwen said as I entered the kitchen. "Any chance our plans involve food? I'm starving." She laughed, remembering our prior conversation about bodies and hunger.

"Coffee first," I said, making my way to the coffee machine to make a pot of coffee and getting two to-go travel mugs ready.

"We are almost there," I told Gwen before backing out of the garage. All the while, thinking, *what have I done?*

Outside the house, it was pitch black; the sun was not due to rise for another two hours. The neighborhood was silent, no cars, no birds…nothing. Nothing but the two murderers driving down the street in their electric vehicle, hauling body parts.

Our plan was simple: get rid of the bags.

As it was trash day, we dropped a few bags in trash cans throughout the neighborhood, hoping that no cameras would catch us as we went about it. Our first stop was to drop off some of the party's trash to place in the recycling bins outside of the 24-hour diner, since we knew there would be cameras there. The lot was dimly lit when we pulled up, and few cars were there. I pulled up alongside the recycling bin, tossing a bag from the backseat into the bin before walking inside.

"Morning, Ladies," A young man in a trucker hat welcomed us as we sat by the window in a booth. "Care for some coffee?" he asked.

"Please," Gwen responded as she opened her menu.

We sat there silently as we perused the menu, placed our orders, and took our first sips of coffee. Outside the window, semi-trucks drove by one by one as they started their mornings. Our food arrived before we knew it, and the young man had topped off our coffees as well. I got the first bite of waffles in my mouth when Gwen's phone rang, making me jump in my seat.

"It's Vince," Gwen said before answering her phone. "Good morning, Honey." I could hear Vince's voice on the other end, but could not determine what he was saying. "I'm fine. I'm getting breakfast with Emma now. We have some errands to run, making it a girls' day."

She continued talking to him, but I had stopped listening. My mind drifted to my children and how they might take this news. I know I did not thoroughly think about the possibility of any consequences. That was clear as day, the only thing that I wanted from this was my husband out of my life. The abuse, both physical and mental, wore me down, but at the same time made me stronger. Made my willpower stronger. I will be just fine, my kids, and Gwen will be okay. We will get away with this.

What if we don't?

My vision began to blur as I stared aimlessly into my plate, watching as the syrup filled the different sections of my waffle. A hand lightly placed itself on my arm, looking up, it was Gwen. She had a slight smile on her face.

"We'll get through this," She whispered.

"How?" I cried.

"I don't know. We will take it day by day, though, you are not alone in this, Emma!" She squeezed my arm even harder. "If we need to, we can always tell Vince. He's a lawyer, and he could help us."

"We cannot go that route; your husband shouldn't know anything about this. The fewer people that know, the better." I told her, taking my arm back from her grasp.

That was the end of the conversation between the two of us while we ate. We were both physically exhausted and needed to keep our energy if we were to get rid of all of the bags in one day. The young man came to clear our plates when we had finished them and asked if we needed any coffee to go. While we waited for our coffees and the bill, the sun began to rise outside our window. I took a moment to breathe fully into my chest and pray, for the first time in over a decade, to survive this.

We managed to drop the bags off in trash cans across three towns and over four bridges that had deep, roaring rivers below, which carried them off to the ocean. As each bag was dropped, my heart raced, my hands shook, and I could not believe the position I was in.

The final bag was dropped off that evening on our way to the movies. We had both agreed we needed a few hours where our brains were forced to think about anything other than what we had just done. Pulling up to the theater, we bought two tickets to whichever movie was to start next, two large sodas, a package of Twizzlers, a large popcorn, a pizza, and some Milk Duds. For the next two and a half hours, we were at peace, we ate every last bit of our food, and even found ourselves laughing at the appropriate times in the movie. It was just what we needed after such a long two days.

I dropped Gwen off at her home, telling her to get a good night's sleep before driving home. I texted our maids that we used after parties and asked if they could come the next day, and then I passed out for the next fourteen hours. I only woke up when I heard the doorbell ring, letting me know the cleaners had arrived.

Chapter Three

"No, ma'am, we haven't heard from him in weeks. He never showed up for the conference." My late husband's secretary told me over the phone. "If you hear from him, make sure he knows he has gotten a lot of phone calls here recently. I have a stack of messages to give to him."

It's been two weeks since Henry was supposed to leave for his business trip. I would not have done my wifely duty if I hadn't checked in with his office. Someone would have called me eventually, and I'm sure of it. A man like him at his job doesn't go unnoticed, according to my husband, although I barely know what he did. I'm honestly shocked they did not reach out sooner. It makes me wonder how often he doesn't show up for the business trips he is supposedly on. But that is in the past, and I need to focus on the future. My children were still away at their camps, and when they arrived home, they were going to start asking where their dad was. I had to beat them to it, give them rock-solid evidence that I had started the search for their dad. Just because I hated my ex-husband doesn't mean I can't be a stellar mother and pretend to help look for their dad.

"This is Officer Brady. Thank you for calling the Gloomridge Police Department. How can I help you?" He asked, half paying attention to the call. I could hear music from a video game in the background.

"Um…hi, I'm not sure if this is the right way for me to call this in or if I should have come in person. Maybe there is a different number I should be calling," I began, intentionally stumbling over my words.

"Whatever it is, I can get you to the right person." Officer Brady interjected.

"Okay, well, you see, my husband left two weeks ago on a business trip and he hasn't come home yet. He should have been home by now. I called his office, and they said he never showed up for the conference, which is very unusual for him." I laid everything out in my best concerned wife's voice.

"Oh, a missing person's report, eh?" He asked, sounding more Canadian than any fellow I have heard in Virginia. "Well, you will need to come in to file that report, ma'am. I'll give the detective a call and let him know you will be coming in today. What time were you thinking?"

"I can come now, I only live seven minutes away. Let me grab my shoes and my purse, and I will be there soon." I said before hanging up the phone.

— ✧ —

"Can we get you anything to drink?" Officer Brady asked as he sat me down behind a desk.

"A coffee would be lovely, thank you," I told him, making a show of wiping a tear from my eye.

He left me alone in a cramped room with only a desk, four metal chairs, a lamp in the corner, and, randomly, a large stack of napkins.

When Officer Brady came back, he had three coffees in a carrier from the coffee shop next door, a brown paper bag, and a man trailing behind him. The man looked to be in his late sixties and ready to retire. His hair was silver in the light, so thick you couldn't see his scalp. He wore a navy-blue suit, a white button-up shirt, and a black tie that appeared to have a deer on it as he unbuttoned his jacket and sat down. The detective looked more like a man who belonged in a tree stand hunting, the very animal on his tie, than in a suit, asking questions about my husband. Officer Brady placed a coffee down in front of each of us, along with another stack of napkins and a piece of coffee cake folded within another napkin. I can tell Officer Brady is the reason for all the napkins before me.

"Thought you could use this, ma'am. Their coffee cake always makes my day feel even slightly better if not completely." He told me as he took a bite out of his coffee cake and took a seat.

"I'm Detective Albert," the man said, then looked at Officer Brady as the young pup who couldn't sit still as he paced back and forth behind me. "Officer Brady tells me you need to file a missing person's report on your husband? Care to tell me the last time you saw him?" he asked.

"The last time I saw him, he was heading to the airport. He left on the morning of August 15th. He travels a lot for work, so I waved him goodbye as he drove away, as I always did." I told him, trying to keep my story short in case there were holes in it.

"Where was he headed?" Detective Albert asked.

"I'm not sure, as I said, he travels a lot for work, so I stopped asking where he was supposed to go." I picked up my fork and began playing with the coffee cake.

"Okay, and how long was he supposed to be gone?" He, on the other hand, hadn't touched his coffee once.

"Two weeks, he was supposed to be home two days ago," I told him, taking a small sip of my coffee.

"Hmm, and when was the last time you talked to your husband?" Detective Albert had not dropped his eye contact, but once to write a quick note.

"The day he left, we usually don't talk when he is gone. I have a job, a house to run, and children to take care of, so I do not often get a chance to call him on his trips." I said, finally taking a bite of the coffee cake.

Detective Albert looked shocked at this information. I took a moment to look at his left hand, which was now resting around his coffee cup, and saw a wedding ring. He must actually love his wife if this is his reaction. They probably talk every day about everything from big life decisions to letting her know he was going to clip his fingernails. That is the marriage I have always wanted, one that is happy and full of love. One that if you were to hear that someone went two weeks without talking to their wife, you would look appalled and suggest marriage counseling, which I would think, if Detective Brady were not present, he would be sliding me a business card for one. Not that he and his wife ever needed one, their perfect remember, they go to counseling to have a third person to bring into their discussions. An outsider's point of view, one that can be unbiased and help break any ties that they have.

"Alright, before you go, I will need you to give me a few more details." He said, pointing to a list he had in front of him.

I answered all of his questions. I gave him all of the information he wanted to know, that is, the information I knew off the top of my head. I did not know his license plate number, but Detective Albert could easily find it if he looked hard enough. He is an intelligent man. Back in his prime, he was most likely one of the leading investigators. Now, he gets put on missing persons cases for a small town. If someone goes missing in this town, they have usually run away on their own accord.

"You were right about the coffee cake; it was really delicious! Thank you for getting that!" I said, patting Officer

Brady's shoulder as he walked me out of the police department.

I spent that evening prepping for the return of my children from their camps. I washed their sheets, vacuumed their rooms, bought the snacks they love, and baked some cookies to hand them when I picked them up. All of this was done to keep my mind off the investigation into the missing person's report. My children would never have noticed if I had tidied up their room or not. To them, the dirtier the better. Socks and underwear are thrown about, toys spaced out like bombs waiting for your bare feet, stuffed animals overcrowding their beds, and water glasses and bottles half-drunk on every surface. Children keep their rooms in what they refer to as organized chaos. To them, the socks closest to their bed are the cleanest, and the further you get away, the smellier.

I love my children with every fiber of my body. I wish they would learn to clean their rooms, especially before they disappear for weeks on end to camp. If I didn't pick it up, no one would, and something would end up molding under their beds. The cleaners requested not to clean their rooms many times, so this chore became my job.

When their rooms were cleaned to my liking and most importantly, my mind was clear, it was time for dinner. I was exhausted and had worked up quite an appetite, so I picked up two different orders of pasta and garlic bread from my favorite Italian restaurant in our town and headed back home. I did not get to indulge in my favorites as often as I would have liked. My husband saw it as being gluttonous.

Slamming the door behind me, I entered my foyer. Placing my bag on the hook and my shoes in the closet. I skipped down my basement stairs to grab a bottle of wine before unboxing my food and relaxing for the night with a movie. A shiver ran across my body as I opened the bottle.

Within five minutes of being home, the doorbell rang. Taking the first deep sip of my wine, I had just poured. I took a deep breath and went to open the door.

"Evening, ma'am. If you could come with me to the station, I have a few more questions for you." Detective Albert stood on the other side of the door, a sly grin on his face, while he took his hat off.

"I just got home with dinner; do you mind if I finish it first? Or you could come inside, and you can ask me your questions while I eat?" I offered up this suggestion, motioning for him to come inside.

There can't be anything he is going to tell me that I don't already know. I would much rather have this conversation from the comfort of my own home. Where I can sip my wine, eat my dinner, and kick him out whenever I need to. I was starving and could barely stand on my own two feet, let alone answer questions from the detective for the second time today.

"The station would be more ideal, ma'am. I can drive you there myself, or you can follow me." He said, motioning for me to follow him to the car.

I could tell there was no way around leaving right now for the station with the Detective. I told him to give me a moment to grab my purse and shoes and headed back into the kitchen, leaving him on my front porch. I offered for him to come inside while I gathered my stuff, but he strongly suggested otherwise. Wrapping my garlic bread in a paper towel, I placed it in my purse to eat at the station. I finished my glass of wine and poured another half glass while I took a few large bites of my pasta. Detective Albert grew impatient and began knocking on the front door again to tell me to hurry up.

"I'm almost ready," I shouted towards the foyer, then closed my pasta containers, placed them in the fridge, and finished my glass of wine. "I told you I had just started eating dinner. I am starving, so a few bites of food before we head out is not going to hurt anyone." Locking the door, I began walking to his car and waited for him to open his passenger door.

Not a single word passed between our lips on the way to the police department. The car was all but silent, aside from the country music playing low through the car's stereo system and the sound of the road beneath us. We pulled in front of the police station; Detective Albert all but jumped out of the car before he put the car in park and turned it off.

I watched him stride into the station in front of me, nodding to each police officer in there as if he had just arrested the FBI's most wanted. I half expected him to start giving out high-fives and kissing babies. Instead, he led me into the room we had been in previously, not asking if I wanted any coffee. Officer Brady stood in the corner of the room, quiet.

"Now, Mrs. Thompson, I have spent a great deal of the day trying to track down her husband's whereabouts. He is not an easy man to find." He stated, a smug smile lining his face.

"So, you found him?" I asked excitedly, feigning the happy wife persona.

"No, if you would let me finish, I can explain what I have found." He said, flipping open his laptop.

I watched as he put his password in "bestdetectiveintheworld1". *Ha! Let's see about that.* People always have the easiest passwords to guess. You would think a detective would know to secure his devices better than that.

"I called your husband's work, and they let me know that he never made it to his conference." As if I hadn't already told him this earlier today, I nodded as though it was the first time I had heard it. "He also never made it onto his plane; he checked in for the flight the day before but never made it onto the plane. You would think a man who was trying to run away would never have bothered to check into his flight. Or at the very least, taken the flight and disappeared in a new state. But that is not what happened here."

He opened the folder on the table, pulled out his flight information, and placed it in front of me. "Since I know you said that your husband did not share any of this information with you, I figured I would give it to you."

"That is very kind," I said, flipping through the documents he laid out in front of me, actually reading what was on them, as I had never known where he was going. Indianapolis apparently.

"Now, this is where the story takes a wild turn," Detective Albert gleefully said and opened a file on his computer. He must not have a lot of cases to be this excited about a missing person's case. I watched as he opened a series of photos. "If you look here, you can see I have followed your husband as he drove from your house, through the town, onto the highway, and all the way to the airport."

Knowing we were going to be looking at a lot of photos here, I reached down into my purse, without breaking eye contact, and pulled out a piece of garlic bread.

"As you might have noticed…" he paused, staring at me as I took a bite. "Where? How? Where did you get that?" he asked.

"Did you forget you interrupted my dinner?" I responded with a bit more sass than was needed, taking another large bite out of the bread.

"Right, okay." He shook his head, trying to remember where he left off. "As I was saying, as you might have noticed, none of the photos we were able to get showed a clear image of your husband driving the vehicle."

The photos before me show Henry's car zooming through the streets, sunglasses on, the sun visor down, what looks to be a newspaper or one of his client folders in his gloved hand, while the other is holding the top of the steering wheel. There was no way to positively identify who was driving the vehicle.

"Does he often drive like this?" He gestured towards the paper.

"He is always driving distracted. While working on one thing or another, he is always on his phone. I'm surprised he hasn't been pulled over yet for it." I laughed, my shoulders shaking, remembering every time I told him to focus on the road, and eventually gave up and let him risk his life if he chose to do that

"He must have been lucky enough to avoid us then. We followed him to the parking garage at the airport. It took us a few hours of searching through the garage to find his vehicle, but we finally found it. When we got his car open, we were shocked. His suitcase, jacket, papers…everything was still in there except for the gloves he was wearing. He left it all in his car and disappeared. Out of sight of every camera at the airport. Any idea why he would do this?" He asked me, closing the folder and folding his hands on top.

I took a moment to finish chewing the piece of bread in my mouth, slowly, to determine what to say next. There are a few different routes I could take; I could play the sympathetic wife and start crying. I could become defensive; however, they would suspect me if I did that. Then, I could take on the curious route and see if there was anything I could do to help them find my "husband". Suppose the detective were to ask around and find out that my husband and I fought now and then, he might see the full sympathetic wife act as a ploy. It's best to stay away from that.

"I am not sure, detective; my husband was a very secretive man," I say, deciding to take a combined approach of the sympathetic wife, but also a wife who is clueless and unaware of what her husband does on a day-to-day basis behind the scenes. Which was not at all a lie, I had no idea what my husband did at his job.

"What was your husband's demeanor like that morning that he disappeared?" Detective Albert asked.

"He seemed his normal cranky self. He was always leaving on business trips and always seemed rather excited or indifferent towards them. That day, he seemed a mixture of both." I said, knowing it was the truth. He was very excited about the trip and distraught with me.

"And how was his and your relationship? Did you guys fight often? Did you guys never fight?" he asked, pen in hand, ready to write down whatever I said.

"I won't lie to you, detective. My husband and I had rough days every now and then, and I would say we fought as much as your average couple. He had his life, and I had mine. The main thing bringing those two lives together was our children and our community. "

"Did the two of you spend a lot of time together?" he asked.

"Not recently, no, as he was on a business trip almost every day this summer," I said. "We would try to fit in date nights every so often, you know, try to keep the spark alive and all." I chuckled.

I could tell from his raised eyebrows that Detective Albert was slowly trying to pin me for this disappearance. However, he has nothing to go on other than an abandoned car and a suitcase. But it's always the spouse, right?

"Are we going to be here much longer? It is getting late, and my children will be coming home tomorrow. I need to prepare for them." I asked, trying to rush this questioning.

"Yes, we can be done for now. But if I have any other questions, I will not hesitate to come and ask," he said, shuffling his papers together and back into his folder.

I rose to my feet, taking the last bite of my garlic bread. Detective Albert was gathering his folder and computer into his bag before standing up.

"I'll be right there," Detective Albert told me as I walked out of the room, pausing just outside the door.

"Poor woman, she must be devastated." Officer Brady whispered.

"That's just it, Brady. Something's off. It didn't feel real, like a woman who truly lost her husband. It felt like she was trying to *make* it look real. I can't place my finger on it, but I will." Detective Albert paused, "Clean this up before you leave." He said louder and headed towards the door.

I quickly ran to the detective's desk two desks away from the room and began fidgeting with the first thing I could grab. Upon closer evaluation, I held a wooden plaque from the Washington, DC Police Department. "Detective of the Year" was etched in large, bold font in the center.

"Ah, the good old days," I jumped as Detective Albert spoke behind my ear.

"Why did you leave?" I asked, turning toward him.

"Um…" He paused, "Politics. Plus, my wife wanted to see me more often. So, we thought taking this job, in your quiet town, would give me less work to worry about." He rushed this, almost as if it were a rehearsed excuse.

"Less to be trusted with, sounds about right for our town." I laughed to break the awkward moment.

"Let's get you home." He placed his hand on the small of my back and began pushing me away from his desk.

On the drive back to my house, I kept seeing him look over at me out of my peripheral vision. His mouth would open as if to say something, but he could never muster up the courage to say it. When you got to my house, I thanked him for the ride and began to get out. There was no real reason for me to be at the police department for that. My guess is he was hoping I would slip up and confess to the disappearance of my husband, and he could handcuff me on the spot. Unlucky for him, that wouldn't happen.

"This won't be the last you see of me," he shouted with an undertone of rage towards me before I shut the car door.

I walk towards and into my house with my head held high, hoping he could not tell his words had any effect on me. I gracefully opened the door with my shaking hands before closing the door and sliding to the ground.

I have never felt such an overwhelming surge of emotions in my life without the influence of drugs or ecstasy, intertwined with profound mental exhaustion. My heart pounded against my rib cage; each thump was loud and clear as if it were trying to escape the confines of my body. My breath came in as short, sharp gasps; they were so rapid I could barely catch up to them. Sweat beaded down my forehead, the cold and slippery layer that made my skin itch. The walls were closing in around me, the air thick and suffocating. I tried to hide the truth about what was really happening to me, each sensation turning the room into a spinning vortex of confusion and fear. Despite the chaos overwhelming my senses, I was exhausted physically. My eyelids were heavy and difficult to keep open. Each bat of my eyelashes pulled me into the darkness. I found myself collapsing, slumped over in the dim light of our foyer, succumbing to an uneasy sleep that offered no proper rest.

The night was a blur.

Flashing light from ahead crossed my vision over and over. Some red and some green. I could feel myself sitting behind the wheel of a car, driving as fast as possible, ignoring the colors and their meanings. The whole night went like this: colors across my eyes and the pressure on my chest of being pushed into a car seat after driving fast. When I woke up, my heart was still palpitating, and there was pounding coming from somewhere close. My eyes were still adjusting, and I came to know that I was still in my foyer: one shoe on, one shoe lying a few feet away. My purse lay beside me; I could hear my phone ringing from the inside. My body and clothes were covered in dried sweat. I could listen to the sound of my shirt crunching with every movement.

"Emma!" I heard shouting from nearby before feeling a thud on the back of my head. "Open up!"

I stumbled to my feet, knocking the other shoe off in the process. As I opened the front door, I realized I had not processed the voice that was screaming my name. *Oh well, the door is already unlocked. Let's see who is about to attack me.*

"Oh, dear lord," Gwen sighed the moment she had a chance to take a closer look at me. "Did you sleep in that outfit?" she asked.

My outfit was from last night, and it is incredibly wrinkled from sleeping on the floor. I watched as Gwen began to take notice of the display of my items in the foyer, putting the pieces together that I had slept there.

"It doesn't matter; your kids are coming home today. We need to get you ready." She said, pushing past me, only to turn back to grab my hand when she realized I had not followed her.

I could hear the door shutting behind me as we walked away, and it did not fully latch. Before this, I would have been terrified about knowing that the door was not latched and bolted shut. The possibility of Henry sneaking into the house without warning me of his arrival used to send pins and needles down my back. But today, I couldn't care less. Today, he couldn't torture me with his sly comments or his tight fist. I had the last say over torture in this household.

Today, the torture is for me, given to me by me. The pain I am giving to myself needs to be knocked out of the way, though. Gwen is here to try to talk some sense into me; she has been here every day since the last book club meeting, trying to help me.

"The busybodies in the neighborhood told me that a cop was here yesterday and that you left with him?" Gwen asked, pushing me onto a stool at our kitchen countertop. "I know you were planning on telling them that Henry was missing, but I figured you could do that over the phone."

I watched as she poured the coffee grounds into our machine and made me the largest cup of coffee I had ever seen. "Here, you look like you need it." She said, handing me the coffee.

"Thanks," I murmured, taking a seat at the dining room table.

She turned away and kept asking questions that I tuned out while she made herself a cup of coffee. I watched as she grabbed a notepad and a pen and began jotting down what looked to be a to-do list. For her? For me? I have no idea. What I do know is that…

The doorbell rang.

"Ah, that should be breakfast." Gwen sprang from her seat and hopped to the front door.

Gwen, my savior. I was starving, but I didn't know it until the smell of bacon wafted into the kitchen.

"What are you doing?" She asked, grabbing hold of my forearm, examining where I had just been running my fingers along a scar. "Where did you get this?" I normally tried to avoid drawing attention to this scar, but I was honestly shocked she had only just noticed it.

"That happened ages ago." I brushed it off, reaching for the bag in her hands.

"Ah, not until you tell me what happened." She pulled the bag behind her back out of my reach.

"I can already tell you know it was from Henry," I paused, trying to consider how much of such an old story I wanted to tell her. "This happened on our honeymoon. We were in the ocean when a fish bit my arm. Henry was certain he knew the fish was poisonous and demanded that he could cut out the poison." Taking a deep breath in as I relived the pain. "He found a piece of glass that had not yet turned into sea glass at the bottom of the ocean floor and cut a long gash in my arm before pushing as much blood out of my system as he could." My fingers ran up and down my arm as I felt the top of the scar on the side of my wrist up my forearm and finished just at the crook of my arm. "Turns out the fish wasn't poisonous after all." I chuckled nervously.

"Dear god, Emma, that is horrible." The bag of food

dropped on the counter as her arms wrapped around me. "You should have left him right then and there."

"Hindsight and all, right?" A dry laugh came bellowing out of my throat, unaware I had even done it.

"Right." She paused. "Now, let us get some food into you while we go over what we need to do today." Gwen nodded as she quietly pulled out box after box of food before sitting down with her to-do list.

A stack of pancakes, bacon, hash browns, and eggs appeared before me, an identical plate to my right in front of Gwen.

"Now," she began as she poured syrup on both of our pancakes. "Your children are coming home today, in four hours to be exact, and we need to be at the airport for them. The last time I was here, the house looked to be in order, so there is not much to clean up. However, your kids will start to wonder where their dad has disappeared to. Any ideas on how to broach that topic with them?" She asked while she cut her pancakes into bite-sized pieces.

"Thankfully, I thought about this yesterday before I was so rudely brought to the police station, and their rooms and the house are completely cleaned! I wasn't really planning on bringing up the fact that their father is reported as missing unless they mentioned it first." I said in between bites.

I really did not know how hungry I was. I had barely any food last night before I was so rudely asked, *more like requested*, to come to the police station. The only thing that sat in my stomach before this meal was half a bottle of wine, a few pieces of garlic bread, and a few bites of pasta. Nowhere near enough food to cover the wine in my system, nor to fuel my body for the day. The greasy food before me and what I hope to be multiple carafes of coffee for the day should do me just right.

"That is not going to be enough. They are at such a curious age. They won't stop asking questions until you give them the answers." She stated.

"Well, I surely can't tell them that we killed their father. And the police have not found his body, so we can't say that he is dead either. So what? I just mentioned to them he went on a business trip, and I don't know when he is supposed to be back. That seems good enough, and Detective Albert can be the bearer of bad news about the poor demise of their father. How about that for a plan?" I asked.

Obviously, there will be no poor demise of their father that he will tell them about. He will never find his body, but he could easily make up a story to scare them. I wouldn't put it past him to do that very thing. That man would do anything to get me to tell him what happened. His intense stare and 'this won't be the last you see of me' intimidation attempt does not scare me.

"Alright, I guess that can work for now. Now tell me about why you were dragged out of your home by a police officer last night." She asked.

"Oh well, that was Detective Albert. He's the old man on the case I told you about. Apparently, he is pretty savvy with technology, or he knows someone at the station who is. He managed to track Henry's car from the house to the airport. He and a squad of officers went to the parking garage and searched for his car before breaking into it and finding all of his travel belongings still in his vehicle. Whoever he has is good because I only told him about Henry being missing, maybe eight hours before he came and got me." I told Gwen in between bites of my food.

"That doesn't worry you? He could get access to your cameras if he wanted to, you know this, right?" She asked, sending a shock to my system. *The damn cameras, why hadn't I thought of that?*

"No, it doesn't worry me a bit. He can pull up all of the cameras he wants. He won't find anything." *I hope.*

"If you say so." She paused to take a sip of her coffee. "How did his car end up at the airport anyway? You never told me."

"That's a story for another time," I whispered, keeping my voice level and my head towards my plate.

Three hours later, Gwen has me fed, dressed, and full of coffee. She began stressing about thirty minutes ago and was continually nagging me to ensure that we left in time, and started pushing me through the hallway and towards the stairs.

Creak

My head whipped to the left, begging to hear where the sound had come from. The staircase was empty, not a soul on it, yet I listened to a creak go from it. I knew which step it was, too, the seventh from the bottom. Henry always managed to step on that stair extra hard, ensuring that it made a noise. Whereas the kids and I barely let our feet float over the top of it, the sound drove us crazy. And here it was again. Just as loud as ever.

"Did you hear that?" I asked Gwen.

"Hear what?" She looked back into the house, waiting for a sound.

"Nothing," I muttered.

I must be going crazy. I'm hearing things. That's it. There is nothing there that could make that noise. It's just my mind making things up again.

We grabbed the cookies I baked and hopped into Gwen's car, the stereo blaring a Madonna song. Typical Gwen. She did not ask any more questions, nor did she even talk to me till we pulled up to the airport.

"Okay, now go get your kids. I will be right here." She said as she put the car in park.

I looked at her, took a deep breath, and jumped out of the car. My children are very different from one another. Raised under the same roof, but were complete and total opposites. Lilly, my oldest, is twelve years old. She fits in perfectly with our friends and their families. A girly girl to the max, dresses and tea parties when she was younger, and now that she is getting closer to a teenager, she keeps asking to start cotillion training. I never had a cotillion, nor knew what it was till I married Henry. My upbringing was a complete 180 compared to my children's. Lilly is a vision and absolute beauty in everything she does in life. It makes me worry that she will end up marrying for status and money and not for love, and end up either hating her life like I do, or like I did, or she will truly love being a housewife. I fear the latter for her, but it will be her choice either way.

Jack is nine years old and an absolute sweetheart. He has been loving and cuddly to me since day one. Always knew when I needed a pick-me-up or when I was mad at his father, he would run up to me, climb into my arms, and give me the biggest hugs. Jack has been my favorite since the day he was born; there was just something different about him. As he got older, he started to look more and more like his father, which scares me. The difference between them was the smile; Jack's smile was authentic and genuine, and his eyes glimmered when he saw me. Henry's smile was sinister, always preparing for his next move.

That's the sweet, innocent smile that welcomes me now as he runs to me through the airport, jumping into my arms.

Chapter Four

Henry's morning routine baffled me. He liked to start his morning doing yoga. I am unsure if he did it to stretch his aging body or help get him in the right mindset. If it were the mindset, I would really like to talk with whoever invented yoga. Henry's mindset most of the time was the opposite of the monks I have read about. Instead of peace and enlightenment, Henry had rage and maybe an enlightenment of his own making. If what he did to our family could be considered enlightened.

This morning brought back many memories of the man I married. As I sat in our bathroom getting ready for the day, I stared deeply into my coffee and began shivering. A flashback of Henry finishing a yoga session and finding me 'clogging the bathroom,' as he put it entered my mind.

"Move out of the way," he stomped in, saying.

I was standing before my mirror in the bathroom; he had his own to use. There is no way I was in his way. My side of the sink was on the far side; he had to go past all of his things, going out of his way just to torment me. When I didn't move, he grabbed my wrist, twisting my arm and submerging my hand in my scalding hot cup of coffee.

"Please," he said, holding my squirming hand as I fought to release it from his grip. When I finally freed my hand, it was more like he had let go to do more damage. He grabbed the mug forcefully and took a sip. "Disgusting, hot tar liquid. You should be drinking something healthier for your body." He said, taking a large gulp before spitting the hot liquid on my face and dropping the mug on the floor. Where it shattered, cutting and burning the tops of my feet. I stopped drinking coffee in the house from then on unless he was out of town.

His hatred for my coffee made no sense to me. He drank energy drinks multiple times a day, and never once did I complain about it. Although if I had, I would get his hand across my face for saying such a thing. I tried shaking this memory as I continued to get ready for the day.

Creak

It's nothing, I tell myself.

Lilly and Jack were sitting at the kitchen island, eating their breakfast, when I came down. We exhausted the topics of everything that happened at their individual camps the night before, so this morning, I walked into a silent kitchen.

"So, kids, school is starting next week. I was thinking we could go to the store today and get you new school supplies and clothes." I mentioned while filling up my cup of coffee, my hand shook, still trying to forget the memory.

"I need a new backpack; mine got ripped at camp. Plus,

the Teenage Mutant Ninja Turtles are so third grade, I need to grow up." Jack started with a mouth full of cereal.

"Okay, and you, Lilly?" I asked, laughing that fourth grade deemed him a grown-up now.

"I have things I could use, too." She said, all the while her face was fixed on her phone screen. Texting away, most likely from a friend she met in camp.

Lilly seemed to have matured while she was away at camp. When I dropped her off at the beginning of the summer, she would spend her days having tea parties with her stuffed animals and would practice her ballet everywhere we would go. But now, she has a certain air to her. When I tried to talk to her about the friends she made over the summer, I got nothing other than their names. Her summer camp was meant for sixth to tenth-graders. She will be entering seventh grade this year, and it made me wonder if the friends she made were part of the older kids instead of her age group. That would explain the new hairstyle and fashion sense she came home sporting. I wouldn't think a seventh grader would be able to give a haircut like that. An older kid who has a cosmetology class in their high school, though, would know how to give a haircut like that.

"Great. Are there any stores in particular that we need to hit?" I asked.

"Sephora, for starters, then H&M. I heard they have the new styles of the year in, and I want to make sure I get plenty of good outfits for this year." She said, not even looking up to speak to me.

"Alright, sounds like a plan. Everyone, hurry up and finish your breakfast and get ready to go. We can meet by the door in an hour." My mind was baffled at what she could need at Sephora. Her "makeup" routine was sunscreen and flavored Chapstick when I sent her to camp.

We went from store to store, gathering the necessities and wants my children needed for their new school year. We had one more store to go into before we could call it quits for the day. My arms were exhausted from lugging around the bags. I was so used to Henry carrying the bags for me that I couldn't wait for Jack to gain some muscle so he could be the one holding the bags for me. Lilly ran into the last store at full force, grabbing things left and right.

"Emma!" I heard someone cheerfully shout from across the store.

I turned around and saw Addison speed-walking towards me. I knew Addison from work, and she was an editor who befriended me when I first started there. I don't work in the office very often, so when we do see each other, she is always in high hopes, excited to tell me anything and everything going on in her life. I loved listening to her stories. She traveled everywhere to see different authors, check in with them on work, and help them improve their novels before we sent them to the printers.

"Addison, how are you?" I asked her, hugging her the best I could with my hands so full.

"Me? I should be asking you that. Word around the office is that Henry is missing. Is this true?" She whispered the last part.

"He is. We haven't heard from him since he left for his trip. The police are trying to find him; the kids have really high hopes they will any day now." I told her.

"Well, if there is anything my team or I can do, please do reach out to us. We would hate for him not to come back. He's a really great guy." Addison said, holding her chest sympathetically.

"He is, isn't he? The kids love him to death, and it would break our hearts if he didn't come back." I told her, beginning to scan the store for my children. "Addison, I should probably go before Lilly runs my credit card bill up. I'll be in the office next week, and I'll stop by to give you an update and say hello!"

"Sounds good, see you then!" She shouted as I walked away, bags lugging behind me.

I quickly caught up to my children as Lilly placed yet another sweater into the cart, while Jack was being dragged behind her. I hugged Lilly and took back over the cart, leading us to the checkout. We quickly left the mall, juggling the bags and the keys through the parking lot. The sun began to dip just below the trees as we drove home. The house was quiet, and the air was thin when we entered. This quickly changed as my children ran into the house, bags ruffling as they ran past me and into the living room.

"You know the drill, let's get the tags off and the clothes in the washer before we do anything else," I shouted as Jack turned on the TV.

One by one, the kids cut the tags and placed them in their own piles. Lilly's clothing was perfectly folded and stacked. In comparison, Jack's clothes were balled up and thrown throughout the living room. I know I need to talk to my kids about their father, especially after being confronted in public by Addison. They were bound to hear it from someone else if I didn't get up the nerve to do it myself.

"Hey kids, I need to tell you something before you hear it from someone else," I paused, muting the TV. "Your father is missing." I blurted out as fast as I could, hating every moment of this conversation.

"What's dad missing? Did he leave something at home that he needs for his trip?" Jack asked, coming to cuddle up next to me.

"What do you mean, Mom? Did he miss his flight? Does he not know how to get home?" Lilly asked, a bit of concern in her voice, with her last question.

"That's not exactly what I mean, kids. Dad left the house and drove to the airport. However, after that, he never boarded his flight. He's gone. And I don't know where he is." My hands began to shake uncontrollably. I tucked them under my thighs to hold them still, waiting for the panic from my children. They both took their time processing what I had just told them.

"I don't understand, where's daddy?!" Jack began to shout as his eyes filled with tears.

"This doesn't make sense, Mom. Dad always follows

his schedule. It's who he is. He would never miss a flight for work. We should call someone! Call the police, have you called the police yet, Mom?" Lilly protested and began pacing the room.

"I have done that already, sweetheart. They are doing everything they can to look for Dad." I said, crossing the room to hug her.

The moment my hands touched her, her knees buckled, and she dropped, just barely smacking her knees into the ground as I caught her. My arms wrapped around her as tightly as I could, and her body began to shake uncontrollably, and I squeezed even harder as I felt her tears hit my arm. Jack sat on the couch, crying his eyes out, as I reached my arm out to welcome him into my embrace.

"Oh, I know, I know," I whispered to my children as I began rubbing their backs to calm them down, just as I did when they were babies. "It's okay, Mommy is here for you. Mommy will never leave you. I will always be here for you."

I feel for my children each and every day, especially today. Finding out that their father is missing was never going to be an easy day for them; finding out that he will never come back will be just as hard. Watching my children cry breaks my heart; it is one of the hardest things about being a mother, knowing your children's sadness and not being able to take it away. I will never leave them, and thanks to me, their childhood will be better with just me for them to look up to. I am all they need; all they will ever need.

—✧—

"Let's go! Everyone out the door, you are going to be late!" I shouted from the front door.

The first day of school is the day every parent waits for and dreads all at once. We look forward to our children leaving the house for hours every day, giving us back the freedom we had lost during the summer. That is, during the times that our children weren't at camp. My summer schedule usually consisted of baseball practices and games, ballet class, swim league, and many birthday parties. We hate to see the new school year come because we know that means our children are getting older and will soon be leaving the house, and that means we are getting older, something no parent wants to admit.

This first day of school also marks the first one that their father will ever miss in their entire life. He has missed plenty of essential things in our children's lives: birthdays, doctor's appointments, and holidays. But the first day of school was the only one that he cared about, and he wanted to be there to make sure his children started the year off right.

"Still no sign of dad?" Lilly asked as she tied her shoes.

"Sorry, sweetie, he still hasn't called. We can try him again on the way to school, how does that sound?" I asked.

Creak

I hate lying to my children, but it is for their own good.

And if that creaking stair has anything to say about it, maybe I won't have to lie to them anymore. The sound of it sent shivers down my spine. I flinched every time I heard it. The image of my husband tumbling down the stairs, thudding like a ton of bricks, is seared in the back of my mind. Hearing the creak made it all the closer to breaking down and telling the truth.

Did the stairs creak when he fell down them? It had to have, right?

As expected, Henry's phone rang and rang and rang, quite possibly bothering the police officer in charge of the evidence lockup. Lilly and Jack tried to hide how sad they were that their father had missed their first day, but I could tell. They sounded like lost puppies on their voicemail, catching their dad up on everything that had happened to them before their first day of school. If their dad were still alive, he probably wouldn't have noticed anyway. But he's not here to say anything. I finished dropping the kids off at school, wished them luck, and drove to Gwen's home. Stopping for coffee and pastries on the way.

"Get in here quick," Gwen said when I knocked on the door. "I have been hearing whispers from the neighbors all day. They have finally put two and two together on why Detective Asshole was at your home. It's fairly common for Henry to be out of town often, but it has been a month since anyone has seen him. There's a lot of speculation about where he is amongst the neighbors."

"So what are they saying?" I asked, handing over

Gwen's muffin and coffee to her.

"A handful of different things, most think you are getting a divorce. They are very popular right now in our neighborhood." She said, not taking a moment to acknowledge the treats in her hand.

"Ha," I laughed, "As if he would have ever let me divorce him! He would have killed me before we ever got to that. He almost did once, have I told you about that?"

"No…when was this?" Gwen's jaw dropped, shock written all over her face.

"About six years ago, do you remember when I told you I was going to Fiji for a month to take a break while Henry went on a trip and the kids stayed with the nanny?" I paused to take a sip of my coffee and to wait for Gwen to nod her head that she remembered. "Well, the truth was I was in the hospital. Henry had come home from work one day in the worst mood I had ever seen him. His clothes were disheveled, and his breath reeked of whiskey. Thankfully, Lilly and Jack were both at their friend's homes for a sleepover. Otherwise, I fear we would have scarred them for life. He came into the kitchen where I was cleaning up for the night, even though it was just me for dinner that night, I had a sink full of water to clean up my mess. I turned around to see him come into the kitchen, tossing his bags on the floor, kicking his boots at the wall, and swearing loudly. I decided that I did not want to be a part of whatever had happened to him today, so I went back to my dishes. Little did I know, this upset him even more, and he was not giving me the choice not to be a part of it. He shouted at me, screaming that if I were a better wife, I would have greeted him at the door, had a drink ready for him, and saved him dinner. But I didn't do that, and quite frankly, didn't want to. All I did was say 'sorry' and turn back to my dishes, hoping he would leave me alone. That was not the case, he screamed, 'Sorry, you think sorry will fix this?'.

"Before I knew it, I was crying, and he grabbed me by the back of my throat, kissed me as hard as he could, and shoved my head into the sink. My head broke the wine glass I was cleaning and cut open my forehead. As I screamed for a breath, I watched my blood and the soap bubbles thrashing around me. I am not sure how long I was held down for, but I was able to grab that wine glass and thrust it behind me, cutting his wrist. That monster still did not let go. I put all of my weight on my stomach, lifting my legs, thrashing them any way I could to hit him. Finally, he let go after a good blow to his balls.

"I escaped through the kitchen and made a break for the front door. Still unable to catch my breath, he quickly caught up. He swiped my legs with him, and I fell to the ground with the weight of an elephant. I tried to turn over to my back so I could see what his next move would be and be able to block it. What I didn't expect was his briefcase to be sitting right next to where I had landed. The last thing I remember seeing was him lifting the case with his uninjured hand.

"When I came to, I was in the hospital. A nurse had

told me I was lucky enough to be alive. A neighbor had come to the door, heard the commotion, and called the cops. Henry lied and said there had been a man who escaped through the back door when he heard the sirens, showing his injured hand as proof that he was also a victim. I had to have my stomach pumped out from all the water and soap that had entered my body. My lungs had collapsed from fighting back. My forehead had the most significant bump any of the nurses had seen. I could see in their eyes that they were worried that it was Henry who had done it, but they were too shy or scared to say anything. Every time he came to visit me while I was still out cold, he played the sympathetic husband to a tee. He would shed a tear or two and beg God to save me. All the while, he was the one who put me where I was. I was surprised he did not end my life in the hospital. It would have been as simple as cutting my breathing tube when no one was looking.

"The hospital had kept me there for two weeks after I had woken up. I spent almost a month in that hospital and yet never told a soul what really happened until today. When I texted you, I was going to Fiji. I would have loved to tell you over the phone, but my throat burned and ached with every attempt to speak. And from what you might be able to guess already, I never did go to Fiji. I checked into a hotel two towns away to recover. I would have stayed longer if Henry hadn't come and literally dragged me home." When I finished my story, my coffee had gotten cold but still tasted good, so I took a sip while I waited for Gwen to respond.

"What the actual fuck, Emma?! This is NOT okay! Wow…um…I knew he was a piece of shit husband…but that? I wish you had told me this way before. I would have begged you to leave him so many years ago." She replied with wide eyes full of shock.

"I know, I thought about it many times," I whispered as I looked down into my hands.

"What reason could you have to tell yourself all of those times to stay with him?" Gwen reasonably asked.

"My children. He would have taken them far away from me. I can't lose them." I began to cry at this point. "They still have faith that their dad is coming back any day now from his trip. I just don't know how to break it to them."

Gwen gave me a huge hug, holding me until I finished sobbing and let go on my own. I moved into her living room, got myself comfortable, and began to eat my muffin in silence as Gwen paced the room. Under her breath, I could hear her say 'okay' every so often. Other times, she would look at me and shake her head. I assumed she was thinking of a plan and kept going back and forth on what she believed to be the right plan. I couldn't take the silence anymore, so I turned on the TV.

"Breaking news," the anchor of our local TV station began, "a prominent businessman of Gloomridge was reported missing by his wife over a week ago. He was last seen driving into the airport to catch a flight. However, he never made it on the flight and was never seen entering the airport.

Police found his car and luggage in the parking garage, but Henry Thompson was nowhere to be found. If you have seen this man or know anything of his whereabouts, please reach out to the Gloomridge Police Department at (893) 742-5678. Any piece of information could be important in finding this missing husband and father." The news then showed the photo I had given to the detective.

Not having many happy photos of my husband, I had to resort to giving them the business headshot he used for his company's website. This realization made me wonder what photo I would display at his funeral. That is, if we ever have one, I'm pretty positive you needed a body and a death certificate for one. I could print out a photo of him from our wedding; it's not like he looked much different from then, anyway. Or I could use the last family photo we had taken. Lilly had been six, and Jack was about to turn three. It was not the best photo of him, but it was the most recent one I could think of. I could see the wives talking now about how I didn't love my husband enough to find a decent and recent photo of him.

I froze. Unsure what to say or do next.

"Looks like you made the right decision to tell them when you did. Otherwise, they would have found out from the news or at school," Gwen stated before throwing herself on the couch next to me.

"I'm fucked." That was all I could mutter.

When I arrived home, a car was parked in the driveway with a man sitting on the hood of the vehicle. As I got closer, I could make out Detective Albert's silvery hair. He was out of his uniform today, dressed instead in a pair of black jeans and a red collared short-sleeved shirt. *Fuck*, I thought as I placed my car in park, took a deep breath and gathered my things.

"Didn't have anywhere else to be this afternoon?" I asked as I climbed out of my car.

"No, ma'am, I even waited for you to return from dropping your kids off at school so they wouldn't be here when I did this." He stated as if he was helping me and not making me feel like a victim here.

"Doing what?" I asked, staying firm in my place in the driveway.

"I need to search your home and get an idea of the lay-out." He said, rifling through his pockets to grab out his search warrant. "It's all legal."

"And I am sure the news today was all you're doing too?" I asked, slightly pissed off. "If you waited for my children to be gone for school, then you must have an idea that I have not told them about the possibility that their father might not come back from their trip?" I asked.

"I had a feeling, shall we?" he said, gesturing towards the front door.

I saw no reason not to allow him in, and legally, I didn't think I had the option. I nodded my head and walked towards the front door.

"I guess we shall start here then," I said as I showed him the foyer and tried to lead him closer to the kitchen.

"I'll take it from here, ma'am. If I have any questions, I will ask you." He said and began taking photos of the home.

Creak

My blood began to boil inside me every time I heard the ominous sound. Following him around the house, I tried not to hover too much or stare at any one thing for too long. I did not want to give him any idea that something had happened here that shouldn't have. He looked through absolutely everything. Nothing seemed to be off limits for him.

He quickly left the foyer and made his way into Henry's home office. It was a pretty standard office and fit into our home very nicely. In the center of the room stood a large, solid oak desk and a leather chair behind it. There were four bookcases behind his desk, stuffed to the brim with books, mostly non-fiction, and many academic books. Henry was a scholar at heart; it might not have looked it, but he could finish a book in one sitting if you let him. And we almost always did. The kids and I knew not to bother him when he was in his office; that was his time to work and do whatever else made him happy at home. Since there was not much that made him happy at home, this was our gift to him. However, our children did not know the whole truth behind why we didn't bug Daddy in his office. They might find out one day, but today was not the day. As I scanned the room, trying to look at it from a fresh perspective, I noticed his golf clubs in the corner, sitting in the same spot when I rushed in and snatched the first golf club, I could get my hands on. I never put the club back with the others, and I hoped and prayed that the Detective was not a golfer himself and would not notice if one was missing.

Detective Albert opened all of his drawers on his desk, rifling through his papers to find any sign of where he could have disappeared. As I stood in the doorway watching his every move, I worried about what he would find. I did not know much about Henry's business, so I wasn't sure if there were anything he would uncover that would point towards fraud, a mistress, or truly anything else. I already had a feeling he could have a mistress, but never once looked for any sort of proof. If this detective found any, would I deny it? Try to save some public face for my husband. Or should I be shocked and play the victim in this scenario? Whatever decision I had made, which I hadn't, I did not get to use it as the detective decided he was done with this room and was ready to move on.

I followed him as he went back through the foyer, into the kitchen, passed through the living room, and got ready to head up the stairs. The sound of the stairs creaking had already entered my mind well before we got close to the stairs. I knew it was Henry telling me he was still alive, that we wouldn't get away with this, that we didn't hide his body well. I began shaking my head to get the sound out as it grew louder when I noticed the detective staring at me.

Creak…creak…CREAK

"Is everything okay?" Detective Albert asked as we got

closer to the stairs.

"Of course, why wouldn't it be?" I asked.

Was I talking aloud before, or did I make a face to make him ask me that? I can't imagine I did. My only job while he was here was to keep a straight face and answer any questions as they came up as truthfully as I could, without telling him what happened.

The first stop upstairs was our bedroom. Detective Albert searched through our things as closely as he had searched through Henry's office, only stopping for a moment to realize how OCD Henry was about his closet. Each shirt is perfectly pressed and in color order. This was a part of his life that he never let outsiders see. He always wanted to appear as the perfect husband who was chill and cool while still being a fantastic provider. What the world didn't see was his obsessive-compulsive attributes, his explosive temper, and his lack of love for anyone in his life aside from himself. His closet spoke volumes about how he was as a partner. His voice, mind, and opinion were the only ones that mattered to him. He refused to listen to anyone else and would never admit if he was wrong on a topic.

"Does your husband keep a gun in your bedroom, ma'am?" he asked.

"No, sir, no guns in our bedroom." I proudly said, knowing this would be the first entirely truthful thing I have told him since we met.

Or was it? Henry could have put a gun in our room and never told me. How would I know? It hasn't occurred to me before that he would have more throughout the house.

We walked out of our bedroom and headed towards Lilly's room when he stopped at the top of the stairs. I could see Henry standing there, anger-induced sweat beating from his forehead, his fist ready to hit anything or anyone in the way, and his perfectly pressed suits shining in the distance. I had to knock myself out of this flashback, *of course, that's what it is, he's not really standing there*, to listen to Detective Albert as he repeated himself.

"What happened here?" He asked.

I walked closer to the handrail at the top of the stairs and noticed where the wood had been chipped. Racking my brain, I couldn't think of when that could have happened. Did Henry reach for the banister to save himself as he went tumbling down the stairs? Did our children scratch it and not tell me? As much as I wanted to believe it was my children, something deep in me knew it had been Henry.

Creak

I froze, shivering where I stood. That was all the answer I needed to know it was him.

"Oh, when did that happen? I'm going to have to have Andrew come and fix that for me next time I go to put together my list for a handyman." I chuckled, trying to keep my fear from escaping my mouth.

He asked what was in the rest of the hallway and decided not to check my children's rooms once I told him.

"Do you have a basement?" He asked.

"Yes, you can follow me." Leading him down the

stairs, sure to skip the creaking stairs, out of habit.

"What was that about?" Detective Albert asked, pointing back towards the stairs.

"What was what about?" I asked.

"That…that thing you did." He muttered, pointing towards the stairs.

"Oh, the whole skipping the step? We have a creaking stair and have had it for years. My children decided to make a game out of it and skipped the step any time they went up and down the staircase. I guess I joined in on their game at one point and didn't notice I had. We have always been nervous it would fall out from underneath our feet." I laughed again.

I tried to keep my cool, but I could smell my sweat as we got closer to the basement. For a second, I had the thought to push the detective down the stairs so this could all be over, but reality set in quickly. Realizing that he had most likely talked to someone at the station and told them he was coming here. If he didn't come back, they would come to me first to question me. As tempting as it was, I refrained.

"This is my wine cellar," I told Albert as we turned the corner and entered my sanctuary. "I have it organized by country, then types of wines, and then by wines that I do not want anyone to touch, and I'm saving for the future."

"My wife got really into wine too for a while, but she fell out of interest in it a few years ago and decided to switch to gin instead. She said it was much easier to drink and get her drunk faster, she loves the feeling right before she gets too drunk." He told me as he perused my wine collection.

"Gin is a great alternative; I have a few gins that I really like as well. If she ever wants a recommendation, I can send her a few. As well as a few cocktail recipes that I personally think are the absolute best." I kept my spot in the entrance of the cellar, trying not to crowd the detective.

"Would you ever switch completely to gin? It seems like you have a lot of wine to keep your attention for a while." He said, wiping the dust off a bottle.

"Never completely, I love my wines too much. Shall we continue?" I asked, trying to get him to stop touching my bottles in case one was to fall off the shelves.

As we moved further into the basement, I watched as he shivered when we moved into the storage room. It took him by surprise to have a temperature change and a style so different from the rest of the house. My wine cellar was already a pleasant, comfortable 55 degrees Fahrenheit, so it was already colder than most basements. However, the further you get into our basement, the colder it gets. You should wear a parka when you are down here, which is why I keep so many blankets in my wine cellar, and I rarely spend any time in the rest of the basement unless I have to.

As we moved further into the basement, my blood began to run cold. I flipped the switch to turn on the lights in the rest of the basement when I stopped moving. My feet froze in the middle of a step. The blood in my face is gone. Leaving behind a pale, ghost-like expression.

"Are you okay?" Detective Albert put his hands on my shoulder.

"Oh yes," I muttered, "just got startled by the shadows. I thought I saw something."

And I did. Not just something, but someone. An all too familiar face stood in the corner. His suit was perfectly pressed, fresh from the dry cleaner. That was the only thing that was clean about him. His eyes were sunken into his skull, surrounded by dark black rings. His face was stark white in comparison to his eyes. Right on his forehead was a gaping hole, the bullet wound that ended his life. I tried to blink my eyes, bring me back to reality when blood began pouring from the bullet hole. His white face was quickly covered in fresh, bright red blood. His all too clean suit, getting dirtier with every passing second.

Detective Albert began walking past me at this moment, his body between mine and Henry's, knocking me back to life.

"Didn't care much for this portion of the house?" He chuckled.

"We use it just for storage, so we saw no reason to get the designer to make this look nice and neat," I said, trying to keep my eye away from the bottom shelf that held the gun safe.

Detective Albert took the room one step at a time. Stopped in front of each container to read its contents. He passed by the gun with no problem as he wasn't pulling items out to see what was behind them, and he had no idea there was a gun there.

"Why is this container empty?" he asked.

Not knowing what container he was talking about, I moved closer to him. He was pointing towards the 'Twine, Rope, and Trash Bags' container. In hindsight, we shouldn't keep all of those things together. It really screams torture house.

"Who knows, I would have to ask my kids or my husband. I don't come into this part of the house very often. My husband used it more than anyone else. I only come down here for my wines." I said, staring through the clear tub to see the one short piece of twine I left at the bottom of the container when I finished tying up my husband. I hadn't thought to fill it back up, and buying a large quantity of these items seemed suspicious now that I thought about it.

A mute, almost inaudible 'mhm' barely flickered across his lips as he moved on through the room. He nodded and took notes about the various assortment of storage boxes we had in our basement. Coming across one labeled 'Tarps,' he did not bother to ask me about it this time, as I'm sure he assumed I would not know the answer to his question. Instead, he wrote down a note with a puzzled look on his face.

Finally, we got to the room I was dreading for him to see. He reached for the door handle as my heart raced, not remembering if I had locked the door or not.

"What's in here?" he asked when the door wouldn't

open.

"That's my husband's room I've never been in, so I wouldn't know what was in there," I said, lying left and right. Let's hope they never ask me to take a polygraph. I would fail tremendously.

"Do you have the key?" He asked.

"No, I would assume there would be one in my husband's office, though. Did you notice any spare keys when you were going through his drawers?" I asked, not knowing the answer.

"No, ma'am, if you do come across a key, though, let me know so we can get into this room. Otherwise, I will have to ask Doug to come and break down the door for me. As much as I enjoy breaking down doors, my doctor has asked me not to use such force in my old age." He chuckled.

The detective is making jokes, really? Did not anticipate this.

"Will do, I won't even open the door without you here if I find the key before Doug makes his appearance."

Chapter Five

"Mom, is the creak in the stairs louder than normal?" Lilly asked one morning. "I swear I didn't step on the stairs, and I still heard it creak."

Hearing this caused shivers to run up and down my spine, freezing in my tracks. This only served to reinforce the possibility that a part of Henry may still be lingering, as though he were attempting to make his presence known.

"You had heard it more, too?" I asked. *I knew I wasn't going crazy; no one else said they could hear it.*

"Yeah, it has been louder since I got back from camp. I hear it at night when I am trying to sleep. I checked the hallway and stairs the first night, triple-checking that the front door was locked. I'm too scared even to do that now and lock my bedroom door every night instead." She said shivering where she stood.

"I knew I wasn't going crazy; no one else said they could hear it." This news had just taken an enormous weight off my shoulders.

"You two are insane. I have heard nothing. I even

stepped on the stairs by accident, and it was silent. I figured you got it fixed while we were gone," Jack shouted from the kitchen, adding to the conversation and my confusion.

"He knows nothing. He's a child," Lilly said skeptically, waving it off.

"Maybe," I whispered, primarily to myself.

I dropped the kids off at school that morning in complete silence. Lilly was fed up with Jack from their small fight that morning, and Jack was in his own world; he did not even consider talking to us. I, however, felt like I was at a rock concert. My thoughts were so loud.

When I walked back into the house, my emotions were at an all-time high, and I slammed the front door as hard as I could; the glass chandelier overhead shook slightly back and forth. My breathing came in shallow, ragged bursts. I balled up my hands in a fist, and began beating at the door again and again and again like my body didn't know what else would release what my voice couldn't say. When my hands began to ache, I stopped and turned back towards the staircase. *Fuck!* I shouted in my mind as I saw Henry sitting on the stairs in his wedding tux. I rubbed my eyes vigorously, hoping the image of him was just that, an image. When I got up the courage to open my eyes again, he was gone.

"Okay, Henry, is this what you wanted from me?" I shouted. "I'm going crazy now. You aren't here, and yet you are all I hear. You are an ever-present addition to our home, and you are not welcome anymore! That's it! I'm getting rid of you, once and for all." I stomped into the garage and grabbed Henry's hammer, which Henry seemed to have used often due to the wear and tear on it. I haven't seen him touch tools in years though, strange. I screamed at the top of my lungs and began hammering on the stairs. Nothing. Not even a splinter. The wood groaned under the hammer, but did not budge.

Creak.

He's daring me to try again. So, I did. I struck it once more, then again. My breaths were sharp and uneven, the hammer slipping in my hand from sweat or rage or maybe both. Finally, a chunk of wood split free from the stairs with a sickening crack. Staggering slightly from the force, I stared at the jagged break.

"Damn you, good craftsmanship!" I cried as making even one hole in the stairs took ages. Finally, swing after swing, that stair looked damaged beyond repair, and I could breathe. This would have to be fixed with new wood, one that Henry could not haunt as he wasn't in the house when it made its way in.

I began walking into the kitchen to make more coffee when I heard it again.

Creak... creak.... creak.

The stairs were creaking louder than I had ever heard. It frightened me, and I dropped the coffee pot, causing the glass to shatter all around me. I hopped onto the kitchen counter to shimmy my barefoot self out of the kitchen to grab something to clean the glass with when I heard it again.

This time, it sounded as if Henry had put surround sound in our home to broadcast that he was there.

CREAK…CREAK…CREAK!

Clearly, he was haunting me, and at least one other person believed me. She knew a ghost existed, even if she didn't know who was haunting our home. And that was enough for me to take the following steps. I called Andrew and asked him to fix my staircase, the scratch on the banister, and all. I begged him to come today and insisted I pay him extra. I lied and said the stairs had fallen out from underneath me, and it wasn't safe for my kids, so I needed it fixed. He promised to be there within the hour.

Andrews's face, upon inspection of the stairs, said it all; he knew I had lied and that there was no way my foot could have caused that much damage. However, he kept his mouth shut and got to work, no questions asked. I excused myself and ran to the grocery store to keep my distance from the construction and, primarily, Henry's ever-present presence. Who knows what he would do in protest of the work? I did not want to be around when Andrew and his team removed and covered up the last part of the house Henry was haunting. I took my time going through the aisles, finding any new fun snacks for the kids to try, and checking out the meat department to see if there was anything that looked delicious that I could put in the oven tonight. As I began my extensive search of the cheese section, I heard my name from the aisle beside me.

"She was screaming at her husband, who is missing,

according to the news. Then I heard a whole bunch of banging and shouting coming from inside. The next thing I knew, a construction crew was pulling up next door, and Emma was greeting them at the front door. Who knows what she is doing, but it can't be good." A woman in the next aisle was speaking so loudly that she didn't care who heard her. Her voice was so familiar, it could only be my next-door neighbor.

"Do you think her husband was in the house?" the other woman asked.

"No, I don't. I have been watching who goes in and out of that house since I saw the news report. Nothing will happen over there that I don't know about." The first woman said.

"What if she has kept her husband locked in her house this whole time? She had lied to the police, and finally, she did something about his presence and needed the construction crew to fix whatever she had managed to do." The second woman began to theorize.

Anger filled me to the brim. I wanted to run over to her aisle and smack the crap out of them for insinuating that I would do such a thing. But I also wanted to leave my cart where it was and head back home. Both of these decisions would mean that bitch Mrs. Finkle next door won. I decided to keep shopping with my head held high; I had done nothing and had nothing to hide. The whispering and gossiping in this town will not be my downfall. I grabbed the rest of my groceries, took my time in the chocolate section, and went to the cash register.

"Oh, Emma, how are you doing?" I heard from behind.

"Mrs. Finkle, Mrs. Ghose, what a pleasant surprise running into you two," I said, putting on my best 'Stepford Wives' smile as I placed my items on the conveyor belt.

"We are so sorry to hear about your husband. I can't imagine what I would do in such a big house, all alone, without my Gary." Mrs. Ghose said, placing her hand on her heart. "You haven't heard anything from him?" She asked.

"Nothing. The last time I saw him, he was leaving for his business trip. I wish I could help the police more, but what can I do, ladies? I'm just a wife." I chuckled.

Anything to get these two bitty bitches away from me.

"Paper or plastic?" The teenager behind the counter asked.

"I have my reusable bags, but if anything doesn't fit, paper, please." Just because I am a husband murderer doesn't mean I throw all of my morals out the window in one day.

"If we hear anything, we will be sure to call the police." Mrs. Finkle stated.

"I'm sure you will. Have a nice day, ladies." I pushed my cart out of the store at an even pace, trying to keep up appearances.

I know they are still watching me from the window, too. I can feel their eyes digging into the back of my skull. The saying that moms have two eyes in the back of their heads could not be more accurate than right now. Before I hopped in my car to drive away, I waved towards the store, not even making eye contact with them, but I could feel in my soul that their heads dipped down so they could pretend they did not see it.

A block away, I pulled my car into an empty parking lot and took a moment to scream. As much as those women infuriate me, I know Mrs. Finkle is the only reason I am alive today. That comment alone told me all I needed to know: 'If we hear anything, we will be sure to call the police.' Just as she had on that faithful day, she has never told me she was the one to save my life; the feeling has just always been in the back of my mind. There is no other neighbor close enough to hear what happens in my home, nor one as nosy as Mrs. Finkle. I should thank her one day, although she will probably deny it, and I will look like a crazy woman. The neighbors probably see me like that currently, anyway, with all the gossip around.

"You really think this ends well for you?" the voice sounded just like me. *Could that really come out of my mouth?*

Oh well, it's time to move on. My life is still mine to live, for now.

"Glad to see you are back," Andrew said, running out to help me bring my groceries in. "This is quite a lot for the three of you."

"You try having almost teenagers in the house. They will eat you dry." I laughed, knowing that most of this was for me. The brownies, the cookies, and the ice cream I hide from my children. It's mom's secret special snacks, moms need that too, right?

I spent most nights wide awake now. Running through the disembodying of my husband, the way we disposed of it, if we left anything that could be traced back to us, and most importantly, what would happen if I got caught. My children would be sent to Gwen's to live, that is, if they don't trace her into this as well. They deserve to at least be with their godmother. I can't get caught; we did everything perfectly. His fingerprints are gone, his clothes have been burned along with my shoes and socks, and our gloves were put in a different bag and tossed separately. We are clean; there is no way they could trace us. We will keep going about our lives as if nothing happened.

"Do you need help putting those away, or would you like to hear about your stairs first?" Andrew asked, carrying four bags in both hands.

"If you don't mind, I would like to have a little drink before I hear about the stairs," I said, turning around and heading for the door.

Andrew followed with the rest of my groceries and placed them on the kitchen countertop for me. I opened a bag of chips and a case of sour cream and onion dip and began munching away while I put the groceries away. The rules for what time of day is appropriate for certain foods or drinks have been abandoned. From the outside, I'm sure I look like a grieving, confused wife waiting to hear any news about her husband and trying to cope any way she can.

Truthfully, they wouldn't be completely wrong. I am grieving. Not the death of my husband but the death of my old life. With my husband gone, no one can stop me from doing anything I want. I have never had this freedom in my entire life. It's frightening.

But I am also celebrating, celebrating being released from his ever-present looming over me, the escape from his torture and snide remarks. I'm celebrating the safety of my children above all else.

"Alright, what can you tell me about the stairs?" I asked Andrew, holding my second wine glass since being home.

"These stairs are a true example of craftsmanship. They are sturdier than any staircase I have ever seen. Are you sure the stairs just fell out from underneath you?" He asked, eyebrows raised, begging me to tell the truth.

"I'm positive that whoever built this home made this one stair weaker than all the rest. We all knew it would fall out on us one day, so we tried to avoid it at all costs." That honestly was not all a lie. The creak annoyed me and the kids, and we knew something would come of it one day. What we did not anticipate was Henry's haunting of it.

"Well, this should be fixed before the end of the day. I covered up the scratch at the top of the banister, but I also wanted to bring this to your attention." He said, pointing towards one of the railings. "If you look closely, you can see what looks like blood. Now, I am no detective, but it does *not* look like this blood would be from your fall today. It looks older. With your husband missing and all, I felt it only right to call the police department and report it." Andrew stated, now with his hands clutched behind his back.

"You did what now?" I began to say when I heard a light knock on the door and saw Detective Albert poke his head into the doorway.

I stood there frozen, unable to move, like a statue. The blood ran dry from my face, the color following suit. I held my breath as a thousand thoughts raced through my head. *Oh god, how could I have missed this? I should have checked the railing. Why did I not check the railing? Why did I have to call someone? It's over, I'm finished. Might as well take me away now.*

"Andrew, glad you called this in. With the ongoing investigation, every bit of information helps us. Thank you for doing your civic duty." Detective Albert grinned as he walked into the foyer and shook Andrew's hand. "Now, Mrs. Thompson, great to see you getting such an early start to your evening." He eyed my wine glass. "This won't take but a moment."

Pull yourself together, Emma!

Detective Albert opened his bag and pulled out a forensic kit. He placed a pair of black nylon gloves on each hand before pulling out a sheet of fingerprint tape. He cut a size small enough to wrap around the railing. Letting it sit momentarily; he grabbed a razor blade from his bag and a few evidence bags to collect the blood. Detective Albert then peeled the tape off and placed it in an evidence bag. Then he cut a piece of tape to have it slide around the railing snug enough to catch any as he scraped away at the blood to gather every last drop. Finally, he took a wipe, cleaned the surface, and placed it in another bag. When he was all packed up and ready to head on, he stopped and looked at me. He had a shit eating grin on his face the entire time.

"This should help tremendously, thank you." He said and took his leave before I got up enough courage to argue with him.

"Finish what you are doing and leave." I sternly told Andrew.

When they had finally left, I sat on the stairs and wept. "Is this what you were trying to tell me, Henry? That you still existed here; your blood was still here?" I shouted. "I get it! I understand what you are trying to tell me. You are forever a part of my life. I can't get rid of you that easily, right? Just tell me what you want from me!"

I continued to sob, tears running down my face. *What am I going to do?* I'm sure that there is plenty of evidence to arrest me. I've seen cop shows, and they arrest on much less. That's it, I'm done for. I might as well start making a list of what needs to be done with my children and the house, just in case. I sat there for a moment longer, waiting for a response. I stood up, kicked the stairs, and screamed when none came.

"Silence, huh? Not even worthy of anything now that

you have been found, huh? Well, we will see who has the last laugh then." I told him, looked at my watch, and realized it was time to pick up my kids from school. I stood up to gather my phone, shoes, purse, and water, and began to walk away.

Creak.

Of course, he would need the last word.

— ✦ —

"Mrs. Thompson, can I have a moment of your time?" the principal of my daughter's school asked me as I approached the front of the pick-up line.

"Of course, what can I do for you?" I asked. Bracing myself for yet another confrontation about my husband.

"If you could park your car and come inside, that would be best. Wouldn't want to hold up the pick-up line." Principal Lightly giggled nervously.

I did as I was told, parked my car, and headed inside to see what could constitute a conversation with me. She led me through the school, passing various groups of middle schoolers getting ready for their after-school activities or to head out to be picked up by their parents. Once corralled into the principal's office, I see my daughter sitting in a chair in the corner. Her head was on her chest, and her hands were shoved into her hoodie pocket. She looked up briefly when we entered, just enough time for me to mouth, 'What happened?' to her before she dropped her head back down.

"Now, we both know this is your daughter's second year at this school. Last year, her grades were exemplary, and they have been so far this year. She is the picture-perfect student for everyone to see and follow suit." The principal began.

As much as I loved hearing the great things about my daughter, I couldn't help but think we were here because of me. Lilly is the best daughter you could ever ask for, stiff as can be, but the best one. She hopes to attend an Ivy League school, meet her version of a prince charming, gain her M.R.S. Degree, and live happily ever after. If anyone would be the problem child, I would think it would be Jack when he gets older and all of the testosterone enters his body.

"Until today, that is." She continued. "A teacher witnessed Lilly punch another student in the face multiple times."

I quickly looked back at Lilly in shock. She pulled her hands out of her hoodie pocket to show me the damage, and I could see blood and a bruise beginning to form around her knuckles, before she quickly shoved them back into her pockets.

"Well, what do you have to say about this behavior?" Ms. Lightly asked as I turned back toward her.

"I would like to know what the fight was about before I put any of my input and thoughts into this," I said, straightening my back.

"You." She said, her face as blank as a canvas.

"That's it. No other context? Mind if I ask my daughter if you don't have the answers?" At this point, I was fed up with this school and, frankly, the principal. I did not wait for her to respond. "What happened?" I asked Lilly, turning around in my chair to face her.

"Some students were saying that you got rid of Daddy, that we were products of another man, and that is why you snapped. I stood up for you, though, Mom. I don't believe a single thing they said. Dad will be back soon; I know it," Lilly said through tears, her voice breaking at the end.

I have never been prouder of my daughter than I am right now. She fought for an honorable reason. But what does this say about her temper? Her father started with a temper like this in school, with little fights here and there for minor things. Maybe when we get home, I will tell Lilly how I know, for a fact, that she and her brother were the 'product,' as the kids said, of her father. Her anger alone should be enough evidence to convince her of that and turn her back to our loving tea party princess of a daughter. However, if I did tell her this, it might have given her suspicion as to where her dad was. And if the kids she bullied were telling the truth.

"I'm sure you have some punishment lined up for her, but frankly, I am very proud of her. She stood up for our family and let them know the truth." I leaned back and grabbed my daughter's bloody and bruised hands, giving her a tight squeeze.

"You're right. We do not tolerate violence of any kind,

no matter how justified by the parent, in this school. She broke the boy's nose while she was fighting. His parents want her expelled. However, since this is her first offense, she will be out of school for a week. Someone will drop off her assignments each day after school. She may return next Monday. Until then, she is not allowed on the property. Given everything going on in your life, I am sure the young man's parents won't want to press charges. So be thankful for that. Until then, put your daughter back on the right path. She strayed a bit too far, and it is time for her to make her way back." Ms. Lightly stood up from her desk and escorted us out of the building without another word.

"A week of out-of-school suspension? Was it worth it?" I asked Lilly when we got back into the car and had the doors firmly shut.

"No," Lilly said, hanging her head low again. "But they shouldn't talk about you or Dad that way. We don't know where Dad is. If we did, we would tell the police, right?"

"Of course we would, sweetie. I miss Daddy just as much as you do. I hope he is okay wherever he is. This is the longest we have gone without hearing from him. It worries me too," I told her.

"Well, at least I can spend more time with you if I am stuck at home for a week," she chirped.

Before leaving the school's parking lot, I told her, "You will also be doing your homework. Being told not to come to school for a week is not a reward. This is still a punishment."

"The real punishment is for Principal Lightly. Being unmarried at her age? I wish never to let that happen to me," Lilly protested.

"Lilly! You don't know why she is single. She could be a widow! Ever thought of that?" I asked her, frankly wondering for myself.

"I guess so," Lilly said, buckling herself up in her seat.

I took a moment to consider what Henry would say about this situation and how I handled it. She is only my responsibility now, and I have to ensure she stays the sweet little girl she is and not let the school bullies turn her. I took the long way to Jack's school and made a pit stop.

"I thought this was a punishment. What are we doing here?" Lilly asked as we pulled up to a drive-thru.

"We are not going to tell your brother the real reason we are getting this treat. But I am very proud of you for standing up for your family, even though it meant getting kicked out of school for a week. Your dad, however, will not react as gracefully as I do. So, the next time you see him, maybe we shouldn't bring this up. Deal?" I asked, putting my hand out to be shaken.

"Deal." She shook my hand and began reading the menu, looking to see what sweet treat she wanted before heading off to pick up her brother.

"Hey, sweetie, how was school?" I asked Jack as he jumped into the car, tossing his bag on the seat next to him.

"Here you go," Lilly said, passing off the special treat.

"Whoa, a milkshake! Thank you so much!" Jack

shouted with glee.

I'm thankful he did not question why he got a milkshake right after school and before dinner. I did not have the energy or willpower to come up with a lie just now. For now, it will be Lilly's and my own little secret. We can drop Jack off at school and not tell him that his sister is really home for a week, because then he will want to be home for a week, too. Then we won't have to lie to him, and he usually gets dropped off first anyway. For now, we will enjoy our milkshakes and head home. It's Friday night; after all, we have pizza to eat and a movie to watch. *A little violence never hurt our family, right?*

The next day, we met Gwen and her husband, Vince, downtown to do some shopping. Downtown Gloomridge was historic, then again, what *wasn't* historic in Gloomridge? Everywhere you go, someone has either fought or died fighting for something, whether that is for our country or because someone slept with another man's wife, which didn't happen as often as you would think. Most of the streets were one-way, which caused the locals a great deal of laughter when we watched a tourist drive the wrong way down the street. Each building stood on the original foundation, and most, if not all, still had the same framework and exterior. The old buildings sell Gloomridge to the history buffs; they simply can't get enough.

Anyway, the kids, Gwen, Vince, and I were hopping in and out of different antique stores. A good ninety percent of the stores in downtown were either antique stores or ones that sold historical artifacts. I am not quite sure how the historical artifact stores stay in business. Eventually, they would run out of artifacts, wouldn't you think? The particular store we were in was crowded that day; a tour group had come through the town and seemed to all end up in the same store we were in. We tended not to buy anything when we wandered through these stores; they sold the same things year-round and very similar items to the other antique stores next to them. I watched as the kids picked up item after item, placing them back where they found them.

"Hey, that's mine," We heard a little boy shout at Lilly, "Mom, it's her!" He screamed even louder, pointing directly into my daughter's face. The little boy in front of her had light brown hair that stuck straight up from his head. His clothes were disheveled, with holes in a few spots. His face was covered in acne and his nose bandaged.

"Hey, knock it off. Leave my daughter alone." I told him, pushing his arm back down.

"Don't you dare touch my child!" His mom came in to defend him, waving her large purse in my direction.

"He started this, and he should not be that upset that my daughter was touching something in a store. We don't want it. You can have it." I picked up the wooden toy train set and passed it off to him.

"He did not start anything. It was your daughter who started this when she punched my poor, sweet, defenseless son!" She said, getting closer and closer to me. Her breath reeked of cigarette smoke.

"Defenseless? Well, maybe you should have taught him to defend himself. That's what fathers are supposed to do." Vince chimed in, poking the chest of this boy's father. He was nowhere near as tall or strong as Vince.

"Oh yeah, and who are you? We know you aren't her dad because her dad is missing. Are you the replacement? You work that fast, huh?" He screamed between Vince and me.

"Just leave it alone, everyone!" Gwen is shouting over us, waving her arms in the air.

The whole store was staring at us at that moment. No one was picking up items, making purchases, or doing their job. If they had something in their hand, they froze holding it. It had been a while since I last caused a scene in public, and I fear it will not be the last with everything going on.

"I'm her godfather," Vince continued. "So, fuck off and leave us alone."

"Or what?" the father asked.

"You don't want to know." He said, "Let's go, guys." He started to gather all of us up in his arms and lead us towards the exit.

"Alright, tough guy, let me see it." The dad shouted as he came swinging at Vince.

The dad lunged towards Vince, sucker-punching him in the back of his head. Vince, a powerful man, always prepared for the worst, anticipated this attack. He swung his body around, hitting the father in his chest and then his face ten times harder than the dad had hit him, knocking him to the ground. I was nervous that Vince would continue the fight and worried about how to stop two grown men from beating each other to death. Thankfully, the store's security guy had heard the commotion and put an end to the fight. He tossed both men out of the store and yelled at them to go in their opposite directions.

"Are you okay?" Gwen and I began asking as we got out of the store.

"I'm fine, maybe a bit dizzy. I'll be fine." He promised, rubbing the back of his head.

"I should probably get him to the hospital and get him checked out, just to be sure." Gwen grabbed her husband by his shoulders. "We'll catch up with you later." She said before walking away.

Jack, Lilly, and I stood in shock in front of the store. We watched as this kid and his mom exited the store and followed the dad as he hunched over against a tree. If anyone needed to see a doctor, it was him.

"Did we learn anything from this, Lilly?" I asked her, pulling my children under each of my arms and walking away before the mom wanted to try something with me next.

"We learned that if Dad didn't go missing, none of this

would have happened." She said proudly.

"You aren't wrong, but we also learned that we shouldn't bait people. Massive grown men, their fists are a lot stronger than yours or that of that boy, and can do some serious damage. Now you are going to pick out something for Vince as an apology for getting him hit in the head. Do you understand?" I informed her, dragging her into the next store we saw.

She spent her time picking out an item for Vince, walking every aisle more than once. Finally, she came to the register with a large, clear bag filled with an assortment of different sour gummy candies, a stack of baseball cards, and a new baseball hat.

"I think he would really like these," she said, placing the items on the register.

Chapter Six

Fall had not yet arrived in this part of Virginia; the sun was beaming over our home that afternoon. Gwen and I took margaritas out in the backyard to lie by the pool and bask in the sun before fall really took over. My fears of Henry did not exist out here; I couldn't hear his constant nagging from here. He stayed haunting the house and nothing more. I was free to be myself outside.

"What are we going to do about Lilly?" Began Gwen. "She's such a good kid, I just don't want her ending up like Henry. This could start her down a horrible path. And you rewarded her with milkshakes! What were you thinking?" She wanted to shout. I could see it, but she didn't want Lilly to hear her screaming, especially not about her.

"Look, I wasn't thinking at the moment, other than I was simply proud of her. She's a great kid; we both know this. I wanted her to know that her decision was the correct one, and that I approved of it even if the rest of society did not. She's an innocent little girl who made one mistake; we can't fault her for it. If she killed someone, then we would be having a different conversation. But she didn't, she only broke a kid's nose, one that I know has been a dick to everyone since elementary school." I told her, taking a sip and lifting my sun hat to make eye contact with her.

"Oh yeah, a different conversation then. Should we have that conversation?" Gwen asked. Her face turned stern, and her eyebrows raised as she began to place her drink down and start what was sure to be a long conversation.

"No, I don't think we…" I began, but got interrupted by the doorbell. "I'll go get that."

"I'll come with you, we are out of margaritas after all," Gwen said, stumbling to her feet.

Passing through the kitchen, I placed my glass on the kitchen counter for Gwen to fill up. I could hear Lilly's music from her room, blasting as high as it could go.

Creak

A shiver ran down my spine. Henry must think whoever is on the other side of this door is trouble. I took a deep breath, grabbed a robe from the coat hook, and opened the door to see a boy about Lilly's age standing there. A cardboard box filled with supplies was on the ground, and his backpack was leaning up against it.

"Can I help you?" I asked, unsure what he could be here for.

"Uh…Hi, Mrs. Thompson," he stuttered to get the words out, frozen in bewilderment.

Creak

"I…I'm here…to see Lilly." He said, shifting from one foot to the next.

Creak

Ah, this is why Henry has been so vocal. This boy must have a crush on my daughter, and with her not in school, he had to come and see her. Doesn't quite explain the box yet, though.

"We are in science class together, and we are supposed to make a volcano. Um… with her not being in school this week, the teacher asked me if my mom could drop me off during my last period. That's when we have science class, ma'am. Then I could come here and we could work on the volcano together. I have to return it to school tomorrow in order for us to get a grade on it." He informed me before looking behind him to the box full of baking soda, vinegar, soap, and an assortment of papier-mâché.

It was at that moment that I realized I was standing before a young, impressionable boy in a bikini. Not just any bikini, but the one that makes my breasts look like they did before I had children and spent years breastfeeding them. I quickly wrapped myself up in my robe while leaning out of the door to see an SUV leaving the driveway. *I guess I have to let him in now, with the mom driving away as fast as she did.*

"Come on in, um… what's your name?" I asked, unsure if he had told me already.

"Eugene, would you mind helping me with this box? My mom carried it to the porch, and I can't get it in the house by myself." He asked while grabbing his backpack off the ground.

I picked up the box and led him past the foyer and into the kitchen.

"Look who I found outside," I told Gwen as we entered the kitchen. If she had been sober, she would have made an attempt to cover herself up, as she had always been self-conscious about her body, but she wasn't today. *Liquor can do that.* "I'll make the kids some snacks while you go get Lilly?" I raised my eyebrow to ask her and hope she doesn't make Lilly feel embarrassed.

I could hear Gwen skipping down the hall towards the stairs. Knowing her, she will walk into Lilly's room gossiping about the fact that there is a boy here to see her. Lilly will probably come out of her room feeling awkward that she had to have her mother answer the door for a boy when she could have done it if only her music were quieter and Eugene had called her in advance.

"So, Eugene, tell me about yourself," I asked while rummaging through my pantry to gather snacks for Lilly and Eugene.

He was just as nervous as he was at the front door. He stumbled across his words and told me about his love for hockey. I handed him a glass of lemonade and a cookie to hold him over while I made sandwiches. Gwen and Lilly were taking more than enough time. I can only imagine that Lilly was brushing her hair, picking out an outfit that would be appropriate, and then trying to talk Gwen into just sending him home, even though Lilly has no idea who the boy is down there, because Gwen never learned his name.

I placed the sandwiches on a tray along with a pitcher of lemonade, four more cookies, and a bowl of pretzels. "You can wait for Lilly in the living room. I'll grab your box after I put this down. Follow me."

Creak

Henry screamed from the only part of the house he had. The sound stopped me in my tracks, and Eugene almost ran into me. Thankfully, he did not; otherwise, we would have more of a mess to clean up than whatever they were going to do with their volcano.

"So, Eugene, how well do you know my daughter?" I asked, taking a seat on the couch opposite him.

"Not super well, we have been lab partners this year, and I heard about her every now and then last year. The whole school talks about you now, actually. Everyone is in shock that your husband is missing; this has never happened in our town before." Eugene gushed as he reached into his backpack.

Everyone in the school is talking about me? Hearing this, my heart swelled with apprehension, unsure of what they had truly discussed. Yet, at the same time, I feel recognized, truly recognized for the first time in years.

"Eugene, do you have any hobbies?" I asked in an attempt to make small talk and steer the conversation away from me.

"Actually, I'm part of the school newspaper. Specifically, investigative journalism. My mother is a journalist at the Gloomridge Times. That's where I got my love for it. She's truly an inspiration!" I froze hearing this. "That's why it was a huge coincidence with Lilly being my lab partner. This gives me the opportunity to have a one-on-one with you!" He said as he pulled a pencil and a notepad out of his backpack.

"One-on-one? What is this about?" I questioned.

"For the school newspaper, of course. I'm the lead investigator on this story. Do you mind if I ask you a few questions while we wait for Lilly?" he asked, basically shaking in his seat.

This story? I don't want to be a 'story'.

"I…um," I began. Thankfully, Lilly and Gwen walked into the room just in time. "Ah, sweetie, there you are. Good luck with your volcano. Call if you need anything." I grabbed Gwen's arm and left the room as quickly as I could, swaying my hips from side to side. I glanced back to watch the interaction of my daughter and Eugene; instead, I watched as Eugene's mouth hung wide open. We made eye contact just long enough for him to realize he was staring and quickly straightened his face out and turned back towards Lilly.

"What did I just walk into?" Gwen asked when we were finally outside by ourselves.

"A little journalist in the making wants to publish my side of the story in their school newspaper. If they don't allow violence, why are they allowing their students to write about anything that is not school-related?" I challenged.

"Plus, if he really wanted my side of the story, there would be no way Ms. Lightly would allow that to be published."

"You would also end up in jail if you let that get published." Gwen reasoned.

"So would you." I insisted.

"Fair, so what are we going to do about this?" Gwen asked, taking her seat.

"Absolutely nothing, we avoid being in the same room together for as long as I can. We also need to put on some clothes when we are around that kid; he stares too much for my liking. Prepubescent teenagers are bound to ogle from time to time, but he couldn't keep his eyes off of me." I said, wrapping my robe tightly around my waist to cover up my body.

"Alright, then we will just move on. We don't say anything to him, and he won't have anything to publish." Gwen reassured.

"Wow, the volcano looks terrific, kids!" I praised them as I walked into the living room. "Do you know if it works?"

"We won't know till we try it in class," Lilly said, cleaning up their workspace.

"Your mom's here, let me help you carry all of this to her car," I said, quickly gathering up their materials.

"Thank you for letting me come over. Please remember that I need to ask you questions for my article. If I don't get to it, I can still publish what I know." Eugene insisted as he hopped into his seat.

Ignoring his sentiment, I placed the volcano in his mom's SUV and waved him goodbye, hoping never to see him again.

Monday could not have arrived any faster. Lilly spent the week following me around the house during the day out of pure boredom and the afternoons doing her schoolwork. By Wednesday, she had decided to practice for her future as a housewife and began baking nonstop. The kitchen counters were swarming with baking sheets, parchment paper, cooling racks, and, of course, flour. The air was heavy with flour. With every breath I inhaled, thousands of particles of the flour that had been floating in the air entered my lungs. I spent the next several minutes running around the house opening every window imaginable. My house was covered in baked goods. Lilly had nearly one hundred mini loaves scattered across the floor haphazardly. It was a delicious minefield to walk through. A minefield that was blocking the path to my coffee machine.

I surely could not have eaten them all by myself; Lilly would nibble here and there, but barely touched her own creations. Jack had no idea there were any baked goods; all he cared about were his pizza bites and chips.

"That's it!" My voice came thundering out of me. "We are taking some to the neighbors!"

"Sure, Mom! Can't wait!" Lilly squealed as she madly ran about the house gathering all the bags, ribbons, and tags she could get her hands on.

We packed up the baked goods that no one in the house had eaten and placed them on our wagon. I got Lilly dressed up in an outfit that screamed a good little girl, since I am sure the whole neighborhood has heard about her time as an MMA fighter by now.

"Hi, Mrs. Finkle!" Lilly exclaimed. "I made you a loaf!"

"Wow, that is so kind of you." She took a deep sniff of the loaf. "Goodness, that smells delicious. What type of loaf is it?" she wondered.

"It's a pumpkin chocolate chip loaf, if you like that, I also have a honey spice loaf I could give you! It's right here in my wagon. Give me one moment." Lilly squealed before turning around to grab a second loaf.

Mrs. Finkle looked at me with wide, doe eyes. I could see the sympathy in her heart. She's wondering what got Lilly into such a kind and giving mood. Most children handle being sent out of school with anger, but not my daughter. However, it could be the grief of her father not talking to her that could also be affecting her behavior. I heard her whispering with Jack last night that their dad was on a secret mission and had to lie low for a while. That he would be back before we knew it, and he would have stories for days to tell them about his wild adventure. Jack hoped these stories were full of chase scenes with cops, flames, and cool motorcycles. I couldn't tell if Jack's excitement was simply from the mind of a nine-year-old or if he genuinely thought his dad was cool enough to ride a motorcycle. For clarity, he is not cool enough to ride a bike. He would pose on one, sure, the actual act of riding one, though, is another story. Henry would pull out the statistics of motorcycle deaths and have them sent to the junkyard to be flattened if anyone even suggested taking a ride, let alone taking a seat on one.

"Here you go! If you want anything else, I have been baking a lot lately and can try to make you whatever you are craving!" Lilly gushed as she thrust the sweets into Mrs. Finkle's outstretched hands.

"Sounds like a plan. Let me at least pay you for these ones." Mrs. Finkle offered.

"Oh no, these are gifts." Lilly jumped in to say before Mrs. Finkle could turn around and grab her wallet.

"Alright, well, any further treats I will pay for." She concluded.

"That seems fair, you have to taste something before you know if it is worth buying after all." Lilly giggled. "Off to the next house, Mom!" She boomed.

"If these actually taste good, get that girl business cards. She is a good saleswoman." Mrs. Finkle suggested while shutting her door.

As we walked up to Mrs. Rhubit's house, I noticed in

the window closest to the front door that she stood there peeking behind the curtain, waiting to see if we would come to her house next. When we made eye contact, she ducked as fast as possible.

"Hold on, she's at my house now." We could hear her say through her front door, unsure who she was on the phone with.

I took a moment to rearrange Lilly's wagon before we rang the doorbell. Giving Mrs. Rhubit plenty of time to gather herself and act as if she hadn't been waiting by the front door for us. Lilly gave her the same speech that she gave Mrs. Finkle, ending the encounter by telling Mrs. Rhubit that she would be bringing around business cards the next time she saw her. I thanked her for her kindness towards Lilly.

"They are leaving now. Have you seen the way she goes about parading her body nowadays? I guess with her husband gone, she has no reason to hide." Mrs. Rhubit told her friend on the phone loud enough to be heard on the other side of her door.

"I heard she has been soliciting young boys, teenagers that her daughter finds for her." The woman on the other end responded.

Thicker skin is all I am going to need for these baked goods deliveries. Thankfully, we only have so many left to drop off; there will be an end to it at least.

"My daughter brought this home from school today. You made the front page." Mrs. Trumpet gloated as she held up a copy of the Gloomridge Times Newspaper. "She brought two home, so you can have this and read it at your leisure!" She handed me the copy, grinning from ear to ear as she saw the color drain from my face.

"Remember, I am taking orders now. Have a nice day." Lilly said before leaving Mrs. Trumpet's house.

It is incredible how quickly a child's passion can turn into a small business. She will end up having more orders than our local bakery if she isn't careful. Once she is back in school, though, I have no idea how she will actually keep the promises to bake these for everyone. Her schedule is plenty busy as it is.

"Great job, Lilly. Everyone really seemed to enjoy their treats. Why don't you go run to your room now and get started on designing your business cards?" I asked her, simply so I could retreat to the basement and read the newspaper.

Gloomridge Times Newspaper
The True Story Behind the Disappearance of Henry Thompson
Written by Eugene Forrest.

In the town of Gloomridge, every day is much the same. The children go to school, the adults go to work, and the wives all stay home and take care of their homes all day. Our police department has nothing better to do with its time than to ticket children who are skateboarding on the sidewalks. The town of Gloomridge is just that, gloomy. Nothing happens here, and we all thought nothing ever would. That is, until Henry Thompson, the father of our very own Lilly Thompson, went missing over the summer. The word around the street is he was supposed to be leaving town for a business trip, one of many he went on that summer. He never did make it to his business trip, let alone on the plane. Thanks to a police department that has not had anything exciting happen in decades, they were eager to talk with an up-and-coming journalist like me. On the day of his disappearance, the police were able to track his vehicle through our sleepy town and onto the highway leading towards the airport. They watched as he drove well over the speed limit. He pulled into the parking garage and was never seen again. When the police found his vehicle, they were shocked when they pulled all of his belongings out of his car. Nothing was taken with him; he fled on foot with nothing on his back. However, it is not clear where he fled to. There were no cameras to capture him leaving the garage, nor have they been able to find him on any other cameras using his latest headshot from his company to search their systems. Henry Thompson has disappeared from the surface of the earth without a trace.

When I went to question his wife, Emma Thompson, she was more than welcoming as I entered her home. In the photo here (captured by Beatrice Forrest), you can see Mrs. Thompson answering the door in barely any clothing. She did not make any attempt to cover her body. With this view, I can confirm there are no visible bruises or injuries on Mrs. Thompson. This helps her case that she has nothing to do with her husband's disappearance. There has been speculation throughout my school and town that Emma Thompson had an argument with her husband that led to his disappearance. However, I feel confident in my statement that she had nothing to do with his disappearance based on the lack of bruises or scrapes on her body.

However, this does not rule her out completely. Thanks to the insider scoop from the police department, I have been informed that there might have been some foul play. Emma Thompson had hired contractors to come and fix a stair that had fallen out from underneath her last week. I had the pleasure of speaking with this contractor, and he informed me that he thought it was incredibly suspicious that she would claim that the stairs had fallen out under her when those stairs were in impeccable condition. Everyone knows the Thompsons' home. It is the largest and oldest in their neighborhood, the craftsmanship alone could rival any company, and their skills today. If this contractor, who wishes to be anonymous, can say for a fact that the stairs should not have fallen out from underneath her, then she had done it herself. But why?

Many may think it has something to do with the blood that was found by the contractor. When I questioned the police department about this, they ensured that the detective on the case had gone to the home to collect the blood sample. They were still waiting to hear back on whose blood it could have been, but I am sure we can all safely say it was Henry's.

So, the question facing Emma now is, why? Why did your husband disappear without a word? Why was she lying to the police and her neighbors about her involvement in this matter?

Nobody has been found just yet, but once there is, the police department states they will be able to make an arrest. It makes one wonder what happened to Henry; it is not easy to disappear a body and have it go unnoticed for as long as Emma has done. When you spend the afternoon in the company of such a vile woman, you begin to think like her. The options of how to murder someone and get rid of their body are endless. The blood found at the scene of the crime might not be enough for an arrest, but it does point to foul play. If the FBI comes and takes my computer in for questioning in this case, I will give it over willingly. A true journalist always has their sources, like the old-school journalists or the ones working deep undercover; they wouldn't have a computer. They would only have their eyes, ears, and their mind as their trustworthy source for a story. I have gone off-topic a bit, but it is all relevant to this story. The story that breaks my journalistic career wide open.

When I went to the suspected widow's home, she welcomed me with open arms into her home. She fed me, gave me something to drink, and even some dessert. I began to question her about the disappearance of her husband, but she refused to answer any questions I had. She quickly walked away, silent in her position to stay away from the media. One might even question why my own mother allowed me into the house of a murderer. Ladies and gentlemen, I am a true journalist. Putting myself in unknown harm's way to gather the facts that only I was able to obtain. This won't be my last attempt. When we have more information, I will try again and let my devoted readers in on my knowledge. Until then, stay vigilant.

Who did this kid think he was? Christiane Amanpour? He is going to have to try harder to rock me. And the nerve of the police department to tell all of this to a twelve-year-old! The only positive thing about the entire article is that the police have yet to determine whose blood it was.

Creak…creak

Shivers ran up my spine as the creaking grew closer. Henry had moved to haunt the basement stairs as well. I leaned back in my chair, taking a deep breath and truly examining my surroundings.

My bottles had moved. *Someone* had been in my basement.

Jumping from my chair, the newspaper falling on the floor, I began searching my shelves. For what? I wasn't sure, but I knew once I found it, I would know. I picked up every bottle in my cellar, looked behind them, and blew off dust from many of them. This cellar held bottles that I have owned since I was in my early 20s. We had bottles from our wedding down here, bottles from every vacation we had ever taken, bottles from the many subscriptions I am a part of, and bottles that friends have gifted me throughout the years. To move every single bottle took hours. It was all worth it when I found just what I was looking for.

On the very bottom shelf, nestled behind a bottle of Rosé that I never planned on drinking, was a camera. I froze, unsure of my next steps. I should destroy it, take it out, and step on it immediately. However, that could make me look guilty. I should leave it there and use it to my advantage by coming into my cellar and crying loudly that I missed my husband. Making whoever put this camera here realize I had nothing to do with it. I quickly put the bottle back on the shelf and continued picking up each bottle and dusting it off. This way, whoever was watching just assumed

I came down to read the paper and decided to do a little dusting. *Problem solved.*

"Family meeting time, guys," I told my kids as we sat down for dinner that night. "As you both know, your father has been missing for some weeks now."

"Have you heard anything from him?" Jack cheerfully jumped in.

"Unfortunately, no, I haven't heard anything from him. However, I have heard a lot from our neighbors and your friend Eugene. The whole town seems to be talking about your father." I watched as Lilly shyly hid her hands, which, for the most part, were healed by then.

"He's not coming home, is he?" she asked.

"I have no way of knowing that, sweetie, but we should be prepared to live our lives if your dad doesn't come home. As horrible as that would be, we don't want to have to do that. I want to prepare the two of you for the possibility that it could happen. It might just be the three of us. Are you two okay with that?" I genuinely wondered.

I never want to hurt my children and make them hate their father. I do want them to be prepared when they fully realize that their dad is not coming home. They are going to be stuck with me for the rest of their lives, and many people might see them growing up without their father as a nega-tive thing. If they knew Henry, they wouldn't think that. Unfortunately, the Henry the rest of the world knew was the face he put on, the kind, sweet, generous man who would do anything to help his fellow neighbor. As I have made painfully clear, he was the complete opposite of this. Having that influence gone during a pivotal time for our children's development is for their own good. They might not fully appreciate it now, but when they get older and are well-behaved members of society and not pieces of shit who abuse others for their own enjoyment. That's when they will be able to let me know I made the right decision all along.

"It will be fine, I guess," Lilly mumbled.

"What would it mean to have just you as our parent? Would Dad come in and be a part of our lives still, or will he be gone, out of our lives?" Jack wondered, his mind not fully wrapping around the concept of his father never com-ing back.

"She's saying he will be gone from our lives for good, Jack. Mom doesn't think he will be back anytime soon, if ever. It will just be you, Mom, and me for the rest of our lives." Lilly explained.

"Oh…" Jack sighed.

"I understand the disappointment. Even though your dad is not a part of your life in true, emotional, meaningful ways, he is still your father. He could be gone for a long time, and we have to be prepared for that." I reassured them, taking each of their hands in mine.

"Okay, so he will miss Christmas, too?" I could see Jack hold back tears as he asked.

It tore my heart into pieces to see him like this, my sweet baby boy. He's one of the last truly innocent children I know. I hope this doesn't change that.

"If he isn't back by then, yes, he will miss Christmas. He will most likely also miss your birthday. There is a possibility he will miss more than just this year. We have to think long term here: elementary school graduation, high school graduation, college graduation, your first relationship, your wedding day, the birth of your first child. I could go on, but I don't want to upset you too much. Your dad will forever be in your heart; that will never change." I comforted Jack by putting my hand on his shoulder and giving it a tight squeeze.

He got up from his seat, walked over to me, fighting back tears, and sat on my lap. Giving me the tightest hug.

"I love you, Mom." He blubbered.

"I love you, too, honey." I cried back.

Lilly came over and joined in on the hug, proving our little princess was still sweet inside.

"If Dad's gone, do we get to keep our house?" Lilly whispered into my ear.

"We should be able to. Do you want to stay here still, or would you like a different home?" I questioned, already knowing her answer.

"I could see us in a smaller house; we don't need all of this space. Plus, this house is haunted." She laughed, trying to hide her fear.

Creak

"Well, if your father doesn't come back, we can talk about moving. I know he loves this house, so it would break his heart to leave this house." I told her, wiping the tears from my eyes and trying to ignore the sound from the stairs.

Creak

I whipped my head towards the stairs and saw that Lilly had done the same. Her father was haunting us both.

You would have to pull Henry tooth and nail from this house; he had always planned on dying in this house. *Technically, I gave him his wish! Go me!* The only part of this house I would care to keep is the cellar, which was my baby. Henry gave me that room to do with as I pleased, he said, back when I think he still loved me. Ever since, my wine cellar has been my fortress. I used my wine collection as my third child; I knew everything there was to know about the wines in our house. Each one was hand-selected and had a purpose in my home. If I ever needed to escape, I knew just where to go. That room was my security blanket. Some days I would go into the room so I wouldn't have to see my husband till I went to bed. He usually stayed locked in his office when he was home, so it was easier to keep my distance even if I was not in my happy place. Often, the times I remember feeling truly happy in our marriage, I had a wine glass in my hand. I know how bad that sounds, but it truly was my escape. The only freedom I had was from a controlling husband. Yes, he spent much of his time away from us, so you would think I had freedom, but every step, every purchase, every move I made, he knew about. I don't know how, but he always seemed to have eyes on me.

"Now, if either of you has any questions whatsoever about what we should do if he doesn't come home, please come to me. If you hear anything new at school or around town, come to me, and I can help ensure you have the correct information and not what the town is spinning in their newspapers, town gossip, or anything else. Is that understood?" I looked at both of my children as I held them in my arms.

"Yes, Mom." They each responded.

The rest of dinner was quiet. Jack would fight back a tear here and there, barely ever making eye contact with me. Lilly stared off into the direction of the foyer, bracing herself for the next sound. At the same time, I stared at myself in the mirror that hung on the wall in front of me. I watched my reflection stand up from the table and walk off in the direction of the staircase. When I blinked, I was nowhere near the stairs. I continued to sit just where I was at the table, fork in one hand, wine glass in the other.

What is going on?

Chapter Seven

"Shred this cheese for me, dear." I handed Lilly a block of cheese for dinner. "Please be careful when you drop the noodles in the water," I told Jack as I watched him hop onto his step stool.

Just then, the doorbell rang. "Jack, honey, will you go get that? I'll take over the noodles."

He hopped down from his stool and skipped to the front door. I could hear a man's voice in the distance asking if I was home. Jack, being the innocent little boy he was, invited him inside without question. His large feet stomping through the foyer and into the kitchen stopped me in my tracks. My heart skipped a beat as my mind fluttered between my attacks from Henry and how he could be walking down my hallway. I held up the knife I was using to chop carrots, ready to protect my family and defend my home against him. When I turned around, it was none other than Detective Albert.

"Mrs. Thompson, good evening. I hope you don't mind me stopping by unannounced; I was hoping I could ask you and your children a few more questions." Detective Albert stated as he walked into the kitchen and stood by my side.

"Of course not, we were just making dinner, why don't you join us?" I encouraged as I walked to the cabinet and took down four plates. "Here, you can set the table. Let's not talk about the case in front of my children; they are very sensitive about it lately. If you have questions for my children and me that are not related to the case, then you may save those for dinner, it's almost ready. Any other questions, you need to save them for when my children go to bed." I whispered, stressing this would be the only way forward if he wanted to stay.

"Alright, let me call my wife and let her know I won't be home for dinner then." He informed me before walking just outside the kitchen to make his call.

The four of us continued our individual tasks. Lilly on the cheese, I worked on the noodles and the sauce. Detective Albert is on the table. Lastly, Jack grabbed everyone something to drink, chocolate milk for the kids and sparkling water for the adults.

"What do you police?" Jack asked, pointing towards the detective's badge, when we all sat down at the table.

"I'm a detective, do you know what that is?" He asked.

"You detect things?" Jack guessed, swirling a noodle around his fork.

"You are very close. I get called in when there is a crime that someone needs help solving. I go through the crime scene and gather as much information as I can to determine who the criminal is and what they did. That way, I can arrest the bad guy. Does that make sense?" Detective Albert asked.

Jack nodded his head slowly, wondering what bad guys he could run around town and arrest. Cops and robbers have always been a favorite game of his.

He and his wife must have had children at one point, or he does a lot of career days at schools to be able to explain his job in such a friendly and easy way for children to understand.

"Who's the bad guy you are currently trying to find?" Jack wondered.

My heart stopped, not even five minutes into dinner, and their father's case was going to come up. *How?* I tried to keep my cool and stop my heart from beating any faster as I braced myself for his answer.

"Well, you see," Detective Albert paused and looked at me, "this is a hard case to crack. There is no bad guy; we aren't sure what to make of it just yet. We are still gathering information that should tell us what we need to know to see if there is even a bad guy."

"So, how often do you arrest people?" Jack inquired, skipping altogether over this bit of information.

"Thankfully, we live in what we call a sleeper town, which means there are not a lot of bad guys in our town. Because of that, I do not get to make a lot of arrests." He explained.

My breathing began to steady as we moved on.

"Okay, but how many have you arrested this year?" Jack pestered.

"This year … let me think … I believe six, no seven. That does not even come out to one a month. Some months, I haven't arrested anyone. The biggest thing a bad guy can do in this town is run a red light or park where they shouldn't be." He sighed, wishing there were more action and danger in our town.

"Wow, and that's because everyone is sleeping in our town? I didn't realize we slept that much." Jack laughed.

Oh, to be a child again.

There was a lull in conversation while everyone began dishing more food onto their plates and taking their first few bites. Detective Albert paused and looked at me when he went to grab a piece of garlic bread, and winked at me. I would like to think that was his way of saying I wasn't a bad guy in his eyes, that I was just a mother trying to take care of my children. That the garlic bread was an inside joke between the two of us, and that's it. Not that the first day he interrogated me, I snuck garlic bread in, and today, which I can assume will be another day he interrogates me, garlic bread makes yet another appearance.

"Have you found my dad yet?" Lilly pipes up.

I dropped my fork onto my plate when 'Dad' hit my ears.

There is just no escaping the topic of Henry today. Instead of asking the detective not to talk about the case, I should have brought up the topic to my children and told them to keep their mouths shut. The last thing I need is for my children to have nightmares this evening. It is a school night after all; I can't risk them having a rough night of sleep.

"No, Lilly, I'm sorry, but we haven't." He paused, letting this bit of information sink further into her mind before continuing. "Do you want to tell me about your dad at all? What was your favorite thing the two of you did together?" He said, switching the topic off of the case just as I had asked.

I lifted my garlic bread and winked at him to tell him 'Thank you'.

"I have a few favorite memories. My favorite has to have been the year he dressed up as Santa for our neighbor's Christmas party. He climbed on the roof of their home and stomped as loudly as he could to get the children's attention. We all ran outside to see him holding a sack filled to the brim with presents. Then he pretended to jump into the chimney. I knew he hadn't actually done that because if he had, he would have been covered in the chimney dust when we saw him later. But also, there was no way he would have fit and made it down safely. After he jumped into the chimney, all of the kids ran inside as fast as they could, and there he was. My dad, Santa for the evening, standing in front of the fireplace, unloading presents out of his sack." Lilly exclaimed.

"Did you ever ask him how he got into the living room

so fast from the roof if he hadn't come down the chimney?" The detective chuckled.

"I did, he swore it was magic." She spouted, sure her father was lying.

"Sounds to me like you don't believe in magic. What is your theory, then? How did he get down so fast?" He chortled excitedly to hear what her explanation had to be.

"I have two theories. One, that another dad was actually on the roof in the costume, and when all of the kids ran outside, my dad came in through the back door and waited for us all to come running back into the living room. This way explains why he wasn't out of breath when we came in. My second theory, less possible though, is that it was my dad on the roof and when he 'went down' the chimney, he really hopped on a ladder and slid down it as fast as he could. Then ran inside from the back door, with just enough time to catch his breath. This one seems less likely as it is harder to pull off and can run into a lot of complications if the kids beat you inside." She explained, her eyes widening with excitement as she told us her theory.

I hadn't realized how much she had been thinking of this; she was ten when her father had done this. Lilly matured in more than one way while away at camp. For starters, Santa is entirely out of the question now, and she went and spilled the beans to her brother, who, to my knowledge, still believed in Santa. She was completely right, though. The neighbor hired a man to stand on the roof yelling 'Ho, Ho, Ho, Merry Christmas' and to pretend to climb into the chimney while Henry was already inside, joking around with the parents who stayed inside to help get him into position. Upon hearing Lilly telling her story, a small smile briefly danced its way across my face, reminding me of simpler and sometimes happier moments during my marriage. A smile that quickly faded. Despite the occasional memorable experiences with our kids and Henry, it does not change the numerous memories I have of Henry's abuse.

"Sounds like you have been working on this case for quite some time. You have wonderful theories there. Both probable." He paused, turning to Jack. "And what about you? What is your favorite memory of your dad?" He asked.

Jack froze, a spaghetti noodle hanging out of his mouth. You could see the gears in his head turning as he tried to pick the very best story possible.

"My dad once took me to a paintball day," he paused, catching my reaction as this was the first I had heard about it. "He told me that I needed to be prepared to shoot a gun one day. There were so many people there, too. On one side was the green team, and we were on the blue team. Dad taught me how to hide around corners and sneak up on people before shooting them. He was really good at being sneaky, and because of that, we won! I left without getting hit once, too! Dad said that was key to the game: don't get hit. Especially since it was just Dad and my little secret, I guess, until now that is." Jack gushed as he used his arms to help illustrate where the teams were.

This adventure of the two of them checked out. Henry

was the sneakiest man I knew. He would often sneak into rooms I was in without me ever knowing. The more of a surprise it was, the harder he laughed when I saw him. I would often jump and scream whenever I saw him stalking me. At the beginning of our marriage, he would do this for fun, and I found it charming. He would jump out from the corner yelling 'Boo', and I would flare my arms and use whatever I had in my hand as a weapon to try and protect myself from being too frightened. As our marriage progressed, the need to defend myself grew. I kept my eyes and ears open as much as possible, waiting for the creak in the stairs, the wind coming inside as he opened the front door, and the sound of the doorknob turning. Anything that would give away the fact that he was home.

"He sounds like an amusing dad." Detective Albert began, "Did he ever get mad at you?" he asked.

"Often," Lilly began, "he does not like it when we interrupt him. If he were in his office, even if the door was wide open, he hated being interrupted. Once, I walked past his office on my way to get a snack, and I made too much noise opening a bag of chips. When I turned around, I screamed. My dad was standing behind me, fuming. I thought I saw flames coming out of his ears; he was so angry. He took my bag of chips and tossed them in the trash before telling me I needed to choose a quieter snack. He can be mean." She sighed.

My children are really opening up to Albert in ways I never thought they would. I fear this may be dangerous later on.

"She's right, Dad can be very mean. I once watched him smack mommy." Jack revealed.

My face went red, and my jaw dropped. Detective Albert turned to see if this was true, but did not even have to ask; my face had said it all. I wish I knew which time he was talking about, so when the detective was bound to ask me about it, I wouldn't tell a different story than what Jack is bound to say to him. He seems to be a fountain of information tonight.

"You know, it's possible our dad never comes back. Did you know that?" He asked the detective absent-mindedly as he took a sip of his drink.

"I did. When someone is missing, there is always a possibility that you won't find them. However, there is always the possibility that you do find him. Keep your chin up and your spirits bright, he just might come home soon." The detective said, calming Jack down and patting him on the shoulder.

Fat chance, I thought. Detective Albert turned his head and looked at me right as I thought it. *Did I say it out loud?* No, I couldn't have, Lilly would have looked at me, too. Just then, Jack began to yawn; his plate was empty, and his milk had all been drunk. Lilly was not too far behind him either.

"Why don't you head upstairs, Jack, and start showering off for the night. Put on your pajamas and brush your teeth. I'll be up to give you a kiss goodnight shortly." I told him.

"Goodnight, Jack." Lilly teased as she got comfortable in her seat.

"It's a school night, Lilly, you won't be too far behind him. Once you finish your dinner, you will be heading to the showers, too." I informed her as she rolled her eyes.

The sass from her fight seemed not to have worn off just yet. I'm hoping it will soon.

Detective Albert and I sat in silence as we watched Lilly turn her last four bites into a thirty-minute ordeal. The two of us had finished our plates, and I was about to get up and start clearing the table when Lilly finally announced she was done. Looks like she realized nothing exciting was going to happen if she stayed up any later. I let her know that I would be up to kiss her goodnight after I saw the detective out. She hopped to her feet and slowly walked away in hopes we would start talking now that she was going to bed.

I waited for her to climb the stairs before I got up from the table. The detective sat there while I gathered up the plates, silverware, bowls, serving utensils, and glasses. His wife must do all of the house duties, so it does not even cross his mind to offer to help clear the table.

"Now that the kids are off to bed, can we talk seriously? Have you found that key yet?" He asked me, jumping right to the point. "I need to know what is behind that door."

"Let's go talk downstairs," I suggested as I dried my hands.

I led him to the wine cellar so that whoever was watching me was not tipped off yet that I had found the camera, letting them know I wasn't avoiding my space. I wanted them to also hear that I was telling everyone the same thing, including the cops. We sat down in my sitting area, trying not to get too comfortable.

"Did you or did you not?" He asked again.

"Before I answer that, I need to ask you a few questions." I paused. He gestured for me to keep going. "Is it safe to say you are the source at the police department who spoke to a seventh grader for the newspaper? Why would you give them that type of information? You should know better than to do that, especially with your tenure. Children's imaginations can run wild, and that is just what happened to that child. Did you read the article he wrote?" I asked.

"I was not the source he was speaking to. Some of our police officers have been there for years with very little action time, so they are not very experienced. If they were to go to another town and take a job as an officer, they wouldn't last very long. Like I told your son, nothing happens in this town. So some of the police get a little jumpy when there is something exciting happening, and they will tell anyone everything they know about it. If the kid had come to me and asked me any questions, I would have told him the same thing I have told many others in this town, 'it's police business and until we have proof of anything, there is nothing to say'. That is what the officer the kid talked to should have told him, that is police standard." He spoke with such confidence that I believed him.

If it wasn't him, then who? There were not many officers within our town, so it wouldn't be too difficult to narrow down who was so easily blabbing their mouths.

"Are there any ramifications we can do with this kid leaking this information?" I asked him, shuffling in my seat.

"Unfortunately, there is not. He has the freedom of free speech, so he can publish anything he wants." He told me.

"Okay, so what about the police officer who leaked the information? He should get fired." I emphasized.

"I agree, but unless the kid is willing to tell us who he talked to, I highly doubt the officer who did it is willing to come forward. If they do, then we can do something. I don't see that happening, though." He got closer to me as he talked.

"Alright, and what can we do about the news? They seem to want to hang me even more than you do." I laughed, unsure if I trusted him enough for this conversation.

"You should already know there is nothing I can do about the press, as I have already told you with Eugene. They are allowed to print and speak about anything they want. Despite having the true facts. I am truly sorry for that." He said, placing his hand on my thigh.

"Thank you for that," I said, pausing to let him continue the conversation.

"So did you find a key, or will I need to get Doug here tomorrow?" He asked impatiently.

I got up from my seat and opened a drawer in the table I kept in my cellar. I took a moment to lift a few papers up and pull out a key.

"I found this in his sock drawer. He had it tucked into a pair of socks that had been rolled up into one another. A great hiding spot, truly. When I shook his socks, I couldn't tell anything was in them until I began unrolling them." I said, shutting the drawer and walking back towards him.

"What else did you find in his socks?" He asked. Falling right into my trap.

"There was a cigar that had been half-smoked in one, with a lighter in the pair directly next to it. There was a small clipping of blond hair held together with a rubber band, very similar to the ones I used to use on my daughter's hair. That one was bizarre considering no one in our home has blond hair." I mentioned.

"Do you still have these items?" He wondered with increasing fascination.

"I do; did you want them?" I asked, knowing he would.

"Yes, please. It would be most helpful to see if I can run the DNA from the cigar and the hair in the system and find out who the hair belongs to." He gushed, quickly reaching into his back pocket to grab a pair of gloves out of the Ziplock bag he had that contained multiple pairs.

There was no way he would find out who the hair belonged to. Gwen gave me a clipping from a doll she had in her attic since she was a child. The cigar, however, I have no idea whose DNA will come back on that one. That honestly was in his sock drawer along with a lighter from a strip club in Missoula, Montana.

"Have you opened the door yet?" He asked when he finished putting the items away and placing them in his pocket. He was as excited as a child on Christmas morning.

"You asked me to wait for you to open the door, and that is just what I did. Would you like to go now?" I asked, gesturing towards the hallway.

Part of the reason I wanted to have this conversation in the cellar was to see if I could catch him staring in the direction of the camera. Even with me walking towards it to grab the key, he hadn't looked even once over there. Either he did not know it existed, or he is just really good at averting his eyes to never look at the camera he placed in my home.

It has to have been him.

He jumped from his seat and left the cellar as fast as he could. Only slowing down to stop and take another look at the storage containers. Everything was exactly as he had last seen it. The tubs never gained more rope, twine, tape, or tarps. I hadn't thought to fill it up, and did not think I would have a reason to need it any time soon. I turned on the lights as we made our way further into the basement and closer to the door. If I didn't know any better, I would think the detective was jumping in his shoes. I don't know what he thinks will be behind this door; there is no way he would expect me to willingly open the door if my husband were trapped in the room, duct taped and handcuffed to keep him quiet. He must have had some thoughts on what went on behind that door, though.

I took my time following him through the basement, never to be too close to him or hover. I fiddled with the key while we walked, making a slight noise as the key hit the keychain. Before I reached the door, I watched as the detective tried the knob once more.

"Why don't you let me do the honors? We don't know what we will find behind this door. It is better if a trained professional is the first one through." He said, bravely asking for the key.

I did my best to hide my laughter. Did he think there was a SWAT team camping out in that room, ready to attack the first person who used the key to open the door? Or maybe he expected there to be a booby trap like in Indiana Jones, arrows flying toward the unknowing victim who opens the door.

Either way, he put the key in the slot and turned the handle. You could see the light from the hallway emanate into the room, but it was not bright enough to make out anything in the room. The detective fumbled along the wall for a light switch before finding it.

I froze in my spot outside the door. Through the sliver of light emanating into the room, I could see blood running down the walls. I saw the rope that held Henry glimmering in the corner. I could hear him screaming underneath the tape, holding his lips shut. *How is he still there? I emptied that room*. I watched as Detective Albert took a deep breath and turned the light on.

A wave of disappointment filled the detective as he saw what was in the room. The room was mostly barren. A folding table stood in the center of the room with two folding chairs on either side of the table. A lamp sat on the edge of the table, pointing towards the chair furthest away. I watched as the detective walked around the room. He looked at the walls, the ceiling, and the floor, trying to find any sign of cameras or a microphone. He flipped the chairs upside down to check underneath them. He turned the table on its side, hoping to find a folder taped to the underside. He turned the lamp on, a spotlight illuminating the chair. It does not pain me to say, he saw nothing. But I saw everything.

"This is it?" he uttered, the disappointment screaming loudly as he talked. "You said you never come into this room?" He asked again.

"Never, I am just as confused as you are. This makes no sense to me as to what my husband could have used this room for." I told him, trying to hide the panic in my throat.

Truthfully, I never knew what Henry used this room for before it became his personal torture chamber. The room looked identical to how it did before I locked him in, minus the soiled and missing mattress that had lived in there. To begin with, I should have questioned Henry about why he had a mattress in this room. Seemed really random but very convenient at the time, so I did not question it.

"Shall we?" He asked, gesturing towards the chairs. "We have a conversation to finish, I believe." I hesitated but ultimately moved into the room, taking the chair opposite him. "Are you okay?" He wondered.

It was a good question. After everything that happened, I wasn't sure what 'okay' even meant anymore. "It's a strange feeling to be in this room. I've been told our entire marriage that I wasn't allowed to come in here. He was very adamant about this. The idea of me standing and now sitting in his private room unnerves me. I half expected the moment I walked in here for Henry to come out of hiding and kick me out of here."

The true feelings I had sitting in this room were exhilarating, even with Henry's blood still dripping from the walls, taunting me. This room is where I gained my freedom. I repurchased my life with my hands, giving me back the opportunity to have any future I wanted in this room. I was never told I was not allowed to come into this room. It was always implied, however, that it was Henry's room to do with as he pleased, and I would keep my distance. I could see why he never bothered to tell me not to enter this room, though, mainly because there was nothing that would give him away from this room. Yes, having a mattress in here was rather strange, but seeing the room as it is now, it's barren. He used this room for the same reason I used it: to unnerve someone. To rattle their brains, mentally and most likely physically. This room was meant to make people confess and give up their secrets.

Looking at this room in a whole new light, I began to wonder for myself how many business trips he went on that his company actually knew about. I could have very well called his company and asked if they had heard from him while he was on his trip, and they could have had no idea that he was supposed to even be on a company trip. Becoming friends with his secretary a long time ago would have been to my benefit now. Unfortunately, I never did. She was an older woman whom my husband would find fat, lazy, and unattractive, so I never saw her as a threat. That explains why he kept her around for so long, though; she must be amazing at her job not to have been fired a long time ago for the next hotter and younger model.

"It sounds like your husband could be a cruel man." The detective stated.

"Yes, if he needed to be, he very well could be," I told him bluntly, not feeling the need to lie now that Jack announced the hitting.

"Your son mentioned he smacked you once. Care to tell me about that?" He leaned forward to show sympathy, but I could tell he still found me a threat.

"Well," I began, trying to pick a time when it was not as vicious as the others. One that if Jack had seen it, he wouldn't feel the need to question it. Just bring it up later on, possibly years later. "As you mentioned, he can be loose with his feelings at times. He has a temper that usually does not last long, so it is easy to see it coming. Henry likes the house to be a particular way; he does not like it to be messy or have things out of place. One day, he came home, and I was baking and making a bit of a mess. School bake sales can do that to you, cause you to bake one hundred cupcakes and deal with the mess afterward. Well, Henry came home in a temper and saw the mess, the cloud of flour, and the sugary icing lying on the countertop, and he lost it. He asked me to clean up the kitchen as fast as possible, but clearly, with one hundred cupcakes, batter, icing, and all of the utensils, I couldn't very well clean it up fast enough. As I began to pick things up, his temper took over, and he swiped all of my hard work onto the floor. He was so angry with himself that he smacked me and told me it was my fault that he had to do that. I had to cheat the bake sale and order cupcakes from a bakery a few towns away, that way no one suspected I hadn't made them." Finishing my story, I sat there in silence, waiting for the detective to say something, *anything*.

"Was," he started to talk, clearing his throat, realization coming across his face, "that the only time he hit you?" He asked.

"Yes." I tried to lie. I could see from the look on his face, though, that I was not very convincing.

"I see. I would assume it is safe to say you wouldn't mind if he stayed away for some time, then? For your children's sake, of course." He slid in the last sentence relatively fast, hoping I wouldn't notice that he understood exactly what was happening.

Detective Albert might be a happy married man, but he

was still in the police force for many years before he became a detective. He had to have seen spousal abuse or domestic violence many times on the job. A man does not give you his sympathy that quickly without realizing what you have been through. Talking to him tonight had been easy; it reminded me of talking with my therapist. I felt like we should be in the wine cellar, enjoying a glass of wine and trauma dumping on one another. Instead, we were in a stark contrast, a bright, clean room, barren of any personality. Very similar to the investigation rooms at police departments in every investigation show I have seen. This man quickly changed from my enemy to someone with whom I felt comfortable. The more cool-headed I am with him, the more I am worried he will find out. Knowing what he was here to do quickly shook the feelings out of my brain, and I still needed to have my guard up. He still wanted to find me as the reason for my husband's disappearance, if not his murder.

"Why don't we end this for the night, then. I can see we are both exhausted, and you have your children to go kiss goodnight." Detective Albert stood from the table, giving me his hand to help me up.

"Yes, I do need to do that. They will begin to wonder where I am. Jack likes to stay up until I come in for a kiss. Once I forgot to, and I found him awake at three in the morning, just waiting." I chuckled and followed him out the door, locking it behind me.

"Strong willpower, that boy." He laughed, imagining

his own children.

I showed the detective to the front door and waited while he put his jacket back on.

"We will find him." He said confidently as I held the door open.

The evening was frigid for October, and a strong, cold gust of wind barreled its way into the house past the detective. The hair on my arms and legs stood up tall, and goosebumps filled my body.

Creak

If only he could stop finding me, haunting my every move in this house.

"Please don't," I whined, before shutting the door.

My heart began racing as I made my way back down to the basement. That shelf felt too exposed. Too easy to find. I stood there in the basement, staring at the gun case wedged behind a stack of blankets. I hadn't touched it since that night, but just knowing it was there made my skin itch.

"I should bury it," I whispered.

My hand hovered over the shelf. That night, I dreamed of dirt under my nails. Of moonlight. Of digging.

I walked up the stairs, stomping on Henry's step with as much force as I could muster, and walked into Jack's bedroom. He was lying down in his bed with his reading lamp on and a book sprawled open on his bed. He had colored pencils laid out as he meticulously picked the next color he wanted.

"Go to bed, honey, you have school in the morning.

You can finish the one you are working on and then turn off your light. If I come back in to check on you and you are still awake, I am taking that coloring book." I ruffled his hair and gave him a big kiss on his forehead. "Good night."

I walked down to Lilly's room expecting a similar image. She was lying on her bed, a book or magazine open. Instead, every light was off, aside from her reading lamp above her bed. She sat up with her arms wrapped around her legs and the blanket draped over her shoulders.

"Sweetie, are you okay?" I wondered as I got closer to her, sitting on her bed.

"Do you think Dad will come back?" She asked.

"Do you want him to come back?" I pried.

"No." She began to cry then.

I pulled her in deep within my arms as the tears became waterfalls. Her heart heaved with each attempt to catch her breath.

"Why not?" I asked when her crying slowed.

"Because he is a bad man, I have seen the way he treats you, Jack, and me. He was only ever truly nice when I was little. The detective asked me today for a moment that I liked with my father, and I could only think of one. Every memory I have of him, he was mean to one of us. He has never been nice to all of us." She squeezed me even harder.

I thought I had shielded her from his torture and mental manipulations, but it seems as though I have failed as a mother to protect my children. She is only twelve; she should not know of the horrors of the world just yet.

"If he comes back, I won't let him back into our home. How does that sound? He can still be your father, just not a part of your life." I squeezed her back.

"I would like that." She released me and smiled.

"Alright, now go to bed. He can't hurt you anymore, sweet pea. Mommies got you." I helped her lie back into her bed, tucked her in nicely, and gave her a big kiss. "I love you so much, I won't let him back. I promise." The one promise I could truly keep.

The next morning, I couldn't remember if I had actually moved the gun or just imagined I did.

Chapter Eight

"**Are** you finally going to tell me how Henry's car ended up at the airport?" Gwen asked as we sat in my bedroom one afternoon while the kids were at school, folding laundry.

"I guess now is as good a time as any to tell you. After all, the detective could arrest me at any moment." I said, folding a pair of Jack's jeans and placing them on the bed. "I should probably start from the beginning, then."

I watched Gwen place a shirt on the bed, unfold it, and get herself comfortable for what she believed would be a long story. Realizing I had never told her how Henry ended up in the basement, I decided I owed her the whole story. After all, she asked zero questions before helping me.

"It all started that morning of the book club. Henry was packing to leave for yet another trip. He was testy the whole morning, complaining that I had smelled like coffee. I had been cautious with my coffee that morning; you know he hated the smell of it. I drank my lukewarm coffee on the back porch in the only blind spot from our bedroom. I hated the extremes I had to go through in order to enjoy a cup of coffee in the morning. A nice warm cup of anything in the morning was something everyone should be able to do if they wanted to. Enjoying life's simplicities." Even though Gwen had stopped folding laundry, I had not. To me, this story was old news, something I would tell as a fun fact about myself when I was eighty. But also, because, in this household, the laundry never ends. "I kept a spare toothbrush and toothpaste in the powder room right near the back door, and I quickly brushed my teeth before I got any further into the house. I cleaned my coffee mug out in that sink, soap and everything. Just to go stick it in the dishwasher so it wouldn't have the possibility to smell like coffee moving forward.

"I grabbed myself a glass of water to clean out my mouth a bit more before heading up the stairs. Where Henry was in his classic, I hated everyone's mood, especially my wife's. I stayed in the door frame while I talked to him, keeping my distance. As he grabbed his bag and headed towards the stairs, I couldn't help but feel everything bubble to the surface. I always had to cater the way I lived to his needs. How nothing I did ever seemed good enough for him. I couldn't take it anymore. He turned around, maybe to hit me, maybe to tell me something. But I didn't give him the time of day to let me know which it was before I began to run towards him at full speed and push him down the stairs. I watched as he tumbled, hitting his head along the wall and on the steps before landing at the bottom of the stairs, knocked out.

"I watched from the top of the stairs, expecting him to wake up and come after me. My heart was racing as each second passed before finally slowing as time went on. When he didn't move, I was able to breathe fully again. I didn't even think. I went down the stairs and grabbed a golf club from his office. Hit him on his head and chest as hard as I could, getting a few good swings in on him before dragging him from the foyer on a blanket to the top of the basement stairs. I pushed him as hard as I could down the flight of stairs to drag him into the room and into the position that you saw him in. I locked the door and ran upstairs. I had no time to think of what to do next; I just did what needed to be done. I knew the girls would be here in a few hours for book club, and I needed to get rid of his car since he was not supposed to be here anymore.

"Quickly, I changed into a few different outfits. I left the outfit I had on as the base layer, double-checking for any blood or anything before I made this decision. I then put on a larger pair of running pants, a balaclava that we used for skiing to keep my hair hidden, a baggy turtle neck, a beanie, and a scarf. Last, I grabbed a pair of Henry's suit pants and jacket, and a baseball hat he often wore. At this point, I was roasting in our home and felt constricted in my attire. However, I needed to make sure I wouldn't be noticed.

"Grabbing his suitcase, briefcase, the jacket he had in his hand when he was initially heading out, and a tote bag. I made my way to his car. Thankfully, the only cameras in our home are facing outwards to watch the perimeter of our house, and there is not a single one in the garage. I reached for a pair of driving gloves and put them on before touching the door handles and putting his stuff inside the car. I put his sunglasses on and the sun visor down before backing out of the garage. I still felt exposed, so I panic checked around the car and saw a newspaper lying on the floor of his passenger seat, and opened it up.

"You wouldn't think holding a newspaper for almost an hour drive would be that exhausting, but it was. My muscles ached by the time I could put my arm down. Since I left my phone at home, my location stayed at home, and I had to drive to the airport based on my memory. It had been a while since I had driven to the airport and not had Henry drive or my phone to guide me, so I took my time before taking any exits. Though I had to drive as fast as I could without drawing the attention of any officers to ensure it honestly looked like Henry was driving the car. That was the trickiest part of the whole thing. Although the police did not know how he drove, I could have driven normally in hindsight. I could have sworn I was getting pulled over at one point of the drive. An officer and I had made eye contact on the highway, a newspaper as high as I could get it, and he never pulled me over. Finally, I made it to the airport and began pulling into the long-term parking garage. I was hopeful there were no cameras inside the garage; I could not see any, but the lighting within the garage was not great. I took my chances and parked the car in the most remote spot I could find. I got out of the car, locked it behind me, and headed for the stairwell.

"The most daunting part, in my opinion, was finding my way home without calling anyone I knew or anyone who could recognize me if questioned in a lineup to blow my cover. Grabbing my tote bag, I began stripping off my top layer and stuffing it in my bag. Henry drove into the parking garage, and another person walked out of it. Wearing completely different clothing and a different body build than what the police would be looking for. I walked to the train station attached to the airport, paid cash for a ticket to take me to our town, and waited patiently for the train to arrive. My foot would not stop shaking, and I had to push hard on my knees to slow them down and stop from drawing any attention toward me.

"The train ride was fine; I was able to keep my distance from everyone. I hadn't yet decided if I planned on stripping the second layer on the train or at my next stop, but I did know I needed to dump Henry's clothes on the train. I hopped up from my seat and headed to the bathroom, checking every possible place to stash it on the way. Every available spot that I thought about ended up being something that someone could come across if they were doing their job or just happened to be bored. This task was becoming more complicated than I thought it would. In the bathroom, there was a panel to the left of the toilet that I was able to shimmy open with a quarter. I dropped his clothes inside this panel, folded the tote bag up, tucked it into my pants, and covered it with the turtle neck.

"When the train had let me off, I still looked like the person who had left the parking garage, which I did not see as a threat to my story. Thankfully, the train station is right next to the grocery store, and many people hop off the train to load up on snacks before catching the next train out of town. That was just what I was going to make this imaginary person do, minus the getting back on the train. I walked into the grocery store and headed straight to the bathroom to remove my second layer. I took my small canvas tote bag that was barely big enough to hold my pants and placed the clothing into it. I shook my bright red hair out, making sure it did not look like it had been in a hat that day, and left the restroom.

"Thankfully, I did have to grab a few things from the store for the book club. I grabbed my essentials, checked out at the register, and placed my grocery items on top of the clothes in the tote bag. Before I left the store, I asked to borrow the teenager's phone behind the register to call a cab. I waited inside the store for a few moments before seeing a taxi pull up, I hopped in as fast as I could and asked him to drop me off a few houses away from my home, so the cab would not show up on my home cameras. I walked the rest of the way home and began to get ready for the party."

I finished my last sentence and my last piece of laundry at the same time. Gwen was speechless.

"You did all of this before the party? And Henry was just in the basement?" She asked when she was able to catch her train of thought.

I nodded my head as I began to get up, put the clothes in their respective drawers or hangers.

"And what did you do with his phone?" She asked, staying glued to her spot on the bed.

"I left it in his briefcase. Saw no reason to take it with me, just to try and find a new hiding spot. The police have it now. Who knows what they found on there?" I shouted from my closet.

"Probably photos of many naked women and their contact information. You know he had to have had women in every city he visited." She shouted back at me.

"I know you are right, but I don't like to think about it," I told her.

She grabbed Jack's stack of clothes while I grabbed Lilly's, heading towards their rooms.

Creak...creak

I heard as I passed the stairs towards the kids' bedrooms, trying to ignore it.

"How do you think Jack will handle being without his father as he gets older? Puberty has to be difficult without a male role model to tell you about the changes in your body. I can't imagine what it would have been like if I did not have my mom or older sister to tell me all about my periods." Gwen reminisced.

"Who knows, I might have another man in my life by

then. He won't start going through puberty for another four years or so. Then he can teach him all about that." I laughed.

Creak

My head snapped towards the stairs. "Not like Henry is here to stop me from dating." I loudly proclaimed so his ghost could hear me.

"I say that's cause to celebrate, let's take the kids out tonight. I'm not ready to go home quite yet either. Vince is watching football tonight, and he is always shouting at the players like they can hear him. I would love a night off from listening to that." She gleefully said.

"Have any ideas?" I asked as we placed the last bit of clothes in Lilly's closet.

"Jack has been talking about a movie nonstop. We could go get dinner, see the movie, and grab some ice cream before we call it a night." She had already pulled up the theater's app and began purchasing tickets for the seven-p.m. showing.

After the theater and a quick stop at our local diner for burgers and fries, we went to the local ice cream shop near my house. Lilly and Jack were both jumping out of their seats in excitement the whole night. An evening spent with their Aunt Gwen out and about on the town was what made them most happy. They loved Gwen; she acted as their second mother in every way. She has always told them when they could and could not do something, always praised them for doing well in school, and got on them when they did something they knew they shouldn't have. Gwen was a true friend; one I could depend upon for absolutely everything. She treated my children as her own and one day might have to be their second mother if I get caught.

When we pulled up to the ice cream place, both kids jumped out of the car as fast as they could. This place had been around for over one hundred years; it was a town staple and had been deemed a historical landmark, so it could not be torn down anytime in the future. It was a small shack that only the employees could enter. The customers ordered through a window after waiting in a long line. The building stood as a beacon with its Art Deco facade. The roof is outlined by the stainless-steel trim, the bright neon lights spelling 'Daisy's Ice Cream' stood on the roof with an equally big ice cream cone that can be seen lighting the way from over a mile away. There is no outside seating, just a few stone benches outlining the front portion of the lot.

By the time Gwen and I caught up to the kids in line, more people had joined behind us.

"What flavor are you going to get?" I asked Jack, already knowing the answer.

"Cookies and cream, it's my favorite. I'm going to ask for sprinkles and a full-sized cookie on the top too!" He jumped with joy.

"What flavor are you going to get this time, Lilly?" She always got a new flavor every time we came here. She insisted on trying each flavor before declaring her favorite.

"I have three more to try before I have had every flavor. I think I am going to do… the cream soda flavor this time." She nodded her head as she continued to think it over, making sure she was making the right decision.

"What are you going for, Gwen?" She went back and forth between two flavors pretty regularly: buttered pecan and maple walnut.

"Good old buttered pecan, you know I can't get enough of it." She said like a giddy teenager. "How about yourself?" She asked me.

"You know I go for the same flavor every time. Honey lavender is my favorite, and Daisy's has the best one I have ever had." I proclaimed.

The line moved extra slowly today. The teenager behind the counter must be new. Daisys only accepts cash, which means the employees have to be quick when it comes to determining change.

"What's wrong?" Gwen asked.

"I feel like I'm being watched," I told her as I pulled my arms closer to my body.

As I look around the line and the people sitting on the benches, I can begin to hear ever-present whispers around me.

"Heard they still haven't found him," a woman mutters

from behind her towering cone of rocky road, not so discreetly nodding in my direction.

"Yeah, and they say she…" A man's voice stops as I move closer to him.

With every customer served, we move closer to the counter, closer to the large mob of teenagers standing around in a circle, staring confidently in my direction. I began to hear them whisper, 'You won't do it,' and 'Watch me,' come from their group.

"Murderer," one shouted, quickly covering their stifled giggle with their napkin.

I kept my eyes on my children, determined not to look in their direction. Gwen, on the other hand, straightened her back, ready to charge the derpy teenagers, their eyes wide with curiosity.

"Just ignore them," I whispered to Gwen.

"Kind of hard to do when they are directing it to you," She whispered back.

"The kids haven't noticed anything, let's just get our ice cream and leave." I sternly told her.

Her calm attitude lasted all of three minutes as the whispers never ended. Her breathing got heavier and heavier, and she was ready to scream.

"Get her!" We heard a scream from a car just too late. An ice cream cone came flying out of the vehicle, smashing itself right on my leg.

This caught my children's attention. My sweet Jack immediately checked on me, "Mommy, are you okay? What flavor is that?" He asked, more curious about the ice cream once he was sure I was okay. "Taste like cherries and chocolate." He was on his knees licking my leg, then taking his finger and scooping up some, he asked, "What do you think, Lilly? You have had all the flavors." And thrust his finger into his sister's mouth.

"That's disgusting, Jack! Don't eat ice cream that you don't know where it came from…" Lilly paused, taking a moment to question the flavor, "That's their Dark Chocolate Cherry Garcia, weird flavor to get just to toss it." She stated.

Gwen ran up to the counter, "Can I have a few napkins?" She asked the teenager behind the counter.

"Is it for the murderer?" He asked.

"No," Gwen stated.

"Sure," he pushed the napkin dispenser towards her, not fully believing her.

"Thanks," Gwen said, taking the whole dispenser, stomping away. "Those little twerps," she muttered to herself as she walked back to me.

"Let's just get our ice cream and go." I stared forward, waiting for each person to finish their order and walk away from the counter, getting us closer to the front of the line. Finally, when it was our turn to order, the teenager in the window stared expressionless at me. Her hair was a neon purple, braided into pigtails that stood off the top of her head. She had a black choker necklace with spikes protruding outwards. Her lips, covered in black lipstick, never moved.

"Can we get two scoops of the honey lavender in a cup, two scoops of the buttered pecan in a cup, a scoop of the cream soda in a waffle cone, and then a scoop of the cookies and cream in a bowl, with sprinkles and a cookie on the top?" I told her my order, watching as she did not bother to enter anything into her computer, did not write anything down, and did not move any closer to grabbing the ice cream. She just stood there.

"Did you need her to repeat that?" Gwen asked.

"Hi, how can I help you?" The teenager asked Gwen.

"I'm sorry, did you not hear our order?" She asked her.

"We don't serve murderers here, convinced or not. It's policy." She stated, nodding her head.

"How dare you!" I started to scream when Gwen put her hand on my chest.

"We will deal with this later, go wait in the car, and we will meet you there," Gwen said.

I had expected flames coming out of her head, knives flying, something! But this is cool, calm, and collected, Gwen. She made sure my children got their ice cream, ordering them two scoops each instead of the one scoop I had ordered for them. Hopefully, Lilly likes her new flavor enough for two scoops; you can never be too sure with these flavors. I rolled my window down to hear what else the people in the line were whispering about me, but all I could hear was the haunting echo of 'Guilty' running through my brain. Of course, I was guilty; I had murdered my husband, but does that make me a murderer if we are never found out?

"Thank you," Gwen said, grabbing the last ice cream from the petty juvenile. "Let me ask you this before I go: how do you know I'm not a murderer, too?" She whispered.

The girl's eyes shot wider than they had ever been before. Gwen followed it up with a laugh and shouted, 'Just kidding,' as she walked away. Though she did serve a murderer without knowing she had. No one knew Gwen had killed, too. I laughed loudly from my car as I heard this transaction.

"Ice cream in the car!" Jack shouted as he hopped into his seat. "Today's been great!"

Oh, to be a child again, Jack reminds me every day about the joys of being youthful. To not worry about money, your reputation, bills, your job, or your love life. The only worry he had was if they had remembered to put sprinkles on his ice cream or if he was to have someone to play with on the playground. I wish my children could stay this innocent for as long as possible, but as Lilly has recently displayed, they are growing up and starting to worry about these things.

When everyone got into the car, I drove away from Daisy's and parked in a parking lot out of sight of the ice cream shop.

"How's everyone's ice cream?" I asked, turning around in my chair to face my family.

"Cream soda is okay. Better played out as a drink,

though." Lilly said, already one scoop down.

"My cookie was still warm when they put it on my ice cream! Can you believe that?" He said gleefully.

"They seem to be doing just fine after all of that," Gwen whispered.

We sat in the parking lot, laughing and joking about what the latest game to play on the playground was and talking about what the kids wanted to do when they grew up. Jack insisted that NASA would allow him to be an astronaut race car driver who drove from space shuttle to space shuttle. Gwen said if you bugged them enough, they might have to, and suggested that they start writing letters to NASA every day to request that they allow him to begin astronaut training at such a young age, making him the youngest astronaut. If Henry were alive to hear this, he would have shut down his dream, insisting that NASA would, in fact, never allow this, and he should just give up on his dreams while he was still young and had time to pick a new one.

Lilly's dreams were simpler. She wanted to be a professional ballet dancer and have two children. I did not want to break the news to her that she most likely couldn't be a ballet dancer and have two children at the same time. She would most likely have to push off having children in order to have a successful career as a ballerina. I could see in Gwen's eyes that she thought the same thing.

When the ice cream had been eaten and the drips from their messes were cleaned up, we headed home. We said goodnight to Gwen as she drove away and headed inside.

Jack was exhausted and said he was going to head to bed early.

"Tomorrow is a big day! It marks day one of the letters to NASA." He said, shoving his pointer finger into the air.

"Can I talk to you?" Lilly asked me.

I led her towards the living room, taking a seat on the couch and pulling her close to me.

"What is it, honey?" I asked her.

"Did you have something to do with Daddy not coming back?" A tear filled her eye as she asked.

The big question is out in the open for a twelve-year-old to ask. She has heard so much from the students in her school and plenty around town. Especially with the ice cream throwing tonight, I don't blame her for wanting to know the truth. Maybe one day I will tell her, the day she fights back, that her dad would have let her do this or that, even though we know that would never be the case. Or maybe I could tell her that if she chooses to marry an abusive man, to warn her about the type of life she is choosing to live. I could tell her on my deathbed as she held my hand and worried if this were the last time she would ever get to talk to me. Who knows, there are plenty of times I could drop this amount of information on her, but right now, at her age, it was not the time.

"Of course, I didn't, honey. Your father was a very peculiar man, never telling us what his plans were. This, leaving us like he did, was something he should have told us. That would have at least prepared us in some way, but he must have assumed we would talk him into staying. Told him how much we loved him and that if he didn't run away, everything would be better." I wiped the tears from her face and kissed her forehead. "I'm always going to be here for you," I told her.

"How do I know you won't run away from me, too?" She said, fighting through her crocodile tears.

"You have my word that I will never leave you," I said, between tears of my own.

"Can I sleep in your bed tonight?" She asked, pushing her way closer into my arms.

"Always," I said, squeezing her tightly.

Chapter Nine

"**We** have to go, Mom," Lilly repeated as she followed me around the house yet again. "It's tradition, we can't miss it!"

"I can drop you off, or you can go with Gwen, but I have things I need to focus on today." I lied, not wanting to face such a large crowd.

"No, Mom. I already told my teacher you would be there; they are very interested in meeting you after what happened the other week." She was still upset with herself after punching that boy, but I am sure the entire teaching staff and all of the parents have seen that article and the lovely photo attached to it, no thanks to Eugene's mother. Who, I'm sure, will be there.

"Why would you do that?" I asked harshly.

"They said they needed to hear from you about something. I don't remember, I just told them you would be there because you are always at the school fairs. I didn't think this was going to be a problem, just go, Mom. Please?" She pleaded.

"Fine, but I am calling Gwen for backup." I quickly grabbed my phone out of my back pocket and called her.

"Yeah?" Her voice sounded distant, and there was a ruffling of grocery bags in the background. She must have just gotten home from the grocery store.

"I need you to come to the school fair with me today. Apparently, I have been promised to go, and all of the parents are more than eager to see me there. Please come." I begged.

"When is it?" She wondered, still putting her groceries away as she asked.

"Today, 4 p.m.," I told her.

"Okay, I can meet you there. I have to go, though, in the middle of something." She said, hanging up quickly.

"She's coming," I informed Lilly and began to get ready for the day.

The school fairs in our town have always been a big deal. All three schools come together multiple times a year to raise money for various things. This year, the high school football team needs new jerseys, so the fair is taking place right on their football field. What they had not considered was that after this fair, there might be the possibility of needing someone to recover the football field after having booths and heels walking around their field. I can't imagine the number of holes from the heels.

The kids hopped in the car, ready for an evening filled with games and surely lots of treats they would usually never get. The high school was the most prominent place in our town to host various fairs, located in the center of the city, you pass it no matter where you are going. *Was the whole town heading to one location, the fair?* I thought as we inched our way through the traffic. It would have been faster to just walk there from our home, but instead, we were sitting in bumper-to-bumper traffic waiting for the parking attendants to get everyone into a spot. When it was finally our turn to park, my kids jumped out of the car as quickly as they could. Jack and Lilly did not look around as they ran through the parking lot; they decided to let the universe determine their fate today, I guess. Because of this, I was left alone walking into the fair. To get onto the field, the town put up the tunnel that the players typically run through before a game to give everyone a memorable feeling of why they were here. As I walked through this same tunnel, my heart beat fast in anticipation of what to expect. My palms felt sweaty as I had to remind myself to breathe long, deep breaths to calm my nerves. In the stands, three banners were prominently displayed, informing everyone when the elementary school choir, the middle school band, and the high school band were going to play. Until then, the school had a DJ playing from their booth at the top of the stands.

The field was smothered with booths and brightly colored banners. I could see vendors selling a variety of fried confections such as funnel cakes and fried twinkies. There were also various smoked meat stands of chicken legs, ribs, and bacon that filled the night with an aroma of mouth-watering yearning. The first booth I walked up to displayed the school's current football jersey and a printed-out poster of what they hope to be the next version. Whoever put this display together managed to pick the very worst of the current jerseys; it was split up the sides, had holes throughout, and was smothered in mud and grass stains. I began to wonder if a parent had tied the jersey to the back of their pickup truck to make it look as destroyed as it did. The new jersey design looked very similar to the current one, from what I could tell through its condition. The main difference was that it was new and clean. I giggled about this and moved on.

I could feel eyes burning into my skull all around me, hearing whispers throughout the air. I decided to ignore it and move on. Gwen would be here soon, and I needed to find where my children had run off to.

"Lose anyone recently?" A stranger asked me as I looked from booth to booth.

"No, I'm good," I told them and kept walking.

"Are you sure you didn't lose your kids like you did your husband?" She shouted behind me as I moved through the crowd. Her voice pierced through the laughs and cheers of the children around me.

I picked up my pace and tried to make my search for my children less obvious. Just then, the school's mascot stopped me. Before now, I thought the decision to make a Reaper our school mascot was hilarious, but at this very moment, I wish it were anything else. I rolled my eyes, steadying my beating chest.

"You look great, if you would excuse me," I told him, and moved to my left to push past him and trek through the fair to find my kids.

Two booths away, I finally spotted my children talking with an adult. With my husband being gone, I hadn't made a point to meet their teachers this year. This person gave off teacher vibes, though, but I couldn't pinpoint if it was elementary or middle school.

"There you two are, why did you run off like that?" I questioned, pulling them in closer to me.

"Mom, I told you we had to meet my teacher." She said, gesturing towards who I assumed to be her teacher.

"You could have done that with me, instead of having me search for you." I scolded them. "Pleasure to meet you, what is it that you teach?" I asked the man standing before me.

"Philosophy. Do you know much about the topic?" The man before me was simple. He wore linen pants and a short-sleeved sweater with pleats down the front. His blond hair sparkled under the sun, and as he talked, the curls on the front of his face tickled his forehead. His bright blue eyes drove into mine like daggers. He was one of the most innocently attractive men I have ever come across.

"No, I honestly can't say I do. What is it that you are

teaching my daughter?" I wondered.

"I help your child explore life's biggest questions. Not to give them answers, but to teach them how to think for themselves. We talk about fairness, right and wrong, truth, and what makes a good life. I help them build the tools to reason carefully, question thoughtfully, and engage respectfully with ideas that matter. In philosophy, they learn not just what to think, but how to think and why that matters," He informed me, standing as straight as a ruler and smiling from ear to ear.

"Is that so, and how well do you think that works on a whole bunch of twelve-year-olds?" I genuinely wondered.

"I would say it is about 50/50, quite honestly." He laughed. "There are students of mine who have gone on to become incredible people in society, becoming lawyers, doctors, and scientists. Then I have other students who just can't quite seem to stay out of trouble, no matter how hard they try." He informed me.

He's older than I thought, if his students have gone through law school or the many grueling years it takes to be a doctor.

"Wouldn't you think, without your teachings, that it would still be a 50/50 possibility to have the students turn out to be great human beings, as you put it?" I questioned.

"Of course, there is always the possibility that their parents are the ones who make them into either bad or good people. It is the whole nurture versus nature argument that has been going on for centuries. I personally believe that if you nurture a child properly, they will become a good person." He smiled at my daughter and could almost be certain that if he were close enough, he would have pulled her in for a hug.

I could feel this conversation taking a sharp right turn.

"So, tell me, how do children who are raised in the worst environment possible for themselves leave that situation when they are old enough and become incredible adults? That would be a winning argument for nature, wouldn't you think? That child was already destined to become a great human being. That same child could have a sibling who lived with them in the slums through a war, drugs, violence, you name it, and they follow the lead of the adults who are in charge there. They become a horrible adult, all while their sibling would be considered a saint in anyone's eyes. How would you describe that?" I pontificated, trying to keep the subject on my side and not against me as I sensed he was getting at.

"I would say there are children who, as you say, are raised in horrible environments that they could never truly escape. Children take the side that is convenient to themselves at that time of hardship; from then on, they are destined to become the good or bad person they choose to be in that moment." He combated, standing somehow even taller.

"Now, once these children are adults, are they able to switch camps? There are many studies about death row inmates who committed some of the worst crimes to end up where they are. Through their time on death row, a lot of them turn over a leaf and become honest, good people who are sorry for what they did to end up where they are. Do you see those individuals as fakers?" I asked, honestly curious, as I had watched too many crime documentaries.

This stumped him for a moment. He looked back and forth between my children and me, presumably wondering how I knew this much about nature versus nurture. Many housewives in our town are extremely simple-minded. If you were to ask them a simple question, it would take them a few beats to understand the question and be able to give an honest answer. Many times, that answer did not make sense for what the question was, but at least they tried. I believe this teacher expected that from me as well.

"I'm not sure this is the conversation for one to have in front of your youngest son here. Don't you?" He copped out and was ready to end the conversation here.

"I couldn't agree more. I wouldn't want him to become a Philosophy teacher based on this conversation. Then he would be debating the ethics of life forever and never be able to come up with a true answer as to what really matters in life." I grabbed hold of Jack and Lilly's hands. "Now, if you would excuse me, I believe I owe my children a corn dog, and we are supposed to be meeting my best friend. I hope you enjoy the rest of the fair." I said before taking our leave.

My children began jumping up and down, shouting 'CORN DOG, CORN DOG', for the whole fair to hear.

Great, now the entire fair was looking at us and listening to what sounded like my children begging for corn dogs, instead of being excited for one.

"Could we get three corn dogs, please, ketchup and mustard on the side, and a small order of fries would be great. Thank you so much!" I said as courteously as I could, not wanting another incident like what happened at the ice cream shop.

While we waited for our food, I took in the fair some more. Aside from the few football-specific attributes, this looked like any other fair in our town. There were games filling every aspect of the fair, from ring toss, basketball toss, balloon darts, hoopla, shooting gallery, fishbowl games, and various different forms of coin toss games, all in the hopes of winning stuffed animals. Many of the stuffed animals were of the school mascot, a Reaper, and lots of various-sized stuffed and real footballs.

"Here you go, ma'am. Enjoy." The man behind the corn dog stand said, handing over our food.

The three of us grabbed the first table we could find and sat down, passing out our corn dogs and placing the sauces in the center of the table for them to dip as they pleased.

"Emma, so great to see you." A brunette woman came up to our table and took a seat. I had seen this woman before at multiple different events, but for the life of me, I either never got her name or I just did not care enough to remember it.

"Here, kids, why don't you take this and go play the ring toss over there?" I handed over five dollars and hoped that would be enough to distract them. As the kids eagerly left their seats to play the games at the booths, I turned back to face this allegedly friendly and familiar stranger.

"I heard about your husband, a shame he's missing. My husband loved playing with him on the golf field." She began to scoot closer to me as she talked.

"I think you mean golf course, not field, and I think you're mixing up husbands here; mine doesn't play golf anymore. His clubs just sit in his office, untouched. He purchased them for the one time his boss took him out golfing, and I have never seen him use them ever again. He despises it and sees no real meaning in the game. Said it was a waste of a lovely morning to stand around with a group of guys, hitting balls around grass." I told her and took my last bite of fries, trying to clean up our mess and excuse myself to leave her.

"No, I'm sure it was your husband. Mine sends me photos from their golfing trips, and I have one here with your husband in it. This was taken over the summer, just a few days before he left for his trip." She quickly swiped through her phone and held it up to me so I could see the photo. *Looky there, my husband is playing golf.* I couldn't believe my eyes. I barely knew any of the men he was standing around with. When did he start golfing? My husband, the man who always stated it was a waste of time, is here on a golf course golfing for what appears not to be his first time, as his monogrammed golf gloves would suggest.

"Would you mind sending that to me?" I asked, stopping myself from grabbing her phone to do it myself.

"Sure, I've already sent it to the detective on the case so he can ask the men any questions that seem necessary. My husband already told me that he seemed to have a pretty solid state of mind that day, didn't seem like he was planning to run away within the next few days at all." She quickly sent the photo to me, and my phone lit up with a text from 'Alice'.

"Thank you for that, Alice. We appreciate all of the help with finding him. I'm going to see how my children are doing now. Have a great time at the fair." I grabbed our trash and walked away.

"You too!" She shouted at me.

This was the moment I wished I hadn't been tricked into coming to the fair. I did not have the energy to talk to all of these people, whom I had only spoken to a few times a year, about the 'disappearance' of my husband. I wish I had brought an insulated coffee mug filled with wine. If I had to speak to these people, I at least deserved to be tipsy while I did it.

How about drunk? I thought, scaring myself as the voice in my head was mean, vindictive, and haunting. And very much, not my own.

"Oh, there she is! The town murderer! How did you get rid of your husband? I would love some tips to get rid of mine." Said a woman who approached me as I threw out our trash.

We needed to leave. I would not let my children hear what our town had to say about me. I stomped my way to the ring toss just in time to see Jack land a ring right over a bottle.

"We have a winner here, ladies and gentlemen!" The teenager running the booth shouted. "What can I get you?" He asked, gesturing towards the pile of stuffed animals behind him.

"The purple monkey!" Jack shouted at the top of his lungs.

"The purple monkey it is, here you go." He said, handing off the monkey. "Hey, Mrs. Thompson, I heard you give help on school projects. You know, I could use some help on my health project. We have been talking about the effects of sperm on smoking hot bodies like yours. Mind if I stop by soon?" He said, ogling me like I was extra credit and miming the world's least subtle jerking-off motion.

I couldn't believe what I was hearing. *What were they teaching these kids?* My face began to redden in embarrassment, but also in anger. Being here, alone, made me question why we came here at all. I needed my backup. I needed Gwen.

"Wow. Still waiting for that puberty glow-up, huh? Good luck with your maturity project." I grabbed hold of my children's shoulders with my clammy hands, ushering them away. My hands were slick with sweat, but I didn't dare let go of my kids.

I gripped their shoulders tighter than I meant to. Jack flinched, just slightly, and I eased up, trying to breathe through the panic buzzing beneath my skin. *Keep it together. Just get to the car. Keep moving.* The crowd was still watching. Still whispering. I could feel it pulsing all around me, like static in the air, under my skin, in the space behind my eyes. My heart slammed against my ribs, too fast, too loud. I couldn't hear over it. Every breath stuck halfway up my throat. There were too many people. Too many eyes. Everything felt too close and too bright.

"Come on," I said, my voice catching. I forced a smile that felt brittle and wrong. "We're heading out."

I steered them back through the fair, my hands still resting on their shoulders like anchors. One foot, then the other. Just keep going. Don't fall apart here. My vision tunneled in and out. I focused on the back of Jack's head. On the curve of Lilly's ponytail, swinging as she walked. I kept my eyes on them and nowhere else. If I stopped moving, I was going to fall apart. If I looked up, I might scream.

And then. A voice. Familiar. Heavy.

"Emma?" I froze. All the air I'd been clinging to left me in one rush. My body stilled, but my mind kept spiraling. I didn't have to turn to know who it was.

"There you are!" Finally, a voice I recognized came shouting behind me.

"Thank God you are here! Our town is crazy!" I said, pulling Gwen into a much-needed hug.

"Tell me something I don't know. What have I

missed?" She asked Jack.

"I won a monkey!!" He cheered gleefully, jumping on Gwen and pushing the monkey into her arms.

"Sounds like an excuse for a celebratory treat!" She said, looking at the kids, "And sounds like you need one too." She said, looking at me, her eyebrows raised.

Jack and Lilly ran to the closest booth that sold all sorts of ice cream treats, mostly chocolate-covered ones. Jack got a cookies and cream dipped chocolate ice cream bar while Lilly went for an ice cream sundae with cotton candy on top. While Gwen was getting the kids their treats, I waited in line for some wine. Keeping my head down throughout the line, I could hear whispers about me from every corner of the fair. The line crawled as glass after glass of alcohol exchanged hands with their customers. Finally, it was my turn. I raised my head to place my order, and Mrs. Trumpet stood before me, looking me up and down.

This bitch!

"Mrs. Trumpet, great to see you," I said, biting my tongue. "Can I get two glasses of Merlot?"

"Emma, you can't honestly believe I can give you alcohol after what we read in the newspaper, can you?" She turned her gaze from me to the person behind me. "Next guest, please!" She shouted.

Thrusting my arm up from my side, I stopped the person behind me from moving forward in line. "I'm not done yet. I am still waiting on my order." My eyes never left Mrs. Trumpet's as I spoke.

"As I said, I can't serve you." She whispered, not wanting to draw attention to herself.

"Look, you really think this one glass of wine is going to cause me to do anything? It's one glass, just give it to me. I'll even pay double if that is what it takes!" My voice was stern as I placed a twenty-dollar bill on the counter. "Then we can go back to pretending like this never happened."

"I'm not sure…" She hesitated. I watched as her fingers hesitated over her tablet, unsure of what to do when a shadow crossed her face. "Gwen! Nice to see you, can I get you anything?" Her attention and demeanor instantly flipped when she noticed Gwen standing beside me.

"I would like whatever it is that Emma ordered; it looks like she has already paid for it, too." She tapped the twenty and pushed it closer to Mrs. Trumpet.

"I can't." She stated.

"Can't or won't? I will start shouting, then you will look like the bad guy here. Do you remember what happened to Jules at the last fair? Do you want to turn out like her?" She threatened.

Mrs. Trumpet hesitated and took a moment to think it over as their eyes stayed locked together. I began to sweat watching this interaction, when suddenly a switch went off in her head. She dropped her eyes and began pouring two glasses of merlot before handing them over to us. Gwen and I each took our glasses, looked at one another, and raised our eyebrows to indicate the heavy pour of wine in our glasses. *Who knew Gwen was so intimidating?*

"Come on, let's go sit in the field and enjoy our drinks while the kids enjoy their ice cream." Gwen led us through the fair and off to a secluded area of the football field and unfolded a blanket before we all sat down.

We watched the festivities from afar, giving me plenty of space from the town. The middle school band had begun climbing into the stands for their turn. According to their banner, they were to start with "Bohemian Rhapsody", which couldn't be more fitting for my current mindset. Our neighbors walked from booth to booth, mindlessly enjoying their day. This town could be picturesque sometimes; today was one of those times. As the evening went on, the sun began to lower in the sky, casting a warm, golden hue over the stands. The light reflected off the band equipment of the soon-to-be teenagers, trumpeting away in the stands.

Jack used his large monkey as a pillow as he lay out on the field, lapping up the last drips of his ice cream. Lilly stared off into the fair, catching the attention of a young boy.

"When you finish your treat, why don't you go catch up with some of your friends. Here's some money." I reached into my purse and pulled out a $20 bill, realizing my daughter no longer wants to be with us.

Hearing this, Lilly sped up eating her ice cream, finishing it off as she eagerly ran off to join her friends.

"What has really been happening before I got here?" Gwen asked, moving Lilly's empty ice cream tray so she could stretch her legs out.

"Did you know Henry golfed?" I asked, showing her the photo Alice had sent me.

"No, but I don't normally keep tabs on your husband's extracurricular activities. What does this have to do with anything?" She wondered.

"Not sure, just a bit of information I learned today. Do you think Eugene's article could have been enough for someone to call me a M.U.R.D.E.R.E.R?" I spelled it out, so Jack couldn't understand it. However, he was lost in his own world, plucking grass blades after grass blades, completely unaware of our conversation.

"He laid out a lot of possibilities within his article, but he is also a twelve-year-old who is talking out of his ass. He has no idea what really happened and did not even come close to the truth. Why are you worried about this?" Gwen wondered as she watched Jack in his own world.

"It's something someone said about me today. I have heard it a few times as I walk around the neighborhood. I shouldn't let it get to me, but it is. I almost wish I had done this a different way, one where we had a body to produce and they wouldn't be questioning me left and right about things they did not know." I sighed and laid down on the blanket.

"If we did have one to produce, how would that make you look? Just as guilty, right? There was no perfect way to do this. We did what we thought was right in the moment." Gwen said, taking her final sip of wine. "Now, why don't we let Jack have some fun, and we will just keep to ourselves the rest of the evening?"

"Alright, let's go." I finished the last sip of my wine as well before getting to my feet.

We spent the next two hours laughing, joking, playing games, and overall having a good time. I continued to hear whispers throughout the fair and got comments from many of the adults and teenagers. For the most part, I ignored them to the best of my ability, and when I couldn't, Gwen helped me through it. Something at the edge of the fair entrance caught my attention as we walked through a crowd. A tattoo I had seen uncovered only a few times poked through the crowd. He was someone I did not expect to see today, and as the crowd thinned around him, he made perfect eye contact with me.

"Whatever you do, do not stop and talk to him," Gwen whispered to me as he got closer.

"Ladies, how are you today. I see you have made a new friend." Mrs. Finkle said, pulling our attention away from him.

"You've met Gwen; she's been a friend of mine for a very long time. I wouldn't consider her a new friend." I said, trying to move past her.

"I was talking about the Reaper. Hey!" She said, looking past my shoulder.

I turned around to see the Reaper standing behind me. Waving like the little creep he was. *How long had he been there?* No one had pointed him out to me until now. The last time I saw him was when he was talking with some of the moms when we were sitting on the field. Had one of them paid for him to follow me throughout the fair?

"Who was it? Who paid you?" I shouted, demanding to know.

He stood there silently, not giving any indication as to who he was. I looked around to see who would be getting the most enjoyment out of this little stunt and saw that the fair had stopped around me; no one was doing anything except looking at me. I saw phones raised, recording me, but I did not care. I was infuriated. I have not been able to go anywhere in this town without having someone talk to me about my husband. Tell me that I had murdered him, made him disappear, that I was a terrible wife, and that is why he had left. I heard it all, and I was done with it. This was the last straw!

"Whoever had him follow me through the fair has had their laugh now, you can go! All of you can go! My husband isn't here to beat any of you up for playing tricks and being absolutely horrible people to me. But if he were, then you wouldn't be doing this to me. Gotta love the irony, right?" I shouted at the crowd in front of me. "But this, this has gone too far. To assume I had something to do with him leaving this town is cruel; to pay for a Reaper of all things to follow me around and make it appear to everyone that I had done something. Shame on you! And for starters, why is our mascot a Reaper? Who had the bright idea to make it a Reaper? Do you not know how high suicide rates are among high schoolers? And you want them to have death itself as a mascot to cheer for at games! Pick a better mascot, people! And ask them to leave me alone next time! I had nothing to do with my husband running away and leaving his family; that was his choice, not mine. My children are already upset enough every day that their father has not come back, and he chose to run away from them. Do you know what kind of trauma that gives a child? Why don't we ask the Philosophy teacher? He seems to know a lot about this topic; he will be able to tell you if what you are doing to me and my family is going to cause my children to grow up and be horrible members of society or not. So why don't you think about that before you choose to ruin their lives? Okay? Now leave us alone!" My lungs heaved as I finished shouting.

My breaths were shallow as I geared up to start screaming again. What would I say? I had no idea. A weight pushed down on my shoulder, pulling me towards it. Gwen stood there, taking a deep breath, asking me to do it as well. After a moment, she drew her eyes away from mine and looked into the crowd, showing me my children. They stood there, shaking with tears running down their faces.

That felt good. At least it was in front of the whole town, I could get my frustration out and tell them all my story at once. If only it were that easy to get them all to really leave me alone. I had called the town out in many ways just now. Most people don't deserve it, but there were many who did in the crowd. Gwen locked eyes with Lilly and motioned for them to follow us immediately. Gwen grabbed

Jack and his oversized purple monkey, and we took our exit towards the parking lot.

"That was quite a show." Detective Albert stated as we passed him on the way to our car. We ignored him as best as we could, but he decided to follow us to our vehicle. "Not sure if that helped your case or not, it seems everyone will be talking about your mental break even more. Giving more of a cause to what everyone already thinks happened."

"Why don't you shut up for once!" Lilly hollered back at him.

He stopped in his tracks, shocked at the violent outburst from such a sweet little girl.

"Everyone, get in the car now!" I screamed.

Everyone, including Gwen, jumped into our car. I slid into the driver's seat and slammed the door harder than I meant to. We left the parking spot as quickly as we could, and Gwen directed me towards her car. She told me she would see us back at my place, and we would figure out dinner from there before shutting the door and hopping into her car. For a moment, I just sat there, breathing. One long, ragged exhale. I said all I needed to say. Finally, what I hope to be no more whispering, no more swallowing down what I truly want to tell everyone. The words had come out, hot and loud, and in public. I began to pull the car away, exiting the parking lot. My breath steadied, and the adrenaline started to drain. That was when the guilt seeped in.

Henry was gone, thanks to me. And whatever monster he had been, I'd still stolen their father from the two small faces that were now watching me in the rearview mirror. Jack clutched his stuffed animal like a shield. Lilly stared out the window, lips pressed thin.

The crowd's voices echoed in my head: accusations, whispers, and disbelief. I'd stood tall when they had shouted at me, but now my shoulders began to curl forward. They weren't wrong. Not entirely. And how much had my children seen? Their mother unraveling or a woman who let her fury take the wheel?

I gripped the steering wheel and blinked hard, holding back tears. I had to pull myself together. I had to be something solid for them, even if every piece of my body felt cracked.

Since the majority of the townspeople were still at the fair, it was an easier drive home. The people who stayed behind were probably still talking about what just happened. As I drove, all I could feel was tired. My body is ready to give out at any given moment, ready to collapse on my bed at home.

"Mom, you might want to see this," Lilly spoke up from the back seat, breaking my thoughts.

"We are almost home, show me then. The whole town is watching me, I don't need a cop to give me a ticket for being on my phone while driving." I told her I wasn't ready to hear what could possibly be happening now.

Gwen pulled into the driveway directly behind me, grabbed Jack's monkey, and helped the kids get into the house. Everyone except Jack piled into the living room. He

went to grab some cheese as if he hadn't already had plenty of treats that were going to ruin his gut. I told Lilly that we needed to order dinner before she showed me whatever she needed to show me in the car.

"Alright, what is it, honey?" I asked her, hanging up my phone after talking to the pizza guy and ordering more pizza than we needed.

"When I went on to my phone during the car ride, all I saw were photos of you." She said, passing over her phone. "I think it would be easier for you just to see what I saw."

On my daughter's phone, I saw photos of me walking through the fair with the mascot behind me, making their rounds on my daughter's social media pages. There were many photos of me, unaware that he was even behind me, some were taken while we were playing games, walking around, ordering food, laughing, and many other opportunities. Others had photoshopped a bikini on me or used the photo of me from the newspaper, others used our Christmas card to put a black 'X' over Henry's face, and placed the Reaper behind him. It was amazing how fast our town could photoshop images and get them posted all over social media. We had only just left the fair when Lilly started seeing these images.

The realization that the whole town had been, in a way, stalking my family the entire time we walked around the fair. Thankfully, Lilly was with friends, most likely that boy, when many of these photos were taken, so it won't hurt her

too much, as children at her age can be even crueler than adults. What will hurt my children is if the town turns into a mob scene and gets me convicted for murdering my husband.

"I think it's time for you to stop using social media for a bit, honey," I suggested to Lilly as I continued scrolling through her accounts.

There was not a single photo of anything else, just me as I scrolled through what was easily over a hundred posts.

"What? Who is supposed to watch what is happening on the socials for you if you take it away from me?" She said, making a good point.

"I can manage it from my account," Gwen suggested, pulling her phone out of her purse.

"None of the kids my age will let you follow them; all of their accounts are private." Lilly countered.

"That's also true. What if I made a fake account and said I was a new student?" Gwen wondered.

"Get real, Aunt Gwen, unless we have met you in person, our generation doesn't just accept invites from anyone. Only I can do this." She said with certainty in her eyes.

"Alright, but you have to keep us in the loop and promise not to respond to what they say. This is not your battle to fight; you can be a part of the army, but you may not go into battle. Is that understood?" I commanded my daughter.

"Yes, ma'am." She replied quickly, hearing the seriousness in her mother's tone. As she promised, I handed her back her phone.

"Alright, let's try to forget about what happened today while we wait for dinner. Everyone, take a deep breath, and Gwen and I will think of our next steps once we are fed." I turned on the TV to put on a mindless show to watch to lift everyone's spirits.

"Yes, it was quite a spectacle that happened this evening at the school's local fair. A local mom, who many believe killed her husband, had a mental breakdown today over a harmless joke. Can you tell us more about this?" The blonde anchorwoman in a purple pantsuit asked on the news.

"We can't escape it!" Lilly shouted.

"A group that has asked to be anonymous paid for the high school mascot to follow Mrs. Thompson around the fair. The Reaper managed to follow her around the fair for at least two hours before she noticed his presence behind her. When she did, she broke down, and she started screaming and yelling at the innocent patrons of the school fair. She even accused our school of promoting teenage suicide because of the mascot, who was an established figure voted for and announced by the townspeople years prior to her residence here in Gloomridge. If we didn't have the mascot follow her around, she would have never questioned the logic behind it. Now that she has, people are actually concerned about what it is representing for their children." The high school's principal spoke out about the event.

"Thank you for informing us of the consequences of her actions." The anchorwoman said before turning her attention towards an all too familiar face. "Now, Detective

Albert, you mentioned to me that you had new evidence against Mrs. Thompson and the case of her missing husband."

"Yes, I do. As many of you have already read by now, Eugene Forrest leaked confidential information on the case." He began.

Yes! I got through to him about the severity of letting a middle schooler publish information about a case, causing a whole town to turn against me.

"As an amateur journalist, he learned a valuable lesson about the ethics of what to report on a case and what not to." the detective continued.

Does he not realize that some of the most famous journalists ignore every aspect of ethics? Maybe a man of his age is remembering when journalists were arrested because of things they would print. Nowadays, journalists can print anything they please.

"In regards to the missing persons case of Henry Thompson, we have had multiple people call in to the tip line stating they have seen him in towns across the state of Virginia. None of the sightings have been confirmed as a positive sighting; otherwise, this case would be closed, and he would be back home with his family, of course, after a few hours of questioning to understand what happened. However, with no knowledge of his whereabouts, we must continue this case with as many possibilities as what could have happened to him. Thanks to the young man's article, everyone has been made aware of the blood found at the

Thompsons' residence. We finally have the results of that blood, and we will be speaking with Mrs. Thompson before we let it get released to the public. Until then, this case is going to be kept confidential." Detective Albert said before he left the interview, not waiting for the anchorwoman to ask him any more questions or thank him for his time.

The rest of the news went on to talk about the success of the school fair and that they were, in fact, going to be able to afford new jerseys for the football players. No one in the house paid that much attention to what the news had to say. Instead, we all went into our own individual panic modes. Lilly began searching every single post she could find from the fair to see if she could confirm who paid the Reaper to follow me. Gwen and I had an outward panic and an inward panic. We were terrified of ever being found out and unsure whose blood could have been found on the stairs. Although I was more than positive, I already knew. Outwardly, we tried to stay brave about the accusations. Gwen was far more convincing of this than I was. The creaking of the stairs continued throughout our panic, which continued to unnerve me even more. And Jack paced the room, waiting for dinner to be delivered, completely unaware that anything was wrong.

Creak

Creak…creak

Creak

    Creak

        Creak

Chapter Ten

Gwen spent the night after the fair so we could come up with a plan. The current plan was for the two of us to keep everything quiet and not tell a single soul about what had happened. This seems like the most responsible plan to me, but sooner or later, this town is going to hang me as a martyr. If we got far enough, the jury would be based on 'my peers', which were the lying, gossiping, biddies that listened to anything anyone had to say and believed them. That was sure to send me to my death.

I stood at the kitchen window; eyes locked on the edge of the garden. *I buried it out there. Didn't I?* I could see it so clearly, slipping outside while the kids slept, shovel in hand, the grass still wet with dew. I remember the sound of metal hitting soil. I remember how heavy the gun case felt. I remember. But I can't picture what I wore. Or what I did with the shovel after. Or even why I chose that exact spot. My fingers curled against the windowsill. What if I didn't bury it at all?

— ✧ —

Creak…SMASH

"What was that?" Gwen asked, jumping to her feet.

"You finally heard it! Thank God, I'm not going insane." I squealed.

"Of course, I heard it, glass just shattered in the front of the house." She said, carefully walking towards the foyer. "Someone threw a brick in your house!" She screamed at me.

I ran as fast as I could to the foyer, "Shit," I screamed, stepping onto glass, not paying any attention to where the glass from the window had spread on my floor, only wanting to grab the brick.

"Emma, stop!" Gwen shouted as I continued to walk across the floor barefoot.

"Those bastards!" I muttered, turning the brick over to see the word 'Murderer' written on the other side.

"Get over here!" She screamed at me. If I didn't move, she would come and get me, risking her feet on the glass, so I did. "Are you okay?" She asked when I reached her.

She grabbed hold of my arms, trying to steady me, though I didn't need it. Taking a moment to pause, a speck of red appeared in my vision. My eyes followed the spot to my feet, where a pool of blood began to form underneath. Picking up my right foot, I stumbled as the weight of my body entered my left foot, causing the glass to twist deeper into the sole of my foot. On any other day, this sight would prompt me to immediately address the situation, but not today.

"My feet will be fine. This, however, is unacceptable!" I said, holding the brick in my hands.

"What should we do? Call the detective and let him know you are being threatened?" Gwen asked.

"Like that would make any difference. Oh no, the murderer is being threatened! He would laugh and put me in handcuffs before I could say anything else to defend myself." I laughed while waving my arms through the air, brick still in my hands.

"Well, alright, let's at least clean up the glass, take care of your foot, and board up that window," Gwen said, her voice calm and steady. At that moment, all I wanted to do was throw the brick back out of the house. Hearing the sound of the glass again. I wanted to break the whole house.

Instead, she made me sit down on the floor, exactly where I was standing, so I wouldn't have to step on my feet anymore. I watched as she swept up the glass, vacuumed to make sure any small pieces were taken care of, and then mopped the floor for good measure. Then she grabbed my first aid kit and got to work on my feet, taking out twelve pieces of glass, pouring alcohol onto the wounds, and wrapping them as tightly as she could.

"If you don't let this heal, we will need to go to the hospital and have them properly do it," Gwen said, tucking the bandage and tying a knot on it to ensure it would not fall off. "Now stay there while I take care of the window, and I will help you get up when I am done." She demanded.

As I sat there cursing myself for not being patient enough to check the brick, I started to rethink my plan. We needed to make the detective make a decision soon about Henry and classify him as a missing person. They obviously have zero evidence.

Creak

Otherwise, they would be knocking...

Creak

down my door this very moment to arrest me.

Creak

And from where I am sitting, they don't appear to be knocking.

Creak, creak

How does Gwen not hear this? He is shouting for the whole world to hear! He wants the world to know he is dead. What else can he magically have the police find within our home? I waited a while before I let anyone know he was missing; his body parts are *clearly* gone by now. Either lost at sea, smashed by a garbage compactor, or sitting buried in a pile of landfill. They will never find him.

Creak

"Shut up already!" I snapped.

Gwen stood frozen in her tracks, "Are you talking to me?" She wondered.

"What? No, of course not." I quickly interjected.

Gwen squinted her eyes towards me, shook her head,

and turned away. I couldn't shake the feeling that, aside from Henry's constant nagging, something was not right.

"Now, who could that be?" Gwen shrieked when a loud thud came from the other side of the front door.

Whoever it was, was not done with me. I grabbed Gwen's wrist as she started to get to her feet. "Don't," I whispered. If the person on the other side of the door had another brick, I could not forgive myself if something happened to Gwen.

"Mrs. Thompson, are you there?" The voice shouted from the other side of the door. "Police! Open up!" He continued when we did not respond.

"I think I should get it," Gwen ripped my hand off of her wrist and made her way to the door.

I gave her one last desperate look when she turned back towards me.

"Oh, Detective," she began, "what brings you here?"

"A neighbor called in a disturbance over here, and since I just happened to be on my way here, I told them I would do both." He looked around, taking in the broken window, the broom and vacuum in the corner, and the bloody bandages on my feet. "Care to tell me what happened here?"

I lifted the brick up in the air, and he raised his eyebrows in interest. Making no effort to approach him, he got the hint and came to sit beside me as I handed him the brick. He scoffed, turning the brick over to read the message, then placed it on the stairs.

"Aside from your feet, did it hurt anyone?" He asked.

"No, sir," Gwen said, crossing the foyer to lean up against the handrail of the stairs.

"Great. Now, will you come down to the police station with me one more time? I promise this should be the last time we have the information on whose blood was on your stairs, and I was informed you had to come in person to find out." Detective Albert stood up, sheepishly giving me no choice but to come with him.

The short ride to the police department was quieter than the first ride, as there was no country music playing this time. The detective's nervous tapping on his steering wheel was the only audible sound in the whole car. I thought to ask him about his wife to ease the tension in the car, but decided against it. He was obviously not in the right mindset to talk about his wife.

After being ushered through the police station, Officer Brady sat in the make-shift interrogation room waiting, notebook and laptop in hand, and a table filled with three coffees.

"Officer Brady, good to see you again." I kindly said, acknowledging his presence as we entered the room.

"Mrs. Thompson, good to see you as well. This is for you." He handed me a cup of coffee.

I took a deep sip and sighed. "You know my weakness, thank you!" I laughed.

"Okay, enough of this." Detective Albert waved his

hands between us. "We need to talk to you about your husband."

The detective opened his folder and pulled out the first piece of paper on top of a large pile. *That can't be good.* I thought as I saw how many pages were in the stack.

"First, we wanted to thank you for coming down here willingly to gain this information instead of having me arrest you to get you down here. We have the results from the dried blood that was found in your home." He slammed the piece of paper down onto the table in front of me. "Can you tell me what this line says?"

There was something in his calm that unsettled me. The kind of patience that comes from already knowing the answers. He'd written it all down, the paper in front of me wasn't a question. It was a confession.

"The forensic analysis of the dried blood sample collected from the crime scene has been completed. The results are conclusive, and the DNA profile obtained from the sample matches that of the victim, Henry Thompson. This evidence supports the ongoing investigation linking the biological material found at the scene directly to the victim." I read aloud my hands shaking.

"Can you tell me what that means?" Detective Albert asked me.

"You are saying that the blood found in my home matches my husband, but where did you get a positive sample of his blood to confirm if it was his blood on the stair railing or not? You didn't get a sample of my blood or that of my children. So how could you possibly be certain that this is, without a doubt, conclusively my husband's blood?" I questioned, keeping my breathing as steady as I could, as infuriated as I was.

"I am not at liberty to say where we got the sample from." The detective responded.

"That is bullshit, I know my rights on this. You cannot say you are certain it's his blood and not tell me where you got a sample from. Have you found my husband? Did he give you a sample of his blood? Because if you did, I would love to see why he left!" I half shouted.

"Ma'am, please lower your voice." Officer Brady asked.

"I will not, do you see what this paper says? You are calling my home a crime scene. What was the crime? My husband running off on us? Yes, that is a crime, and his children would also like to have a word with him about leaving them. Did you know he missed their first day of school? He never misses their first day of school. He could have at least waited till school started before he disappeared, but I had to deal with two crying children on the first day of school. That is a crime." I rambled, trying to get them to change the subject.

Officer Brady expressed his sympathy, noting, "Yes, ma'am. We understand your pain. However, we can't tell you where we obtained the blood sample for your husband."

"Let's move on, shall we?" Detective Albert asked.

"I thought that was all we were waiting on. What else

is there?" I asked.

"What else is there?" He mocked. "Emma, Emma, Emma, my dear. There is plenty more to talk about." He laughed. "Let's talk about the room in your basement. When I was in there, it was wiped perfectly clean; I could smell the chemicals that had been baking behind that locked door. Any idea why it was like that?" He asked.

"I have no idea. Henry must have wiped it clean before he left us. As I have told you before, I have never been in that room aside from the day we toured the house and just the other day when you came over and stayed for dinner." I pleaded.

"Very likely story. So, you are telling me that your husband, who had packed a bag for a trip he was never planning on actually going on, took his time to empty a room in his basement and douse it in chemicals? Then what, drive to the airport and leave with nothing but the clothes on his back?" He wondered.

"I guess." That is all I could think to say.

"Alright. Do you want to know what theory I have?" He asked.

"Sure, I am assuming you were going to tell me either way," I said, taking a sip of my coffee.

"I think you murdered your husband in that room, got rid of him, and cleaned up the room, thinking we would not find out. How's that for a theory?" He asked.

My heart was pounding. How could he possibly have guessed that? *Alright, deep breaths.*

"There seems to be a flaw in that idea of yours. Have you looked at my body recently? There is no way I could lift my husband; he was easily a hundred and fifty pounds, and I barely hit a hundred and ten pounds myself." I countered.

"That's a good point, Albert," Officer Brady piped up.

Detective Albert eyed him down, telling him who the boss was in this situation. I could see his brain starting to work through the pieces, trying to figure out if it was possible for me to do it.

"And why would I possibly want to murder my husband?" I asked, curious to hear what theory he had for that.

"Well," he paused, "you said it yourself, didn't you? Your husband has hit you before; maybe that was enough to set you off." He said, trying to convince himself of this motive.

"If that were the reason, wouldn't I have wanted to do it years ago when he hit me the one time?" I challenged.

"She has another great point there, sir." Officer Brady insisted.

If the detective's eyes could kill, we would be putting him in handcuffs from the look he gave Brady. I knew I liked Officer Brady not just because he fills me with coffee.

"Okay, well, how do you explain these?" He boomed, throwing pages upon pages of photos of my car outside of multiple locations the night we tossed his body. "I followed your actions for the two days after your husband drove himself to the airport. What I can't seem to figure out is this blip of time here." He pointed at the photo of me walking out of the grocery store and into a cab. "You see, I was able to get a pretty good picture of your whereabouts during this time frame; however, I do not have access to your home cameras, so I am missing a chunk here. I did not see when you arrived at the grocery store, but my main question is why you took a cab instead of your own car." He questioned.

I have never been so scared in my life. Detective Albert had actually done his research, although I am still skeptical about the blood. What else was he going to find? If he kept at it, he might be able to guess everything that we had done and have me hanged without a trial. Gwen too.

"That was the night of my book club. It was my turn to host, and hosting that many women for book club can be extremely stressful, so I had a few drinks while setting up, thinking I was not going to have to leave the house. However, I had run out of a few necessities for the event and called a cab since I was not in the mindset to drive." I stated confidently.

"Likely story, I will have to ask your neighbors for their camera footage to corroborate your story. They will likely have footage of a cab driving through the neighborhood about, say, an hour beforehand?" He asked me, making a note on his tablet as I spoke.

"That sounds about right. The stores are not far from my home, and I spent some time wandering the aisles and figuring out exactly what I wanted. Didn't want to have to call another cab if I forgot yet another thing." I laughed, sweat pouring out of my armpits.

"Interesting story. Would you like to hear what I have to say?" He paused, not waiting for me to answer. "I think you needed an alibi. I think you made an appearance at a public place to get a confirmed alibi for the timeframe shortly after your husband arrived at the airport. However, a train ride from the airport to the grocery store would put you right around that timeframe, wouldn't it?" He asked me.

"How would I know?" I countered, trying to keep my sentences short so he could not see the rate at which my chest was rising.

"Have you ever taken the train?" He grilled me.

"Ever? In my entire life? Yeah, I have ridden a train before. But that is like asking if I have ridden a bike or walked down a sidewalk; everyone has ridden a train at least once in their lives." I explained, feeling the sweat pool down my legs and onto my bandaged foot.

"You know what I am asking, have you ever ridden the train from the airport to our town?" He asked again.

"No." I lied.

I had taken the train to the airport a handful of times when I didn't want to pay to park my car when it was just me traveling. I never did it with my children, though; it would take much longer than just driving to get them all loaded up and into a train.

"Alright, let's leave that as it is and move on. Can you tell me why I have photos of you and your friend stopping at dozens of locations from the early morning all through-out the day after your book club, was it?" He asked, pointing at each photo.

"We had lots of errands to run, and we like to run them together. We get an early start so we can hit all of the stores and not think about how long we spend in each one." I told him yet another lie.

"And that's why you were at a diner before the sun even came up?" He doubted.

"Yeah, an early start requires being fueled," I stated.

"You stopped at a diner, four department stores, a pharmacy, a coffee shop, a spot for what I am assuming was lunch, and the list goes on. At each stop, you took a bag out of your car. What was in those bags?" He asked, tapping each photo as he named off locations.

"Trash from the party. My trash would not be picked up for almost a week, and we had way too much to put in our normal trash can. So, we put the wine bottles, those girls drink a lot, in one bag and put it in a recycling bin around town, we put the trash in other trash containers around town as well." I quickly came up with the lie.

He has more information about my whereabouts than God if they were watching. I continued to sweat through my clothes, leaving what felt like a pool of sweat in my shoes. The room begins to heat up as the fluorescent lights beam down. My hands are clammy, resting uneasily on the metal table, and I force them to stay still, though every nerve in my body screams to flee the room. Flee the investigation.

I should have kept my mouth shut and my actions quieter.

"When you put everything together, I could tell a pretty solid story about what happened. Your husband lashed out one more time, and you told yourself you would never let him hit you after that one time. Or maybe, just maybe, you lied about that, too? Your husband was physically abusive to you, maybe even to your children. He went to hit you, and you snapped. You murdered your husband and somehow got rid of him. I haven't figured out how you did that quite yet, but I will. You then dropped his car off at the airport and rode the train back, thinking no one would know. You called a cab from the grocery store to get back home and prepare for your party. All the while, the blood of your husband had seeped deep within your fingernails. Into your very pores. Does that sound right? Sounds very convincing to me. I think a jury would think the same thing. We have his blood as proof that something happened within that home. Now, we just need to get it before a judge." He said, bullying my every fiber.

"Are you not missing one detail?" I asked.

"What's that?" He asked, wondering himself.

"No one has seen my husband or his body, if you are trying to say he's dead. How can you prove anything without a body?" I wondered.

"Technically, we cannot consider her husband dead for at least seven years if he is still missing. However, with the blood results coming back as her husband's, the timeline for this could be moved up." He clarified.

"I've read enough books in my career to know that the little amount of blood found on the stairs could not constitute enough blood to consider he died. This could easily have been a prick on his finger that he rubbed on the stairs while making his way down them one day. You would need gallons of blood or stains to be able to conclude that he was, in fact, dead or had died in our home. And if that was the case, I had nothing to do with it, and I do not know how he could have died as I watched him leave the house and drive away to the airport. Which you have as proof of, from the first time you dragged me to the police department to question me. Isn't that right, Detective?"

I watched as he stumbled through the papers on the table, trying to shuffle them back into place. Sweat poured down his face as he contemplated this bit of information. Most likely, believing me to be just a little housewife with no other skills or knowledge outside of dishes, laundry, and hosting. I've been in this room for hours, having the same conversations over and over. Rehashing my whereabouts, trying to trip me up to admit I killed my husband.

"You have been reading too much fiction; that is not how it works in the real world." He laughed. "This is enough information and evidence to arrest you for life."

I laughed a little too loudly at the absurdity, the sound echoing oddly in the room. "You think that proves anything?" I protested, but my voice shook, letting my panic shine through.

The room began to feel smaller, the air thinner. "I need

a break," I finally gasped, the words spilling out in a desperate rush before I could stop them. They left me alone in the overly hot room, my head buried in my hands as I tried to stifle the sobs breaking free. This surface of calm is crumbling fast, and I'm on the verge of being swallowed whole by my own deceit. I can't let them take me. They don't have anything tangible. They know it.

"Arrest me then." I calmly said as they walked back into the room, my mind made up.

"We technically can't, I have been asking my boss to let me arrest you for weeks now. However, we can hold you for mental instability, which you have clearly shown to us. Don't you think, Officer Brady?" He asked.

"She seems pretty upset to me, but who wouldn't be when you have been accusing her of such heinous crimes?" Officer Brady calmly stated.

I knew I had liked him from the beginning.

"Although, maybe a night or two would give her enough time to reconsider her story. Maybe she will tell us the truth about what happened to her husband. He was a man who did not deserve what had happened to him. After all of that, doesn't he deserve justice?" Officer Brady continued.

On second thought, maybe I don't like him after all.

"So, what is it going to be? I have children to get home to and get dinner started." I asked.

"Well, you should have thought about that before you went and murdered your husband. We are going to give you one phone call to find suitable arrangements for your children, and then we are going to take you in." Detective Albert stated.

"You can follow me," Officer Brady gestured for me to follow him out of the room. "You can use this phone to make a phone call."

"I need to use my phone to get the number, I don't have it memorized. I might as well just call from my phone, then, right?" I asked, plunging my hands into my purse.

Officer Brady looked at his feet, kicking up dust. "It's policy that you use our phone; we need to have a record of your conversation and who you spoke with."

"If I am not technically under arrest, does that policy even apply to me? How about we let this one phone call slide and save you a few bucks from your phone bill?" I suggested and began searching my purse.

"You do have a point there. I would rather you just use our phone, though, can you just do that?" he pleaded.

"Sure, I can do that," I said, grabbing my phone out of my purse.

Officer Brady excused himself to check if my accommodations for the night were ready and to see what they would have for dinner. I took a moment before moving, waiting to hear his footsteps recede. Unlocking my phone, I opened Gwen's contact card and questioned if I should do as I was asked. I decided against it, I'm not under arrest, so I hit call on my phone and placed it underneath their black telephone.

"Hey girl, what's up?" Gwen asked.

"I need you to listen quickly and do not ask any questions till the end. I am staying the night at the police station. I am not under arrest, and they have plenty of stories about what happened. I need you to pick up the kids from school and tell them they are having a sleepover at your house. Please feed them dinner and don't tell them why I am missing for the night." I finished.

"How many of the stories are correct?" She asked.

"Too many of them, but no evidence to prove anything," I told her.

"Okay, good news then. You will have to tell me why you are staying later, but for now, do you think you should call your attorney?" she wondered.

"I don't want them to think I'm guilty. If I call an attorney, I will look guilty." I whispered.

"You're staying there overnight; it already sounds like they think you are guilty. Have you used your one phone call?"

"I'm on it now with you," I said.

"You called me from your cell phone, hang up and call your attorney on their phone. Send me your attorney's number so I have their information just in case. Do it fast. I am assuming there are no officers near you. You don't want them to walk up to you and find out you are using your one call to make two calls. I love you, and good luck." She said and hung up.

She was right, I should call my attorney. He loved my

husband, and they were always talking on the phone together. I'm sure we covered the cost of his new house last year with the number of times they spoke. I never knew what they were talking about; I just assumed it had something to do with his company. The few times I have had to speak with our attorney, they made me feel as though I was an idiot and should have Henry handling my affairs as the other housewives had done. I swallowed my pride and pulled up his contact information and slowly dialed his number on the thick black police phone.

"Hi Bob, I have some information I need to catch you up on. For the short version, I am in our town's police station and need representation. I'm not under arrest. If you could stop by, I can fill you in on all of the details." I asked, unsure of the response I would get with the little bit of info I gave him.

"I'll be right there," Bob uttered and hung up the phone.

Officer Brady had not come back yet, so I took the time to make one more call from my phone.

"Bob's coming. Wipe the footage from your security cameras." I demanded of Gwen and hung up.

Quickly, I placed my phone back into my purse and waited for Officer Brady to come back. It did not take long. They must watch when you hang up from your call.

"Are you ready, ma'am?" He asked as he came back into my vision.

"As ready as you can be," I told him.

I followed him through the police station, down a long, dark corridor only lit by the small sconces spaced throughout, and down the stairs to the basement. The cells were completely empty. Not surprising since our town is so strait-laced.

"This one's yours," Officer Brady said, unlocking the last cell on the right. "Someone will come by for dinner soon. Try to get yourself comfortable." He started walking away and paused. "I need to take that from you." He gestured towards my purse.

Holding my purse tight against me, I watched as his eyebrows lifted to explain to me what I already knew. He was going to take it whether or not I wanted him to. I released my grip and handed over my purse.

I went inside the cell, stopping in the center to take a look around before taking a seat on the bench to the right. It was going to be an uncomfortable night; there were no pillows, no sheets, and no cushions on the bench. Just solid wood that stank as though many inmates had peed themselves lying on the bench, frightened by the unexpected events that lay ahead of them. I sat there accepting the fate I had given to myself on the soiled bench. My mind raced over whether I had made the right decision or not to ask to be taken in. As shocked as I was to be taken in, honestly, I did ask for it. Now I just wait, wait to see how this plays out. Wait to see if the detective comes up with enough to pin me. Until then, I worry about my children, Gwen, and myself.

"Here you go. Not like you deserve it or anything, husband murderer." An officer shouted at me as he slid my dinner into the cell a little too aggressively, rocking the glass of water and sending the sandwich to the floor. He was the number one contender for who leaked the information to Eugene now.

He disappeared before I could even thank him. I picked up the sandwich and put it back on the tray before lifting up the bread to see a slab of tuna. It looks like I will not be eating dinner tonight. The tuna had a stench to it that rivaled the bench. I took a sip of the water before taking a seat back on the bench and dozing off against the wall.

"Emma," a man shouted, scaring me awake.

"Oh, Bob, so great to see you!" I cheered, wiping my eyes to make sure he was really there and not just my imagination.

"Are you doing okay in there? I see they brought you dinner at least. It doesn't look like you touched it. I'm glad I brought you this, then." He said, lifting up a bag from the steakhouse around the corner. He took out each individual box and slid them through the bars as best as he could. "They wouldn't let you have a knife." He said when he saw me open one box to see a steak that had been precut into bite-sized pieces for me.

"Can't imagine I'm that much of a danger to them to have a knife taken away from me." I shook my head as I spoke. "Whatever, at least I have a proper dinner. Thank you for this!"

"Now that you have food, can you tell me what happened? Why are you even in here?" Bob asked, rightfully so.

I caught Bob up to speed on the situation, minus the part that I did, in fact, murder Henry.

"He's missing? Are you certain about that?" He asked.

"Positive, I haven't seen him since he left. Do you know anything about the room in the basement?" I wondered.

"I know a lot about that room. I'm not sure how much I can really tell you if he is still alive, though." He muttered.

"What does that even mean?" I asked in between bites of potatoes and steak.

"It's client confidentiality; I can't talk about it." He whispered.

"I'm his wife and your client, too. Does that not give me the right to know about what you two are always talking about?" I questioned him.

"No, unfortunately, it does not. Your husband was involved in a few different businesses that were not always legal." He whispered, unsure what the cameras surrounding the cells could pick up. "Because of that, I cannot talk to you about them, especially not in a police station. If he is found, then maybe you can ask him about them, but until then, or he shows up dead, I can't tell you about them." Bob said regretfully.

"Alright, fine, but what are we going to do about me and this situation?" I gestured widely to my cell.

"The first thing I am going to do is get you out of here.

Why in the world would you even suggest that they arrest you? You did nothing wrong. But that is beside the point right now." He shook his head. "Once we get you out, we are going to make sure that this detective you are telling me about cannot do anything to ruin your reputation. That means a lot to you, and it would be a shame if being accused of this ruins that." He spoke.

"I fear we are far past that; my neighbors have been spying on me and whispering throughout town. At this rate, the whole town probably thinks I did this." I replied, remembering the scene at the fair.

"Well, whether that is true or not, we need to fix this. Sit tight for me and let me figure out what to do, okay?" He asked before getting up, collecting my trash, and walking away.

I nodded my head, and he took his leave. My lawyer officially thinks I am clear and has nothing to hide; however, he does not know the true story. I wonder if I will need to tell him what really happened to Henry, or if Gwen and I will be taking that to our graves. I hope the latter.

Just then, the cool, musty air enveloped me in its silent embrace. The bars of the cell stood cold and indifferent, teasing me. I wasn't under arrest, not technically, but being held in this suffocating space felt just as binding. The faint creak of the old wooden stairs outside the cell was torturous, each groan and echo teasing my frayed nerves. The sound was hauntingly familiar, too much like the daily and nightly creaks of my house. With my eyes closed, I could almost believe he was there, descending the stairs after one of our countless arguments, his shadow looming in the doorway. My heart raced, and my breath hitched in my throat, the boundaries between past and present blurring dangerously.

As panic took hold, I wrapped my arms around my shivering body, the cold seeping into my bones. *Could he really be here?* My mind raced with paranoid thoughts, each more illogical than the last, but fear has a peculiar power in the dim shadows of an isolated cell. Gasping for air, the walls seemed to close in around me. In my heart, a tempest of regret and terror raged, my thoughts a whirlwind of what-ifs and should-haves.

My mind darted to my children, the innocent bystanders in the chaos of our lives. The weight of my next breath felt unbearable as I confronted the darkest of my secrets. Would it have been better to confess to the murder of my husband? To cleanse my soul of the bloodstained night when I had silenced his threats forever? Maybe then the shadows would cease their torment, and my children could escape the curse of his hidden tyranny.

But as the creaking continued, a sinister lullaby I knew all too well, I curled tighter into myself, the cold floor a harsh reminder of my reality. Alone in the grip of my encroaching madness, I realized there was no escape from the echoes of the past that chained me just as securely as the bars that held me.

— ✧ —

"Wake up! I have a question for you." Detective Albert shouted as he banged on the cell bars.

I jumped to my feet, knocking the rotting tuna sandwich across the floor. My eyes took a moment to focus to see who had frightened me awake. *What time is it?* I thought as I watched Detective Albert sway in front of me.

"I have a question for you." He repeated.

Unsure what to say, I stood there silently, waiting for him to respond and taking a closer look at him. His once straight uniform was wrinkled. His jacket was hanging off one arm, his tie was loose around his neck, and his shirt was unbuttoned enough to see the stained undershirt beneath it. His shoes were untied, and one of his pant legs was tucked into his socks.

Was he drunk? I wondered.

"Why did you do it?" He sloppily asked.

"Do what?" I asked him, already aware of what he meant.

"Murder him? How could you do that to your husband?" He sputtered.

"I didn't do that." I sternly said.

"One day you think you are in the perfect marriage, and the next you are dead on the side of the road. How does that happen? How can a woman decide to end it like that, out of nowhere!" He screamed.

"Not every marriage is perfect; that is why divorce rates are so high," I answered, unsure if we were still talking about me.

"What could you possibly know about divorce rates? You murdered your husband; you are a widow now." He paused. "Unlike me, I am going to be a divorced man soon. My wife came to the same conclusion as you did. You did not want to spend any time with your husband anymore; you couldn't stand him, maybe you didn't love him anymore. She decided I was too much and she was going to divorce me. At least she didn't kill me, right?" He cried, shaking the bars of my cell.

"I'm so sorry to hear that. How long were you married?" I asked, wanting to know as much as I could.

"Forty-three years, best forty-three years of my life, too. That woman was my life. I loved her more than anything else in the entire world. Did you even love your husband?" He asked.

"I did, when I married him, he was a very kind man, over the years, he, as you guessed, got meaner. I still love him, though." I concluded, catching myself before I spoke too much out of line.

"Well, if you want to give my wife any tips on how to kill me, I am sure she would more than welcome it." He laughed too loudly, losing his balance.

"Let her know I can't help with that if she asks," I told him. "I think you should go home. It looks like you have had too much to drink tonight."

"I don't have a home anymore. She wants me to move out. She's taking the home. She said, and met a life coach who told her this was her year to become something of her-self. It was the year that she would make a change and get everything she wanted when she was younger. Which means she never really wanted me; she just settled. That's what she told me; she was in love with me, but she was settling. She could have gone off and married a Spaniard who lived off the coast, and they could have lived their lives drinking wine and having as much sex as they wanted. She said she's going to sell the house and move to another country." He blabbered on.

"Albert, can I call you Albert? Why did you come here?" I genuinely wondered.

Just then, he sat down on the floor, placing his head in his hands, and began crying.

"I don't have any friends, your case, and my wife are the only things I have going on in my life. I just came from a bar where I sat alone, drowning my heartache in as many whiskeys as the bartender allowed me to have before he cut me off. When I was told to go home, I didn't know where to go. So I came here, to my job, my other life. You want to know a secret?" He slurred. "I lied to you. We never had a copy of your husband's blood to test against the blood in your house. We have no idea whose blood that is, and will probably never know." He whispered and then burst out into uncontrollable laughter.

His confession shocked me for the mere fact that he

told me what I had already known. They hadn't found his body, and they would never find his body.

Chapter Eleven

Detective Albert left the police department, unsure of his next move. He had let it slip that he lied about the blood and needed something else to help pin the murder on Emma. Hopping into his police-issued vehicle, he began driving aimlessly through town, only to wind up at Emma's house. Checking the doors and windows for an entrance, he stumbled across an open window in the living room. He lifted the screen and climbed in, closing it behind him.

"Hello?" he half-shouted, half-whispered as he wandered throughout the house.

When he had determined he was alone, he made his way to the basement. He stopped at the top of the stairs, gripping the railing tightly. The air that wafted up from the wine cellar was cool and pungent with the scent of cork and fermentation, a scent he had avoided for the last seven years. His throat tightened.

He took one step down, then froze. *Not yet.* Instead, he turned back, pacing the hallway. He opened a kitchen drawer, pretended to look for clues, then circled back to the basement door. His hand hovered over the knob.

"Just get in, grab the key, and get out," He muttered.

Still, he didn't move. Finally, after a few deep breaths, he descended the steps. At the threshold of the wine cellar, he stopped again. The rows of bottles stared back at him like a wall of temptation. A bead of sweat slid down his temple. He stepped forward, then back. Then forward again.

"Don't even think about it," he warned himself. But the tension in his chest grew heavier. His fingers twitched. He reached for a drawer instead, pulling it open, then slamming it shut. Again and again, rifling through the room. But with every failed drawer, frustration and craving built.

Finally, he grabbed a bottle. The cork popped like a gunshot. He didn't use a glass. Just tilted it back and drank. One bottle became two. Stumbling through the cellar, he made his way to the cold, bleak part of the basement. The door to the back room loomed ahead, daring him to come closer. He grabbed the nearest object, a book, and hurled it at the door. When it didn't open, frustration flared. He began pulling containers off the shelves around him.

"That bitch must have moved it!" He muttered.

One by one, Albert pulled down every container, dumped their contents onto the floor, and searched for the key. He doubled back on a few of the bins, questioning whether he had missed it. Then he found it: a gun case, tucked on the bottom shelf and surrounded by dust bunnies. Tossing the wine bottle aside, he sat down and tried to open the case.

"Okay, kids, be quick. Vince is waiting for us to start the movie. Grab what you need for the night. Jack, do not forget your toothbrush!" Gwen called from upstairs.

Footsteps echoed above him, reminding him that he was no longer alone. He grabbed the gun case and rushed to the stairs, easing the basement door open. From the crack, he watched Jack pack snacks, one for now and one for later. Albert slowly began closing the door again, hoping to stay hidden.

"What are you doing here?" Jack asked as the door caught his attention.

Albert froze. He glanced around, then gave a quiet laugh when he realized Jack was talking to him.

"I need to ask you a few questions. Police business about your father," he whispered, motioning for Jack to follow him.

Jack hesitated. He knew not to go off alone with adults he didn't know well, but Albert had been over for dinner. That seemed like enough. He followed him down the stairs.

"Did you find him?" Jack asked as they entered the wine cellar. "What happened in here?" He asked as he took in each drawer still open and objects cluttering the countertop.

"Nothing, don't worry about that," Albert said quickly.

"So, did you?" Jack pressed.

"Did I...?" Albert paused. "Oh, find your father. No, I haven't. But I have some questions that might help us locate him."

"Okay. Do I get a detective badge like yours?" Jack asked, pointing to the one clipped to Albert's jacket.

"I can get you one," Albert said. "What I really want to know is what your dad did down here. Do you know about the room in the back?"

"I don't know," Jack answered.

"Not even a guess?" Albert asked, his speech slurring.

"Well, he used to come down here after work sometimes. Wouldn't let us in when he was here. Trust me, I tried. He was serious about keeping it private," Jack sighed.

"Did you notice anything different about this room?" Detective Albert pressed.

"I've never been in it, so I'm not sure. But I did see a woman who worked with my dad leaving from the basement a lot." Jack began looking back up the stairs, trying to find the polite time to walk away.

"Anything else?" Albert pried.

"She always wore really nice suits. I asked Dad once why they didn't go to his office upstairs, but he told me it was none of my business. So, I stopped asking." He shrugged and began to turn around.

"Were these women always alone?" Albert grabbed Jack's shoulder, stopping him.

"No. Sometimes big men came with them. They always had briefcases." He paused. "What happened down here?" He wondered again.

"Police business, son. Thanks for your help." Albert held up the gun case. "Have you seen this before?"

"Once. I was really little. Dad brought it home and scared everyone. I haven't seen it since. I thought Mom got rid of it." He paused. "Can I go now?"

"Of course. You've been here too long. Someone might notice. Go on." Albert whispered.

The detective watched him head up the stairs, then held a finger to his lips in a silent "shh." Jack nodded, but planned to tell his mom the moment she returned.

Albert waited for the sound of footsteps above to fade before moving again. He counted four distinct sets: two light ones, probably Jack and Lilly, one with the clicking rhythm of heels, and one heavier, slower tread. Unsure who else was home, he stayed put.

He stretched out on the wine cellar couch and let the wine lull him.

"Women, huh?" He muttered. "Why bring them down here? Were they prostitutes? Was Henry running something on the side?"

His mind spiraled with theories, each one darker than the last. Eventually, he passed out. When he came to, it was 3 a.m., and the wine bottle dangled from his hand. His mouth was dry, and his head pounded. He sat up slowly, blinking against the dim cellar light. The mess hit him all at once. Papers, containers, and drawers were left open, with wine splattered on the stone floor. He groaned and reached for another bottle, removed the cork, and took another long swig. One more wouldn't make a difference now.

He stayed on the couch for a few more minutes, letting

the wine settle and staring at the chaos he'd created. Then he got up and started cleaning. Slowly, unsteadily, he returned items to the drawers, though not always to the right ones. He stumbled over himself twice, knocking over a half-filled bin and swearing under his breath.

After clearing the cellar floor, he returned to the shelves. He grabbed another bottle. Telling himself it was just to help him focus, he drank as he reorganized the storage bins. Thankfully, the labeled containers made that part easier, though he mixed up more than a few.

He wiped smudges off the counter with the sleeve of his jacket, mopped up a puddle of spilled wine with an old towel he found stuffed in a drawer, and took another drink. The cellar looked marginally better by the end, though not close to how he'd found it.

His hands trembled as he placed the final bin back on the shelf. He took one last swig, set the empty bottle beside two others, and quietly let himself out. The wine cellar would be disorganized for quite some time thanks to him. He left the house quietly, gun case in hand, and headed back to the station, new theories simmering with every step.

Chapter Twelve

As I stepped out of the police department, the morning sun blinded me. I had been locked in the dark cell for what felt like too long, even if it were only a day. My car was back at home, and Gwen had my children; the only option for me was to call a car service. While I waited, I went next door to the bakery to get some coffee. I would not be seeing my children after the night I had without some form of backup, even if it was mainly for my emotional support. A shot of espresso down and a nitro cold brew in my hands, I was ready.

The car pulled up in front of the police station just long enough for the driver to get bored and start scrolling on his phone. I knocked on the door and placed my phone up to the window to confirm I had the right vehicle before hopping into the back seat.

"We can leave in just one moment. This is getting good." He motioned towards his phone.

He held his phone in his left hand just above the steering wheel. I could not hear what was playing on his phone since he was wearing headphones, but the images on his screen were of me. He swiped to the following video, and a woman came on to talk about me. So far, the driver had not turned around to notice my face and make the connection, and I prayed he never would. I began to sink into the seat, becoming one with the car and trying to blend into the surroundings.

"Have you been hearing about this as well?" He shouted back towards me. "This woman might have killed her husband! He's been missing for a while now!" The car pulled away from the curb, and we began the short drive back to my house. When I did not answer his questions, he turned around to ask if I could hear him. His eyes searched every visible part of my body, then began to widen with recognition. "You're her!" He screamed, slamming on the brakes of the car in excitement.

"Let's just get home. I miss my kids." I pleaded, taking a sip of my cold brew to help block my face.

Putting the car in park, he unbuckled his seatbelt and turned fully around in his seat. "I have to know what happened! No one is able to get a quote from you; everyone is talking about you on social media!"

"Please, can you just take me home?" My eyes felt the heaviest they had been in a while, my heart sank in the back of the car, and I was ready to disappear.

"Do your children know what happened?" He continued bombarding me.

I grabbed my purse and placed my hand on the door

handle. "You are not getting a good review from me."

"Wait, wait, wait! Don't go. I'll stop." He turned back around in his seat and kept his promise and continued driving.

Once the car got above forty miles per hour, he broke that promise. "So, the Reaper was he in on it, too? I heard your children are starting to fight in school, too. Have they always been like that, or did it only come out since their dad went missing? How did you do it? Did you do it?"

His questions continued, but I stopped listening. The car was going too fast for me to jump out, and he was getting closer to my house. Ultimately, I stayed silent. My nerves shaking uncontrollably, I placed my coffee between my thighs to keep from spilling as we turned into my driveway. Before he could put the car in park, I pulled the lock and jumped out of the car, slamming the door behind me and racing towards the front door.

Creak

Welcome home.

I walked around the main level of my home to see what condition I had left it in and if it was still in the same condition. With the detective as drunk as he was, I would not have put it past him to ransack my home, knowing my children were not here and he had the house to himself.

"Shit!" I screamed. I ran to my basement as fast as I could to check the back room, practically throwing my body towards the knob. "Still locked," I said, sighing.

The shelf looked exactly the same. The same dusty

blankets, same broken lamp beside them. But the space behind them? Empty. I pushed everything aside. Pulled the whole stack onto the floor.

Nothing.

The gun case was gone. For a few seconds, I just stood there, blinking like it might reappear if I looked hard enough. I tried to remember moving it. I could almost see myself carrying it outside. The weight of it in my hands. The night air on my skin. But I couldn't be sure.

"You buried it," I said out loud, to hear the words. "You did."

But if I was wrong. What if someone else had found it? My mouth went dry. I backed up a step. Then another. *Maybe I never moved it. Perhaps someone else did. Or maybe I'm losing it altogether.* I stood there for too long, staring at that empty shelf like it might confess something. But it didn't. The next thing I knew, I was back upstairs, shoving the back door open so hard it slammed against the siding. The garden glared at me in the early morning light, quiet, still, mocking. I remember burying it. *I do.* I told myself I couldn't keep it in the house. I know I went outside. I know I dug a hole.

Didn't I?

I didn't bother with gloves or shoes. The ground was cool under my feet. The shovel leaned against the shed like it had been waiting. I started by the hydrangeas. That's where I thought I remembered digging. One scoop. Two. The sound of metal scraping the earth. My breathing got louder than the crickets.

Nothing. I moved to the fence line. Dug again. Faster this time. Dirt flew behind me in frantic, uneven bursts.

"You put it here," I whispered. "You put it here, Emma."

But the hole stayed empty. I dropped the shovel and clawed at the ground with my hands. My nails bent. My fingers stung. Somewhere behind me, a dog barked. A porch light clicked on. I didn't stop.

"Where is it?" I said, louder now. "Where the hell did you put it?"

My heart pounded so hard I thought it might crack something inside me. And then I heard him.

Henry. Soft, smug, right in my ear: "You never buried it."

I froze. My hands, caked in soil, trembled in my lap. That voice wasn't real. It couldn't be. But it felt real. The garden swayed. My vision blurred. I couldn't tell if I was crying or just dizzy. I looked around at the holes I'd dug, the mess I'd made, the dirt on my skin, and felt the weight of it all pressing down in guilt, grief, fear, and now this: *madness*.

Grabbing my phone out of my pocket, I dialed Gwen.

"Did you take the gun out of the basement?" I asked Gwen the moment she answered the phone.

"Hello to you, too," Gwen answered dryly, slightly annoyed by the seriousness in my tone when she called. "And no, I did not take it. Why would I take it?" She asked disbelievingly.

"I don't know, but it's gone. When you and the kids were here, did you let them out of your sight at all?" I asked.

"No, I sent them to their rooms to grab some clothing, and I stayed downstairs waiting for them. They never went near the basement." She promised me.

"I need to find it. Thank you for watching the kids. Can you drop them off after school today?" I asked.

"Of course," Gwen promised.

I thanked her and hung up the phone. My hands trembled slightly as I glanced around the ruined yard before me, and the memory of the cluttered basement, tools, and old photo albums scattered everywhere. I couldn't stand the sight or the memories any longer. With a heavy sigh, I turned and ran inside, each step feeling heavier than the last.

Creak

"Shut up, Henry," I screamed as I walked past the stairs and towards his office.

The door to his office creaked ominously as I pushed it open, the sound slicing through the silence like a warning of what was to be found beyond. I hesitated on the threshold for just a moment before entering. The air inside was thick with dust and stillness as if even the room were holding its breath and waiting for its owner to come back. It had been his sanctuary for so long, and now he was gone. The reality sent a shiver down my spine. I moved to his desk, the hum of the computer greeting me. I took a deep breath, knowing I would not have luck getting in this time. I have not been able to get in yet.

I stared at the login screen like it might offer her a clue, something I missed in my earlier attempts. But there was nothing, just his stupid face smiling at me from the wallpaper in the background. I had tried "password123," "Harvard," "Ferrari," and "JackAndLilly." Four failed attempts. One more and I'm locked out.

No dice.

My hands hovered over the keyboard. He was arrogant. Vain. Obsessed with appearances. Of course, it wouldn't be something sentimental. Of course, it would be about him. I typed it slowly: HenryJamesThompson.

Enter.

The screen flickered. The desktop loaded. I let out a sound; half laugh, half gasp. He made his password his full name. Middle name and all. *Because, of course, he did.* Because who else would he think of first?

I had to see what was happening in our house, and I needed some semblance of control over the chaos that had unfolded while I was away. My fingers flew over the keyboard, logging into the home's security system. The screen flickered to life, displaying various angles of our house, all of which were exterior.

There they were, my best friend and the kids, stepping through the front door. Each face was tight with concern. Gwen used Lilly's key to get into the house after she spent a considerable amount of time looking through her purse for her copy of my house key. Jack ran into the house as quickly as he could, leaving his bookbag on the front steps for Gwen to bring in.

I continued to watch through the motion detections, heart sinking, as my lawyer appeared next. His expression was grim as his brow furrowed and his jaw tightened as he rang the doorbell and was greeted by Gwen. After a brief exchange where barely any questions were asked, she let him in. When he left, his arms were burdened with a mountain full of files. *What was in those?* He didn't stay long, just long enough to gather what he needed and disappear.

But it was the detective's presence that tightened the ever-growing knot in my stomach. He arrived quietly before anyone else, sneaking into my home through an open window, his movements surprisingly methodical and precise for how drunk he was when he left me that same night. When he left after Gwen and the kids had been gone for some time, my gun case was under his arm, a silent testament to the gravity of the situation. I leaned back in the chair, overwhelmed, the ghostly echo of my husband's laughter haunting the edges of my mind.

What was he doing here for that long? I wondered, leaning back in Henry's office chair. I looked around his office for truly the first time since we bought this house. He had plaques and awards from his career posted around the walls, and the bookcases were filled to the brim with books stacked on top of one another. His first edition copies of books had been placed in a more organized portion of his bookcase. He had a propeller that looked to be two feet wide hanging above the door to the office. I hoped he had that hung just right; an earthquake would be all that was needed for it to fall off the wall and onto someone's head, killing them instantly. He had an Eames chair sitting in the corner with a copy of "Ulysses" by James Joyce lying over the armrest, open to page 420. Henry had noted his thoughts throughout the book in pen. On the table next to his chair, he had a chess set whose pieces were made out of marble. The game appeared to be half-played. On his desk, he had a globe in the corner, multiple fountain pens stacked onto leather-bound journals.

Opening his drawers next, papers and files came billowing out the further I opened the drawer. Many of the documents had the letterhead of the company he worked for, so I ignored those. However, there were some that had the acronym 'MSF' across the top. I knew nothing about this company and began collecting all of the documents that had to do with it. All in all, I only came across three pages. I started to wonder if the files that Bob had walked out with were all from 'MSF', and he just happened to miss a few, so I gave him a call.

"Hey Bob, I saw you stopped by the house while I was away. Anything you want to tell me about what you did when you were here?" I questioned, leaning back in the office chair.

"Emma, great to hear you are out. No matter what I tried, they wouldn't let me get you out quickly enough, so sorry about that. A full day at the police station must have been a nightmare." He paused, noticing I was not responding. "Yes, I was at your home. Your friend Gwen and the kids were there too, I never saw Jack, though, but I was promised he was there somewhere."

"Did you take anything while you were here?" I asked.

"Yeah, I did. Let's see, what did I take?" He said, dragging out his answer. "Oh, I grabbed a few files from Henry's office. Nothing crazy, just things I did not want the police to get hold of if they happened to stop by." He finished trying to end the conversation there.

"Did those papers have anything to do with 'MSF'?" I interrogated.

Bob started to sweat; the secrets he had been holding for Henry were slowly beginning to unfold. The sound of a pen hitting his desk could be heard as he cleared his throat before speaking.

"Where did you hear that name?" He asked as innocently as he could.

"You left a few of their papers behind when you took the others. Based on these papers, I feel like I can make a pretty clear understanding of the other businesses that my husband was a part of." I told him.

After a moment of silence, Bob sighed, realizing there was no use in hiding it from me.

"Henry was a part of many businesses, but 'MSF' was a special one to him. He started that one from the bottom many years ago, shortly after you two got married, actually. That is where he gets most of your money from; however, you can't claim any of that, otherwise, you will have to start paying taxes on it. That is why I didn't want the police to find those files. You would owe a lot in taxes if this ever came out." He said in a hushed, quivering tone.

"Right, okay, so if Henry is gone, what happens to this business?" I asked, needing to know now more than ever.

"Well, it's written down that if he were to die, disappear, or be incapable of performing his duties within this company, his best friend and you would take over the operations." He told me.

"Does he have a best friend?" I laughed before I could stop myself.

"Yes, I'm sure you have met Sylvester once before. He has a deep voice, he's about six feet tall; the guy looks pretty big and like he goes to the gym a lot." He implied.

"That Sylvester?" I squealed. "He delivers packages to our house. My husband's best friend was a package delivery guy? That's sad." I said sorrowfully.

"No, he wasn't a package delivery guy. He often delivered packages to your house filled with files that Henry would need for the next few days. Aside from that, they were together all the time. He worked for 'MSF' but also with Henry at the company you know of. That is where they were able to conduct MSF business during the day and still bring in an income for the IRS to see." Bob explained.

"Are you telling me that my husband was what exactly?" I asked, unsure what he was trying to tell me.

"Until Sylvester sees a need to bring you in on the business, you will not know what your husband was. Sylvester will send you your portion of the business. Henry made a pretty penny from this company. This will make sure you and the kids are well taken care of, and you will not have to find a serious job. You just need something that shows some form of income, so the IRS doesn't question anything. Does that sound good?" He advised me.

"Are you forgetting I have a job? I work at the publishing house in town." I told him.

"Oh, right, Henry told me you got yourself a job. Good for you, keep it." He spoke.

"What do I do now, then? The police still think I had something to do with Henry going missing." I complained.

"I will take care of it. Just put those papers in an envelope, and I will call Sylvester to have them picked up from your house. Have a good day, Emma." He said, hanging up the phone.

"Mom!" Lilly and Jack shouted as they ran into the front door. "We missed you!"

"I missed you, too. How was school?" I asked as they both fell into my arms.

"Great, we painted a photo of a turkey in art class, do you want to see it?" Jack asked before he began rifling through his bookbag.

He pulled out a piece of paper with a wild burst of reds, oranges, and browns all mixed together in a way that only a child's uninhibited imagination could manage to call a turkey. I chuckled softly to myself as I took notice of the oversized body parts, the massive legs needed to carry such a large turkey, and the feathers, each a different size and style. Jack's imagination truly was something else. Children are filled with the pure creativity needed to come up with a turkey whose small, dotted eyes stared into my soul.

"It's beautiful, honey. Why don't you go hang it on the fridge?" I asked him, giving him a kiss on his head before he ran off.

"And what about your day?" I asked Lilly.

Lilly looked down when she replied. "Not as good as his." She said in a somber tone. "The kids would not stop talking about you. I heard many of the teachers whisper in the halls that you were arrested. Is that true?"

"That is not true. I was not arrested. The detective asked me to help him on the investigation with your dad and needed me to stay while we figured out what happened." I told her, catching Gwen's eyes across the foyer.

"Thank you for letting them stay at your place. How were they?" I asked her.

"Perfect little angels as they always are." Gwen smiled.

"Well, we need to go talk. Lilly, why don't you go unpack your bag and talk to your brother about what you would like for dinner?" I asked her.

Lilly skipped off and up the stairs. She hated having a packed bag lying around her room from any trip, so I know I can trust her to get everything unpacked and placed in her laundry basket properly. Gwen and I walked into the kitchen and saw Jack admiring his turkey painting.

"Sweetie, can you go upstairs and unpack your bag. Then go check with your sister about what you want for dinner." I asked him and waited for him to leave the room.

"Okay, so really, how was it?" Gwen asked.

"Not as bad as I had expected it to be. The first hour was the hardest, sitting in that cell with my thoughts running wild with what could possibly be happening outside. I was worried they had found anything to tie you to this, that they had found the bags and could determine it was him, the fantasies ran wild in my head." I told her. "It was difficult to get past the stench of the cell. I'm sure thousands of men had peed in the cells in the police station's basement."

"Sounds horrible." Gwen sighed.

"The strangest part was that the detective came to me and told me his wife wanted a divorce. He showed up plastered, I have no idea what time of day or night it was, either." I laughed.

Hearing this, Gwen raised an eyebrow. "He what? That doesn't sound very professional. Do you think it was a tactic?" She asked. "You know to get you to lower your guard because he might be too drunk to remember it."

"I honestly didn't think of that, but I don't think it was. He was agitated. I can't imagine he could have faked that."

I told her. "What really makes me think that is that he told me he was lying to my face. He faked the blood analysis report he showed me when he was questioning me, and then later told me he lied about it. Although that could have been a tactic, now that I think about it." I confessed, and a new worry washed over my mind.

"Whatever it was, I am glad you are out of there. The town went crazy with you in there. I was nervous someone was going to start rioting in the streets and breaking down the police station to get a chance to see you behind bars or worse." She uttered, realizing she had begun speaking too loudly and the kids could possibly hear her.

"That's a little dramatic, Gwen. Now, enough about that. I need to show you something." I told her.

"Okay, let's go then." Gwen began moving, not knowing any direction to go.

"No, you need to go by yourself. I found something when I was searching my house the other week. Go into my wine cellar, and in the far-left corner, you will see something behind a few bottles of wine. When you find it, don't make it obvious that you did, just grab a bottle of wine from somewhere near there and head back upstairs." I instructed her.

I waited patiently in the kitchen, pacing back and forth for her to come back upstairs. She had been taking a while down there. When she finally did, grief ran across her face.

"You saw it, didn't you?" I asked, noticing she did not have a wine bottle in her hand.

"Oh, I saw it, Emma. We need to talk." She grabbed my shoulder and ushered me to take a seat.

"I know, it's insane that someone would put a camera in my house. I haven't been able to find any more, but I figured with your help, we could find the others." I cheered.

"No, Emma. No one put that camera in your house." She spoke.

"Yes, they did, you saw it! How did a camera get there then? I have never seen that camera there until recently," I told her.

"When I went down there, it was not difficult to spot what you were talking about. I couldn't believe it myself either, I got so angry I did not listen to your instructions," she said

"Clearly." I cut her off, pointing to her empty hands.

"Well, I decided to look even further and moved the bottle of wine in front of it." I froze at the mention of the camera being exposed. "Thinking whoever was watching this would not know for a fact if I had seen the camera or not. Even though it was very obviously placed. The camera was sitting on its side, up against the shelf, where I could get a perfect view of underneath the camera." She paused then, unsure how to tell me the rest. "Emma, there was a label on it that read "Property of Emma Thompson". You put the camera in your own house. If there are any more cameras, you put them there yourself." She said, disappointedly.

"No, that's not true. There was no sticker on it when I

went down there." I told her.

Right?

"Did you move the bottle in front of it?" She asked.

"Well, no, I didn't want them to know I had found the camera, so I left it where it was," I informed her.

"I think it's better if you see it for yourself then." Gwen grabbed my arm and began to pull me towards the door. "This is for your own good."

I followed Gwen down the stairs with my head held high, so sure that I was telling the truth. Why would I put a camera in my own house? That sounded ridiculous. I was not insane either, so obviously, she was lying. Gwen took the lead when we got to my wine cellar; her movements were sharp and purposeful, and she walked as fast as she could to the far back left corner.

"Look for yourself, it's right there." She pointed to the shelf, a mixture of confusion and concern in her voice.

I squinted, my brain refusing to make sense of what she was showing me. The camera was labeled clearly with my handwriting, 'Property of Emma Thompson'. But that couldn't be right. I had told her about feeling watched, sure, but installing a camera *myself?* Impossible.

"Emma, do you not remember putting this here?" Her questions were a direct hit to the chaos brewing inside me.

I reached out, fingers trembling, and took the camera in my hands. The label was unmistakably my handwriting. As I turned the camera over, examining it, flashes of memory sparked deep within my mind. I saw myself buying the camera, the fear that had consumed me after… after we had done the unthinkable. The truth of what had been done was murky, something the outside world would never know about.

Nausea rose up as the realization hit me hard. I had put the camera there. Not out of fear of someone else, but out of fear of myself, of what I might do if pushed again, or what I might discover lurking within my own shadowed corners. I sank to the cold basement floor, the camera falling from my limp grasp. "I... I had to know if I was still safe, even from myself," I murmured, the words barely a whisper. Gwen knelt beside me, her presence a sudden warmth in the chill.

"Safe from what, Emma? He's gone. There is nothing to worry about," she said.

How could I explain that every time the stairs creaked in the house, every footstep or door closing, every whisper of wind, felt like a ghostly accusation? How could I tell her that the man we killed to save myself still haunted my every moment? Tears blurred my vision as I grappled with my fractured reality. I had been living in a self-made prison; one filled with the paranoia that caused me to install the camera.

"I'm not okay, Gwen," I confessed, the fight draining out of me. "I haven't been okay since that night. I see him... in shadows, in dreams. The camera... I thought it would prove I was alone, that it was all in my head."

Gwen's hand found mine, her grip firm and grounding. "You're not alone, Emma."

As we sat in my basement, the weight of unspoken truths and unresolved grief pressed down. Acknowledging the camera and my doing it was just the first step. Dealing with the lurking fears and the specters of our past actions would be my next battle. I needed to get help for my children. I couldn't leave myself alone.

"I need you to stay with us. Tell your husband he can join too. Tell him the truth: the loneliness of the house has weighed heavily on me, and I'm afraid to be alone right now." I cried.

"I'll make sure he joins. Having a strong man here could help you." She hugged me harder than she had ever hugged me before.

"How does he feel about everything going on? I never asked you." I cried, hugging her back.

She let go of the hug, keeping me within reach by holding my forearms. "He is your number one supporter, no matter what you do. However, the rumors around town have been making him nervous about our friendship. He's hoping none of it is true, but since the two of us know it is, let's hope he can stay away from the rumor mill some more." She whispered. "I should be getting going now. I'll be back in a few hours." She gave me one last hug and a kiss on my forehead.

I sat in the wine cellar, coming to terms with the realization that I had been frightening myself in my own home. The fear of Henry coming back to life and injuring me for good was not rational. The creak in the stairs, however, was real. Lilly heard them too. I just needed to get rid of this house; it was settled, and I couldn't live here anymore.

When I got back upstairs, the children were throwing around take-out menus, trying to decide between Chinese or Italian, so I let them pick both since we had more company coming for dinner than just the three of us.

"Can I ask you two if anyone had come over when you came over to pack a bag with Gwen?" I asked when I hung up the phone after ordering the food.

"Yeah, the detective was here!" Jack piped up.

"No, that was the lawyer, Jack." Lilly contradicted.

"Not it wasn't!" He shouted. "I know what the detective looks like. He was in the basement and asked me questions. I'm getting a police badge for it!"

"Mom, tell him he's wrong. The lawyer was here, you can ask Aunt Gwen!" Lilly shouted back.

I stood frozen in place, catching my breath. "Jack, are you certain you saw the detective and not the lawyer?" I got down to his level and asked.

"I'm positive, he was even wearing a police jacket. It was the same guy who had dinner with us." His certainty made me calm, but pissed off Lilly even more.

"The lawyer went into Dad's office, not the basement. He even left with some of his files!" Lilly fought back.

"That's enough, both of you. Go do something in opposite rooms, please, until dinner gets here." I watched as they both left the room, slumping into the closest chair to me.

My body is heavy, the weight of the day pressing down on me. I poured myself a glass of red wine, taking a deep whiff of the wine, the rich aroma briefly distracting me from the turmoil in my mind. For weeks, I thought I was being haunted by Henry or that someone, mostly the detective, was tormenting me from within my own walls. My heart was a constant drum of paranoia. But as I sit here, the wine swirling in my glass, a cold realization has dawned on me. If I put the camera there, the truth still sends shivers down my spine, sharper than the crisp air outside. Why would I do that and not remember? My mind races through possibilities, none of them comforting. With the creeping dread came a spark of curiosity. *There has to be footage, right?* Recordings. Evidence. Proof of whatever I thought I needed to capture or protect myself from, even if from myself.

The thought of waiting for Gwen to arrive to see the truth together stopped me for a moment. I needed answers now, though. I jumped up, my wine glass teetering, then steadied myself. I rushed to my bedroom, skipping the creaking step, booted up my computer, and began searching for the files that had to be there. I braced myself for what I was going to see: the act of putting the camera in my sanctuary and the mental state I was in when I did it.

I pulled up the first file and began watching one after another. The first was two months ago, just a week after Henry's death, when I had put the camera up. My laptop was leaning against a chair while I learned how to set up the camera. Two bottles of wine were empty and lying on the floor beside me. My eyes were two hollow holes in my mind, nothing comforting coming from them. I moved my body around as each limb weighed more than my total body weight. I couldn't watch it anymore and moved on to the following video.

For a while, most of the videos were me running down to grab a bottle of wine, or Gwen and I hanging out in the cellar, chit-chatting about nothing and everything. They were all very casual. That was until the video of me finding the camera. Every video after that, I stood and sat as straight as I possibly could; not a single ounce of relaxation flew through my body. I had tightened every muscle in my body, I stopped smiling, and would come down to sit on the couch simply so the imaginary person who put the camera there would not be suspicious that I had found it. If anyone watched these videos in order, they would have been able to tell something was up.

The detective showed up in a few videos; the one I did not care to watch was when he had first entered my wine cellar. The monotonous conversation about his wife and wine did nothing to entertain me. I truly needed to know the truth. The later videos did just that.

"That's what I was looking for!" I muttered to myself. "That bastard is going down!"

I grabbed the closest flash drive I could and began downloading the videos of the detective searching my wine cellar and talking to my son without a search warrant, and him drunk and sleeping on my couch in his uniform. *Yes, something I can use against him to get this case closed.* I thought.

Chapter Thirteen

The next morning, I woke up to the smell of breakfast being cooked and a pot of coffee being brewed. I took a large whiff of it from my bed and was instantly transported to heaven. Nothing was more satisfying in this moment than the prospect of a breakfast that I did not have to cook on a school morning and a fresh pot of coffee. The empty bed and the smell of my home reminded me that Henry was absent.

I jumped out of bed, throwing the sheet to cover up the space where Henry used to sleep, grabbing my robe and slippers, and heading towards the heavenly smell from downstairs.

Creak

"Good morning to you, too, Henry," I said as I walked down the stairs.

"Good morning," Vince greeted me with a full cup of coffee as I walked into the kitchen.

I held the coffee cup close to my chest, comforted in the knowledge that I was safe. "What a good morning it is,"

I said.

"Did you sleep well?" Gwen asked, flipping pancakes on the stove.

"The best night of sleep I have had in a long time. Thank you, guys, for that. Truly, it wouldn't have happened if you weren't here." I took a seat at the table and waited to be told breakfast was ready. It was not every day that someone cooked breakfast for me in my own home, and I was going to savor this moment.

"How long do you think you will need us to stay here?" Vince asked me.

"Not sure yet, I'm not quite sure what is going on with the case. I need the detective to realize I had nothing to do with this, so we can move on with our lives. Who knows when that will really happen?" I sighed once again, filling my nostrils with the wonderful smell of the coffee in my hand.

"Maybe you should see a therapist, Gwen told me about the camera, and that fear came from somewhere deep within you to do that. You need to speak to someone about that; otherwise, you will be terrified in your house forever." He took a seat opposite me.

Gwen's head whipped around to make eye contact with me. She raised her shoulders and motioned towards Vince with the spatula, to say 'sorry, you know he hears about almost everything'. I returned her gaze by looking towards the basement stairs and back at her. Her eyes went wide, and she immediately began shaking her head no, letting me know that the secret would never get to her husband.

"Maybe, I just won't have this house for much longer. Do you think changing houses will help? All of the negative energies haunting me can stay here, and we can get a fresh start elsewhere." I said, taking the last sip of my coffee.

"Maybe," Vince said, shrugging his shoulders. "Are you completely sure that Henry is not coming back?"

"I can't be completely sure, but it's been months. If he wanted to come back, he would have by now. Don't you think?" I asked him before I caught Gwen's eye contact. Raising my eyebrow and looking towards Vince and back to Gwen, I let her know I was ready to move on from this line of questioning.

"Alright, enough of this topic," Gwen said, placing a plate in front of Vince and me with pancakes, bacon, and scrambled eggs. "Emma had a very lovely morning. Let's not ruin it with your many questions."

Gwen and I subtly shared another look of acknowledgment, as though she could read my mind, quietly reassuring me that she's got my back.

"I should probably tell you before we end this topic that I found this taped to your front door when I went to get the newspaper." Vince held up a note that read:

I have news, meet me at the station at noon.

- A

That is one ominous note. It could only be from one

person, though.

"Want me to come with you?" Vince asked.

His unwavering support took me aback. Initially, I thought of declining it, but decided otherwise. "Honestly, that would be very nice of you. I would love your company and support." I reached my hand across the table, found his hand, and gave him a nice squeeze.

The rest of the morning was rather relaxing. Lilly and Jack did not fight once during breakfast. I was not sure if it was due to their argument the previous day, plain exhaustion, or the appearance of Vince in our kitchen. The kids did not see Vince nearly as often as they saw Gwen, and still acted shy around him. I sat back admiring the usual banter between Gwen and Vince as they rehashed the story of how they met to the children for the hundredth time.

"And so there I was, sitting under a tree bawling my eyes out when Vince came walking by…"

When breakfast was over, Gwen offered to drive the kids to school while I got ready for my menacing meeting. I called my lawyer, Bob, to make sure he was present for the meeting as well, just in case. Then, I placed the flash drive with the camera footage into my purse. Vince and I said goodbye to Gwen, checking with her to make sure she was okay with watching the children if we weren't back before they got out of school.

The drive to the police station became one that I knew all too well. Three stop lights and a stop sign, two right turns, and then a left into the station. My mind was focused on the mundane task of driving, well, watching Vince drive more accurately. We stayed silent during the ride, only exchanging a brief look as we turned into the station.

"Any idea what this could be about?" Vince asked as we pulled up to the station.

"I have a hunch." I put the car in park and got out. "Bob, thanks for coming."

He stood in front of the police station waiting for us and shook my hand, then Vince's when the introduction was made. We all looked from one to the other, waiting for someone to make the first move towards the door. Vince broke the spell, walked to the front door, and held it open for the two of us.

"You got this," He whispered as I walked by.

The police station was buzzing with excitement as I walked in, a stark contrast to what I had experienced during my previous visits. Officers were at their desks screaming and shouting into their phones, at one another, and just generally in the air. They were getting ready for something, something big. Could it be the arrest of a murderess? Or something else? No one had run up to us and thrown handcuffs on me just yet, so I took it as good news, for now.

"Mrs. Thompson, so great to see you! It looks like we will need the conference room instead. Come right this way, I will see if it is available." Officer Brady greeted us in the lobby.

"What's going on in here?" Bob asked.

"We will get to that." Officer Brady said, leading us toward the conference room. "Looks like we are in luck. Go in and have a seat. We will be right with you."

From the inside of the conference room, we could see out to the rest of the police station. The conference room held a long table big enough for twenty-six people to sit in. The two smaller ones each had a projector screen on one and a large monitor on the other. The wall that faced the outside of the police station was all glass windows staring deep into the forest that the police station backed up to. The last wall was also fully glass and stared directly onto the desks of the police officers. Through the large glass windows, we watched as one officer after another gathered their papers, jackets, and coffee mugs and headed out of sight, presumably out the door as well.

"Where do you think they are all going?" Vince asked.

"I don't know, but I don't have a good feeling about this meeting." I sweated. Wishing I had given my children a tighter hug and more kisses, and told them every second I saw them this morning how much I loved them.

We were left alone in the glass conference room, watching as each and every officer had left their desk and gone out of sight. A few moments passed, and finally, Officer Brady and Detective Albert entered the room.

"Sorry, that took so long, we brought coffee." Officer Brady cheered.

Officer Brady and Detective Albert both had sweat dripping down their foreheads, their chests were rising at a fast pace, and their white button-up shirts had sweat marks under their armpits.

"This seems to be your strong suit, Mr. Brady." I winked.

"Now, this is a full room. Who did you bring with you here, Mrs. Thompson?" Detective Albert wondered.

"This is Bob Solsen, my attorney." Bob stood up from his seat on the left of me, dressed in a black suit.

"Nice to meet you, sir." Detective Albert reached out to shake his hand.

"And you," Bob replied.

"This is Vince Harrison. He is my best friend's husband and here for moral support." Vince stood up from his seat on the right of me.

"Great to meet you as well." He said, shaking Vince's hand. "Well, I am sure you are all wondering why we asked Emma to come down here today."

"What we are really wondering is why you asked her with a note to her door. Why not call her? What if she hadn't gone out her front door at all today? Would you have come to arrest her for missing a meeting with you?" Bob grilled the detective.

"No, but we would have come to your house to escort you to this meeting." He told them.

"Please have some of your coffee, what we are about to tell you might be shocking." Brady chirped while pushing the drink carrier full of coffee towards us.

What could be more shocking than them telling me

that they are arresting me for the disappearance and murder of my husband? I think the whole town is waiting for that to happen. I sat, heart racing, for them to continue talking. Instead, everyone took a sip of their coffee.

"Could you please tell us why we are here, then, instead of wasting all of our time?" Bob broke the silence.

"Right, of course. As you are all aware by now, Henry Thompson went missing a few months ago. Well, with the help of his wife," The detective pauses to point at me. "We think we found him."

My heart sank, hammering in my chest, a frenzied beat that screamed for me to run, to hide, to disappear into the ether before they could tie the knot of guilt around my neck. Panic clawed at my chest, but I forced a mask of calm despair onto my face, the face of a distraught wife who had just received the worst possible news.

Bob leaned in beside me, "Stay calm, answer only what you're asked, and let me do the talking." His voice was steady, as if he expected this.

As the detective laid out photos before me on the table, my mind flashed back to the night we disposed of his body throughout a few towns. Had they found one of the bags with half of his head? Had I accidentally placed it in one of the green recycling containers? Had one of the large dumpsters not yet been emptied, leaving behind the rotting carcass of my husband? I had been so confident at the time as we placed each bag in its new location. But now, doubt crept in like a thief, stealing that confidence. I took a moment to try and catch my breath and look at the photos lying before me.

"Well, technically, we haven't found him. We only have a hunch." Detective Albert said.

I let my breath out louder than I had anticipated, causing everyone to look at me.

"It will be okay, Emma," Vince said, holding my hand.

"I have been gathering information on Henry for the past two months. Information that I have gathered from Emma, your children, neighbors, Henry's boss, and coworkers. Pretty much anyone who has ever talked to you or Henry. The blood taken from your home led us nowhere; there was no way to prove that anything happened to him with that sample. So, we had to scratch that idea." He spoke.

"I told you that," I muttered.

"Calm yourself," Bob whispered into my ear.

Detective Albert continued, "I had the theory that you had enough time to murder your husband, hide his car, and make it back in time for your party as well. However, that theory also had to be scrapped as all of the photos were clearly Henry driving, and your cell phone never left your house that day, even though you did go to the grocery store. So that part is still up in the air."

"So far, it sounds like my client is not going to be charged with anything," Bob stated.

"We are getting to that. Please give him more time to explain our thought process to get to our conclusion." Officer Brady asked.

"Thank you. I talked to the women who attended your party. Most of them mentioned that you seemed like your normal self, bubbly and happy to be with your friends. They noted your lack of appetite during the party and that you did not answer their questions as fast as you normally would. But, otherwise, you were your normal self. None of them said you seemed in the mindset to have just killed your husband."

I waited patiently for the ball to drop as I held tightly onto my warm coffee cup. My armpits were sweating, and I worried that Bob and Vince could smell the truth on me.

"Then you found the key to the room in your basement. The room was a game-changer and led me to search harder into Henry's career and side jobs. When you were here, locked in our cells, I went to your house and found your gun case. I originally went to get back into the room and swab it down while using a blacklight to examine the floor and walls to see if I missed anything. Unfortunately, I couldn't find the key. However, I did find this," he said, placing the gun case on the table.

"I already knew that," I said, placing the flash drive on the table, "On this is footage of you lying to my child about the reason why you were in our home. You are searching my wine cellar, looking for what I now understand was the key to the back room. I planned on turning this in to your superior to get you taken off of my husband's case; you are obviously too obsessed over this."

"You should have told me about this." Bob scolded

me. "Did you have a search warrant to enter my client's home?" He asked Detective Albert.

"Yes." He proudly said.

"I am asking if you had one for the time that you are on camera searching her home. Did you have a warrant for that time?" He asked again.

"No." Detective Albert whispered begrudgingly as his jaw tightened in response. His fists balled on the top of the table, as a vein on his temple appeared to bulge.

"Then this is ours, and anything you found out about it is no longer relevant and cannot be used to file any arrests," Bob said, grabbing the gun case and flash drive off the table and placing them in the chair to his left.

"That's fine; we couldn't get it open anyway. The only thing we could determine was that Emma's fingerprints were on it. *When* did they get on it? That we could not determine." Officer Brady piped in.

"Then I spoke with your son, who really got the ball rolling on the information for my theory. If you look at the photos before you, I began searching the airport garage footage to see if any suspicious vehicles left the garage shortly after Henry parked his vehicle. One car stood out." He said, pointing towards a photo of a white van.

Bob elbowed me in the ribs at this. When I caught his eye, he quickly looked at the photo of the van, then back towards me. He placed his phone on the table, opened to a note that read 'That's Henry's van'.

This is finally starting to look up; I had nothing to do

with this white van. If Henry did, what does that mean to me? And all Jack had told them was that Henry had people coming and going from the house. Was this news to me? Yes, but I can't imagine what Detective Albert took this as.

"When I pulled the information on the car, it was found that the driver had been arrested before for kidnapping, drug use, and involvement in a gang. Our police force is on the way to his home now to search for Henry." He spoke.

"Do you think he was kidnapped?" Bob asked.

"It's the only logical answer once you throw out the idea that Emma here killed her husband. We have not found a single trace of Henry starting a new life elsewhere, and we have looked! If he did manage that, he is very good at staying away from cameras or had his face surgically altered, which seems unrealistic." Detective Albert explained.

"So what are we doing now, then?" Vince asked. "If Emma is cleared, why are we still here?"

"You are here for Emma's protection. You see, we followed this van from the airport all the way to his house. On the way there, he stopped to pick up a few things. He placed a barrel of gasoline in the van; those aren't easy to buy. Then he stopped for lunch, getting way more food than just for himself, and he took the back roads as often as he could. The times he did not, that is what you are seeing here." He pointed at the images on the table.

The three of us looked at one another, trying to determine if the detective and his officer had gone a little crazy.

These people didn't kidnap my husband; I kidnapped him. I bit my tongue to stop myself from coming out and telling them their theory was insane, because I knew if I did, it would be the end of my life.

"So, when they finally got to where they were going, he parked the car in his garage, so we are not sure what happened once inside." Officer Brady explained. "What we do know is that just a day later, he took that van out and drove it to the middle of the woods. We don't know what he did there, but we have a team and cadaver dogs searching the woods now."

Listening to Officer Brady explain where they were in their thought process, my body began to tighten. I could feel my hands unconsciously tighten around my thighs, my fingernails digging as I squeezed even harder.

You have got to be shitting me. I actually got away with this. I thought to myself.

Vince grabbed my hand off my thigh and held it with his left hand, and began patting it with his right, reminding me to take a deep breath. I was unsure how to feel in that moment; I was both shocked and confused. Where were they going with their findings? What had they found? Had I truly gotten away with this? My body began to relax slightly as the optimistic feelings surged through my body.

Officer Brady turned on the screen in the conference room and began to work on getting his laptop to cast onto the screen when a woman walked in with bags of food and a tray of beverages from the burger joint down the street.

"Ah, thank you, Janet!" He said, thanking her and placing his credit card back in his wallet. "I figured we were going to be here for a while, and since it was lunchtime, I took the liberty of ordering us lunch. I guessed at what everyone would want, so feel free to trade."

His cheery disposition was a stark contrast to how he had treated me previously. He must not get to raid an innocent person's home every day; this excitement he feels most likely tops any joy he had at his wedding, when his children were born, or his first arrest. The disappointment he is going to feel when nothing comes of this, though, is what is going to bite me in the ass.

Officer Brady got the video to work and hit the volume button. The screen was split into two different events; the left side showed men walking through a forest and cadaver dogs loose, searching for what they believed to be my husband's buried body. The right side showed a SWAT team in the back of a vehicle gearing up for the raid.

"Please, please, everyone dig in." Detective Albert requested as he unwrapped a burger for himself.

They had gone all out for this; we each had burgers and fries and a soda to help wash it down. If this lasts for very long, I can imagine him sending out for ice cream or milkshakes to go with this. I nibbled on my fries while I watched with every fiber in my body, waiting for them to discover something. Bob and Vince finished their meal with excitement as they watched what felt like a movie to them. This, though, was my life. If they find anything, it will come back to me. I had no appetite for anything.

We watched with tense anticipation as the SWAT team exited the vehicle, making their approach to the house. The air in the room was thick with anticipation. The SWAT team stood at the ready, waiting for their team leader to complete their final checks. He looked over his shoulder, ensuring every member was in their position. The room was silent between the video and us, our eyes searing into the television. The silence was broken only by the leader whispering through his radio, "Stack up," his voice steady and authoritative. His team swiftly jumped into action, ready to ram the solid wooden door down.

We listened as the leader raised his hand, signaling for the imminent action. "On my call," he muttered into the microphone. You could see the team tense under the pressure, ready to perform their job. The leader lowers his hand in one swift, firm motion, shouting, "Breaching! Breaching! Breaching!" The words pierced the air in the conference room, where everyone was holding their breath. I took a moment to look away from the screen and saw the woman who dropped off our food staring into the room. I tilted my head, motioning for her to come in and join. It's not fair for her to be the only one on the outside of this if the whole police department was in on it. She entered the room just as the team shattered the door with the ram's strength. The team poured into the house, ready for whatever awaited them inside.

They passed through a dark, dingy living room, spotlights covering every aspect of the room. With no one in the living room, they moved on to the next room, maintaining the tight formation they had entered the house with, prepared for any possibility. Room by room, they shouted, "Clear!" letting others know the room was empty and not a threat. We watched from the leader's camera as their teammate opened the next door, tossing a smoke can in at the same time. They quickly made their way into the room, and when the smoke cleared, a man was sitting on his bed, frozen in the act of trying to cover himself up. They approached with caution and quickly lifted the man out of his bed and led him out of the house. Someone lifted the sheet up and saw bags and bags of cocaine lining the bed.

This was enough for the leader. He followed his teammates out of the house with the man while the rest of the team continued searching the house. The men lowered him to the ground, face down, and handcuffed him behind his back.

"What's your name?" The leader asked as his team turned the man around to sit on the ground.

"Tommy." He said, spitting in the direction of the leader.

"Who do you work for?" The leader shouted.

Tommy sat there silent, his face unwavering. Sweat poured down his cheeks. His clothes were filthy with holes throughout, unsure if they were there before or after the team had ripped him out of his bedroom.

"You are bound to tell me eventually. With the little I saw in there, I know we have enough to put you away for life. So why not just tell us now who you work for?" The leader pleaded, trying a nicer approach this time.

"Can I use it to lower my time if I tell you?" Tommy asked, starting to settle on the ground, barely needing the officer's hold on his arms anymore.

"I can see what I can do." The leader responded.

"MSF." He cried.

Bob squeezed my hand, yelling at me not to turn my head or make any notion that I knew that name. What type of business was my husband involved with? I was dying to turn around and start berating Bob with questions, but I knew better.

"NSF, did you hear that too?" Officer Albert asked us.

"Yeah, that is what I heard, NSF." Bob piped up, hoping to stop any questions about the name.

"You are coming with us; we have more questions for you." The leader said, gesturing for his team to pick him off the ground and toss him in the back of one of the officers' vehicles.

If I did not have an appetite before they found Tommy, I for sure do not have one now. We watched the right screen as they continued to go through the house, pulling pieces of evidence from every room. The left screen was still searching through the forest for my supposed husband.

"So, what does this mean for my client?" Bob asked Detective Albert.

"Right now, the suspect has been apprehended. There does not seem to be any immediate danger to Emma. We would like her to stay here still to watch as we gather more information on her husband's whereabouts." Detective Albert told us.

"Do you mind if we take a break while we wait for more news? I would like to speak with Emma privately, and I am sure Emma would like Vince to call Gwen and give her an update. Would this be okay with you?" Bob said, getting up from his chair in preparation for his response. Ready to walk, no matter what their answer was.

"Of course, Brady, will you show them to a room?" He asked.

"I think we will just go outside and get some fresh air; it's such a nice day, after all." Bob quickly interjected, pulling me from the table and out of the room.

"Get in," he said as we walked up to his car. "Whatever happens in there, I need you to keep your cool. They have found out way more than I would have ever expected them to. I need to cover Henry's tracks and keep you out of this. Otherwise, you and your children will have no income. You have enough to live on for a few years, but we don't want the feds to take anything from you. I don't care how much you and Henry hated each other; you need to keep this business a secret for the rest of your life. Do you understand me?" He spoke rapidly, trying to cover it all in as short an amount of time as possible.

"Of course, I understand," I told him.

"Great, now go next door and get you and me a coffee. You need to relax. Grab yourself a treat or something while you are there. I noticed you didn't eat much back there. You are going to need your energy if they do end up finding something." He handed me his credit card before saying. "I have a few phone calls to make, and we will go back in together."

I did as I was told. The walk to the coffee shop next door felt good. A light breeze filled the air and my lungs as I took in a deep breath. "This is a good thing," I whispered to myself before walking into the coffee shop, hoping to believe it myself.

I ordered myself two cappuccinos, one for here and one to go, and a black coffee to pick up on my way out for Bob, and grabbed a blueberry muffin and a slice of coffee cake since the last time I had it, it was so delicious. I took a seat to enjoy the food, but mostly to calm my nerves. Coffee was not the traditional drink that is used to calm nerves, as it helps raise your heart rate, but I drank it as fast as I could. The coffee cake, however, eased me more than anything. The calm atmosphere of the shop was also a great help. It was empty, aside from the employees who were minding their own business, giving me the personal space I needed to process what had just happened.

An innocent man, well, I guess not as innocent as he could have been, was just arrested because of me. My husband's, and I think it's mine now, too, business is at stake if they figure out the correct name for it. I'm going to have to ask Bob the next time I remember what MSF stands for. This man is going to go to prison for the rest of his life from the number of drugs he had in his home alone; if they manage to pin a murder on him as well, he will be looking at multiple life sentences.

"There you are," I heard Bob say as he got closer to my table. "I sent you to grab something and come back. They will be wondering where we are. Grab your stuff, we need to go."

The employees heard Bob and brought over the second cappuccino, his black coffee, and a bag for what was left of my baked goods. I thanked them and headed on our way. I was mainly thankful that they hadn't talked about me once while I was in there, at least not in earshot. Thankfully, the whole town will be talking about something other than me murdering my husband very soon. I should be able to ignore these types of conversations a lot easier than I had been able to with the previous story.

"Get in here, quick," Officer Brady shouted when we returned to the conference room.

Officer Brady, Detective Albert, and Vince were leaning forward in their chairs, excitedly listening to the officers searching the forest. The cadaver dog was digging in the ground and looked to be about a foot deep in the dirt. The officers who had never once been in this position before froze, waiting for the dog to discover what he smelled deep in the ground. I took my seat back at the table, squeezing my coffee mug as tightly as I could. It was bizarre to have gone from such a stressful event to finally calming my nerves at the coffee shop, only to have them ramped up again in a matter of minutes.

"Whatever they find, Gwen and I are here for you," Vince said, taking his attention off the screen for a moment to squeeze my shoulder and make me feel supported.

When we turned back, the dog had stopped digging, and the officers began pulling the dirt away. The more they pulled the dirt, the more they uncovered human bones scarcely layered with bits of flesh.

"Oh my god," I uttered, turning away from the screen.

I expected them to find nothing, not a human body that looked as if it had been burned to a crisp.

"We can turn it off if it is too much for you, ma'am," Officer Brady mentioned, reaching for the remote.

"No, I need to see this." Detective Albert burst with excitement.

I began to wonder why he wasn't in the field watching this. If this case were so much of his life, as he had once told in the cells, you would wonder why he wouldn't want to be there actively pulling this body out of the ground. Maybe his enthusiasm is looked at as a negative by his superiors, who think he would be a danger to the other officers in the field. So they told him to stay here, watch me, and make sure I was here to see what they believed happened to my husband. Whatever it was, his excitement made me sick.

"Albert, if you are there, this body is beyond recognition. There is no sure way to conclude that this is his body right now. We will have the medic wrap him up and bring him back to the lab to see if there is any way for us to identify him positively. We are cutting the feed now and will call you with any other updates we have." The man from the forest informed us, then cut the feed, sending the left side of the screen to black.

Thank God they cut the feed. I have no idea who is on the ground, but it sure was not my husband. They don't know that and possibly won't know it ever. I couldn't watch any more of it, though, and was thankful they ended the call.

"Is there a way to check in with the team at the house so we can end this viewing session and we can all go home?" Bob asked.

"Give me a moment," Detective Albert said, stood up, and left the room.

The room fell silent again, waiting for his return.

"This is good news!" Officer Brady shouted, breaking the silence. "Sorry, we accused you of murdering your husband; we can see now how very wrong we were."

His voice fell quiet near the end of his sentence. I always felt like Brady was sure I was innocent, but had Detective Albert whispering in his ear about me, trying to convince him otherwise. He began questioning his abilities as a police officer and whether he was ever ready for a detective position.

"Okay, everyone is good to go home. They informed me that they were able to pull a few fingerprints from the inside of the van and would keep me updated on whether

Henry's prints were in there or not. That should be able to help us identify the body as well. We will know more in the next few days. Until then, don't leave town." He warned me.

We took our leave as quickly as possible before he changed his mind.

Chapter Fourteen

Detective Albert closed the door behind him as we entered his office at the police station. His face resembled the sadness he had when he told me about his wife leaving him. I had never been in his office before. They must have upgraded him after the whole 'Tommy ordeal'. He previously only had a desk with the rest of the officers. It had one window facing the parking lot at the rear of the building, the sun shining through, casting shadows across the desk as the evening sun began to set.

"I owe you an apology," he started, his voice unexpectedly quiet.

Every muscle in my body tightened, unsure of what he would say next.

"We tested every surface in the back of the van for fingerprints, along with multiple items within the house. As you already know, your fingerprints were not found anywhere within the van. Henry's, however, were everywhere. They must not have done a great job at tying him down if he was able to touch so many parts of the inside of the van and still not escape." He sighed breathlessly.

I exhaled my own breath, which I hadn't realized I had been holding, a strange relief I did not know if I should feel. I kept my face as neutral as possible, hoping that nothing crossed my face that would give away my true feelings of relief. "And the body we found in the forest," he went on, his eyes drifting away briefly before locking back onto mine. "We can't identify him beyond confirming he was male, most likely older than twenty-five. There's... there's nothing directly tying you to his death, though."

I nodded slowly, maintaining the face of one who is a grieving widow. "I can't imagine who would do such a thing. My husband was a good man, no matter the fights we had. He was a contributing member of our town. He deserved more," I murmured, my voice quivering just enough to display sadness to the best of my ability.

Detective Albert watched me, the lines of his face etched with conflict. "I suspected you," he admitted, his voice barely above a whisper. "And I'm sorry. The evidence... it... seemed to point in your direction at first. I shouldn't have assumed you killed him. It's just that most people say to look at the spouse first. And I guess I leaned on that harder than I should have,"

His coming to me at this time should have filled me with glee, knowing how expertly I had covered my tracks and his body. Knowing that Gwen and I had escaped his investigation. Yet, all I felt was the hollow victory. "Thank you for telling me," I said, my throat tight. "It hasn't been easy."

"I can only imagine," he said, his words weighted with genuine remorse. He took a step closer. His overbearing presence felt imposing yet strangely comforting. "I wanted to tell you myself to apologize for the distress I've caused you during this investigation." His office was silent for a moment, save for the faint ticking of the clock on the wall behind him. I looked up at him, meeting his gaze, pushing down the dread.

"Why have me come here to tell me this?" I asked curiously.

"I guess I needed to see you, to explain things in person, and to make sure you were alright." He paused, his eyes searching mine.

"Thank you, Detective," I said, my voice soft but steady. "I appreciate your honesty. It's more than I can say for most."

He nodded, looking as if he was about to say more, but instead chose silence. After a moment, he turned towards the door. "I'll walk you out," he said, pausing as he stood at his desk. "If there's anything you need, or if you remember anything that might help, you have my number."

"Of course," I replied, offering him a weak smile.

As the door to the police station clicked shut behind me, the smile dropped from my face, replaced by the grim mask of reality. I was free from suspicion, the detective's guilt ensuring he would not probe further, yet I was bound forever by the deed I had committed. I had won, but at what cost?

The part of me that could sleep at night, laugh without guilt, and look my son in the eye without flinching. That part was gone and buried with him. I thought surviving meant freedom, but now it just felt like walking barefoot through glass. Quiet. Careful. And never really safe.

"Can you believe it? They found someone else in the woods!" Gwen gleefully cheered as she spoke.

The two of us sat in the wine cellar, catching her up on all of the aspects of the case after we left the police department. It had been two days since they found that body, and the police had found out more than I would have ever expected them to. Because Henry's company owned the van, his fingerprints were all over the inside of the van. Giving the police plenty of evidence to say that yes, Henry was, in fact, kidnapped by Tommy. He then killed him and burned his body with the large barrel of gasoline, dumping and burning his body in the middle of the woods. The chief of police was more than satisfied with this and told them not to dig any deeper into 'MSF' or, as they knew it, 'NSF'. Which left my family out of the line of fire from what I am sure would be a mountain of information and evidence leading straight to us.

"I wouldn't have believed it either if I were not there

to witness it," I told her, topping off our glasses of wine.

"What are you going to do now?" She asked.

"I don't know yet. The rest of my life is ready for me to write it. It is just a matter of what I want to fill it with." I mentioned. "For now, I want to fill it with cheer." I lifted my glass to propose a toast, "to living each day as if it were your last."

"To our last days, let our lives be worth them!" Gwen cheered.

The next day, the news hit every stand and television station in our area. I stumbled across it for the first time at the grocery store when I was standing in line to check out.

"I knew you hadn't done it, Mrs. Thompson. You have always been so nice to me. I could never see you do that to your husband." The teenager behind the counter told me.

"Thanks," I muttered as I finished my transaction and headed towards the exit.

This was not the only encounter I had that day of people coming up to me to swear they knew I was innocent. Mrs. Finkle ran across her yard to tell me as I pulled into my driveway. My hairdresser said she could see me doing it, but knew I didn't. The mailman took it upon himself to write a letter to me and left it in my mailbox for me to find. If only the people who had sworn, I was such a good person knew the truth.

"The housewife who was wrongly accused of murdering her husband has had all accusations dropped due to the police finding his body and linking it with mob-related crimes." The news anchors all said, following it with an anecdote about a time they had run into me and believed me to be a person of upstanding moral character. There was only one person who could have gotten the news anchors to lie on set about meeting me, so I gave him a call.

"Was this your doing?" I asked Bob without even saying hello.

"Which part?" He countered.

"The news anchors are telling lies about meeting me. I've never met them in my entire life. Why are they saying this?" I asked him, shaking the remote in the air after I had watched one too many news anchors lie.

"You once told me that the way you were perceived in society meant the world to you. I am simply making sure everyone knows you did not do this and no one other than that detective truly ever suspected you." Bob told me.

"Well, thank you for that. What else have you done?" I asked, recalling his initial response when I inquired about his role.

"I might have made a few calls to the chief of police, threatening a lawsuit on your behalf. Claiming your reputation has been defaced can lead to lost opportunities and potentially cost you the job you love. That's just what a good lawyer should be doing for his client. Especially one of your magnitude." He concluded.

"Anything else you have been meaning to tell me?" I asked, double-checking my bases.

"It took a lot of back-door transactions, but I have managed to continue to get you payments from MSF. Ones that are completely untraceable by the IRS, police, or any of the feds. You will receive an envelope from Sylvester once a month filled with cash, and you can only deposit enough to cover your bills. Anything else must be kept in cash or invested properly. I will get you in touch with a banker who can help you with all of this. If you need anything, I am always your lawyer. Call me whenever you need me. I have to go now." He informed me before hanging up.

MSF wasn't just a name whispered in basements. It sponsored the town's fall fair, had its logo printed on the back of youth baseball jerseys, and hosted annual charity galas at the golf club. On the surface, it was just another moneyed foundation. Clean. Corporate. Untouchable. The real work, the sanctioned parts, was kept hidden in deep, firewalled compartments. No one person ever knew too much. Not even Tommy. And if one part of the machine went down, the rest would adapt, reroute, and move on like nothing happened. My life was about to get better in so many ways.

Epilogue

It has been nearly a year since Henry died, a time that was marked with suspicion, interrogations, and the ever-present whispering neighbors. I had reached a turning point of my own, spending each day as if it were my last. At the end of the long two months that I was under constant scrutiny from everyone, the police closed the case and concluded that Henry had been a victim of mob violence. They saw Henry as one of the members who stepped out of line, one to be punished with his life, following suit in the hundreds of years-long traditions of getting rid of the trash. They weren't too far off. Henry was in charge of MSF, which I later learned stood for "Managed Syndicate Funding." I was able to let go of that chapter, finally focusing on peace and the future.

In the late evenings, I spent many restless nights watching as the rain softly pattered against my bedroom window. I wonder what my life would be like if Henry were still alive today to control us. Would I even be here? Henry had managed almost to kill me once. Why wouldn't he try it again?

You might think you know my story by now. A tragedy, a crime, and a moment of madness. Henry and I were the perfect couple in everyone else's eyes. But behind closed doors, it was a different story. It was all a performance, one that had been practiced for fifteen years. Beneath his charming exterior, Henry was the most controlling man I have ever met; he was a master of subtle threats and sharper fists. I lost large pieces of myself, slowly and quietly, until I didn't recognize the woman in the mirror. I was trapped, suffocating under the weight of his dominance. The morning it happened, something inside, deep within, broke. It wasn't planned; it usually isn't. It was the culmination of years of suppression and fear, the constant need to shrink myself to fit the mold he cast for me. Murdering him, taking him out of my life for good, a part of me felt... liberated. The other part of me is thankful for the income that is still coming in from his side business. Without it, I would not have been able to spend this year finding myself, nor would I be able to continue enjoying my life. For this is the only thing I am grateful for that Henry did for us.

Living in this suffocatingly small town during the investigation, where my every move and word were watched like a hawk, made me wonder for just a moment if I had made the right choice. The rumors of what happened after Henry had disappeared were endless, most of them directed at me. I had to learn to ignore the whispers, the threats made in my direction, and the constant feeling that I was being watched.

Thankfully, I had Gwen, and she was my rock. She has always been there for me through thick and thin. If Vince had allowed it, I would have liked to marry her instead. She helped me get rid of the ever-threatening aspect of my life and stood by me as the town single-handedly attacked with as much force as a fire hose. Instead of making me feel inadequate about the choices we had made, she reminded me each day that what we did was necessary for my family's well-being.

As time went by, I began finding joy in the little things. My coffee in the morning without the fear of smelling like it, the evenings spent at home in my cellar reading a good book, and play dates with my children at the park. Eventually, the town moved on from the shock that my husband was in a mob and got murdered for it. Bigger news came and went, overcoming each story until my life only came across people's lips for good things. I began to breathe again without the fear that someone would come into my house and hurt me or my children.

My children were thriving, too. They did not know the truth of who or what their father was, but they were there for the oppressive atmosphere that his presence gave every day. They learned to become individuals who were better every day than they were the day before. They were more outgoing and cheerful every day. My children knew they could come to me to talk about their feelings openly and without fear, which they did often.

I killed Henry. It's a truth I'll carry to my grave. But I

won't let it define me. I am more than my actions, more than his victim or his killer. I have been reborn from the ashes of my past life, seeking redemption and peace each and every day. I do not identify as his widow, not as a murderer, but as a survivor. I will live with my guilt, yes, but I will also live with purpose. To help, to heal, and to hope. Maybe, just maybe, I can turn this tragedy into a testament to change for myself and for others.

"Ready, Mom?" Jack shouted from the car window.

"I'll be right there," I yelled back.

"This is it, then?" Gwen asked.

We all needed a change of scenery. Our home still creaked when we did something Henry would not have liked, and we still heard the one-off comments about him throughout the community, especially in Lilly's school. Where children hold on to the worst parts of your life and torment you about it till you cry, Lilly had stayed the ever-loving little girl I always knew she would grow to be, but she still struggled with this every day. I needed to take my children away from an environment that knew about the worst event in their past, especially before Jack grew old enough to have his peers bully him for this.

"Looks like it," I told Gwen as we both stared towards the house.

The largest house in the neighborhood has now been fully emptied, each painting taken off the walls, each glass wrapped nicely and neatly, and all of my wines packaged. We took all of Henry's belongings and donated them to Goodwill. All except his Eames chair, which Jack requested to move into his bedroom in the new house, and a fountain pen that Lilly asked to keep. The walls have been repainted and the house scrubbed clean. All ready for the new home-owners to move in next week.

"I'm really going to miss you. Are you sure you don't want to stay?" Gwen asked for the millionth time.

"I'm sure. We will stay in touch and make sure to visit each other as often as we can. But I need a new lease on life, as they say. I can't stay in this suffocating town anymore." I cried.

"Could we go back to painting again when we get to the new house?" Lilly asked.

I told her maybe tomorrow. I hadn't picked up a brush in months. I was going to miss Gwen with all of my heart. I wouldn't know what to do without her, but I was going to have to find out. We purchased a home in New Mexico, a cute one-story ranch. There was no way I was allowing stairs into our house ever again.

Authors note

About five years ago, I was driving an hour and a half away from my home. I didn't have any music playing, no podcast, and no audiobook in the background. It was just my thoughts and the sounds of the road. That day, I couldn't get the image of Emma out of my mind. I wondered what it would be like to be suffering in a marriage. I had just gotten out of a long relationship at this time, so as you can imagine, my mind wasn't in the most stable place emotionally. She wouldn't leave my mind. I ended the trip with a voice memo on my phone of her suffering and how she was emotionally. Over the next year, I continued to dream of her, but I kept putting her story off because I was working on my second novel, Adeline, at the time. I slowly built her story's outline every time I could think of something to add, until last year, when I finally felt ready to write her story. I was seven months pregnant with my first child when I sat down to write the first chapter. I sent the chapter around to friends and family, and everyone kept asking for the rest of the book, but that was all I had. Fast forward to when I was three months postpartum. My maternity leave at work was about to end, and instead, I got laid off. I had told myself that I would not wallow for too long; I had Emma's story to write. I had to prove to myself and my son that in times of crisis, I could persevere. The story you just finished reading was not the original outline I designed for Emma. As I came to know her better, her choices became clear to me. The twist ending came from the months of trying to figure out what Henry did for a living, as you probably realized, I never decided what he did outside of the mob.

I'm incredibly proud of this novel and the fact that I completed it while pregnant and postpartum. It truly demonstrates how mothers are capable of more than just caring for their children. They may need a village to help and a few hours of peace to complete the edits. But we end up getting there. I hope you enjoyed this novel as much as I did when I wrote it.

Megan Eik
6/17/2025

About The Author

Megan Eik writes emotionally charged fiction that explores the weight of womanhood, the complexity of survival, and the haunting consequences of the choices we make to stay free. Her stories blend quiet intensity with psychological suspense, drawing readers into the minds of women who bend and sometimes break under the pressure of what's expected of them.

She is the author of Louise, Adeline, and The Steps She Took, a slow-burn psychological thriller that examines what happens when the façade of the perfect life starts to crack.

Megan lives in Virginia with her family, where she writes in the in-between hours, surrounded by books, baby monitors, and whatever's left of her tea. You can find her on TikTok @meganeikauthor, on Instagram @authormeganeik, or visit meganeik.com to learn more.

Other Works by Megan Eik

Louise

A story of love and murder creates a serial killer. Louise grew up as an only child, surrounded by friends and family. In college she started to separate herself from others until she met the love of her life. Growing up in a future world, with new technology and different ethics she tried to stay true to her self until her life took a drastic turn and she finds herself among a dozen dead bodies and a life sentence.

Adeline

After escaping death, Louise found refuge in a small town. Upon meeting new people, she changed her identity and now goes by Adeline Fower. For years, her perfect small-town life was never threatened. That is, until her past came to find her. With the anniversary of her murderous rampage approaching, her life, family, and friends could all be in danger.